NEVER HAD SHE FELT SUCH FIRE IN HER VEINS, SUCH EXQUISITE TORMENT.

Never had she known the release, the fusion into one body that occurred. They were truly one, forever joined. She knew that even after she returned to the East, even after she returned to another life, she would be fighting the pull of Jake's arms.

Yet they couldn't be together, she was convinced of that. She would still return East. She must go back.

But she would think about that later . . .

Montana SUNRISE

MARGARET CARROLL

HarperPaperbacks
A Division of HarperCollinsPublishers

This is a work of fiction. The characters, incidents, and dialogues are products of the author's imagination and are not to be construed as real. Any resemblance to actual events or persons, living or dead, is entirely coincidental.

HarperPaperbacks   *A Division of* HarperCollins*Publishers*
10 East 53rd Street, New York, N.Y. 10022

Cover illustration by Jim Griffin

First printing: April 1992

Printed in the United States of America

HarperPaperbacks and colophon are trademarks of HarperCollins*Publishers*

❖ 10 9 8 7 6 5 4 3 2 1

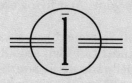

Her name was *Ellen Brandon Stanwood, not an easy*
name to forget. Perhaps, she thought, a new
name with the same initials might be the
answer. Elsa B. Stone, or Elise Burton Starr, or Elsie
something. She had read that criminals who
change their names often get caught because they
retain the same initials out of habit. In her case,
she mused, there'd be big savings in the cost of
monograms alone.

She laughed ruefully to herself. The mono-
grammed sheets and towels, the engraved silver,
the Porthault linens, were no longer a part of her
life. She could not help but believe, after what she
had gone through over the past few months, that
she would never again live the exciting and comfortable life she had come to expect would be hers
forever. The chauffeured limousine, the live-in
maids, the spread in *Architectural Digest,* certainly
had seemed to be the simple wages of hard work,
and she still found herself feeling twinges of
resentment now and then that she should be here,

flying west to a new—and what she suspected would be far less pleasant—life, with all those necessary comforts gone. And flying economy class, at that.

Ellen Brandon Stanwood had always been a star. As an honor student in high school, an active and successful undergraduate at Smith, at the top of her MBA class at Harvard, as a woman to watch on Wall Street. She was known as E. B. by that time and was watched from a distance more often than not, because most men were unwilling or perhaps afraid to make the effort required to catch her attention. On the surface she was all business, and more often than not her passions had been directed at the challenges of the stock market—the boardroom rather than the bedroom.

She had often wondered why success meant so much to her. Certainly she had the looks to attract a man and the intelligence to keep him; why then did she feel such an urgent need to compete with—and outperform—men in their own milieu? She certainly had never felt inadequate; on the contrary, much of her impatience was directed at the men who just could not seem to keep up.

Her father had often commented that she was the son he never had, and she was certainly aggressive enough to be a son of his. Her father had been a successful and hardworking businessman himself, and some of her best early memories were of Saturday mornings spent sitting at a desk in the corner of his office, watching him work and mimicking his actions. By the time she was in high school, she knew what he was doing and why, and from time to time she contributed surprisingly good ideas herself.

She always knew her place would be in the world of business, and that she would succeed. It was expected of her. Her parents had watched the early days of her Wall Street climb and had been proud of her, but their death in an auto crash several years ago had spared them the humiliation of her downfall. She never could have faced her father after failing him so miserably.

Why did it have to happen? She'd worked so hard—she deserved her success. She was one of the best. Was there ever a time when she could have stopped and changed course? No, that course was set the day she'd walked onto the floor of the stock exchange. . . .

1982

It hit her the minute they walked through the glass doors and were enveloped by the noise and excitement—the feeling of the place. It had to play a part in her life. Never had she encountered anything that made such an impression on her as this crazy, confused, yet totally organized chaos that was the trading floor of the New York Stock Exchange.

A carnival, a casino—those were the impressions that hit her. The wood floor was strewn with scraps of paper like pink and white confetti. Video monitors were piled on top of aging trading stations. Green jackets, blue jackets, and the somber hues of the specialists mingled and separated in some incomprehensible dance.

It was a dance of dollars—millions of dollars changing hands, fortunes being made and lost, through the actions of these calm-faced men. And they were mostly men, of course. But no matter. She knew that despite the excitement and the ever-present risk of what went on here, the real power lay with those who orchestrated the action—those unseen men and women who were initiating this frantic activity through the banks of phones lining every scrap of wall and every post.

It must have been fate, she thought, that prompted her trip to New York at just that time, that caused her to bump into an old friend of her father on the street, visiting New York with his teenage daughter.

"Ellen, I'm sure you're busy, but could you do me a gigantic favor?" he had asked. "You could save my life. Meg is doing a report on the stock exchange for one of her classes, and I arranged with a friend of mine who's a floor broker to actually take us onto the trading floor. It's a pretty big deal—not many people get to do it, and it's really the highlight of her trip. But I'm stuck with a conflicting appointment I can't get out of. Could you take Meg over there for me? You'd probably enjoy it yourself. I'll take you both to tea at the Plaza afterward."

She had laughed at the idea that she might enjoy a guided tour of the stock exchange. With only a few months left to her MBA degree, she had already planned her future in business. So it was only to make Meg happy and do a favor for a family friend that she went—and saw her future.

They'd all laughed about it later over tea at the Palm Court. Meg, who had been so excited about the prospect of visiting the stock exchange, had disliked everything about it. "It's terrible. How could anyone stand to work there all day?"

Barney Ellington, the floor broker who'd shown them around, tried to explain it to her.

"The level of activity is addictive in a way—the split-second decisions, the challenge in every trade. When I go shopping with my wife it drives me crazy. I'm used to making a decision in seconds, and if she takes more than five minutes to buy a car, I get jumpy."

Ellen understood completely. At that moment on the floor she'd begun revising her carefully designed career plans and setting her goals along a totally new and far more exciting track. While Meg stood surreptitiously checking her watch, Ellen and Barney talked excitedly, stopping only when Meg finally cleared her throat pointedly and motioned to the clock.

"Dad's waiting for us, Ellen. I hate to interrupt, but we probably should get going." The young girl was puzzled by Ellen's reaction to this very confusing place, but like any well-brought-up sixteen-year-old, she had learned not to question the vagaries of adults—at least not openly. Ellen, and Barney, and Meg. Their lives became entwined that first day—touching lightly at first, but gradually woven into a pattern Ellen thought would never be torn apart.

Meg's own future lay in New York, but in a New

York very different from Ellen's. Acting became her life, far removed from the world of Wall Street. In the years that followed, a wary friendship developed and ripened between the driven Ellen and the younger girl. Ellen helped her find her first apartment and watched over her while she learned about men and the city and the disappointments only an aspiring actress can know.

When she looked back across the rubble of her ruined career, humiliated and beaten, needing friends but too proud to seek them out, Ellen simply could not face Meg. Nor could she face the other friend and associate she'd first met that wonderful long-ago day.

Barney Ellington, who'd demonstrated to her how the floor broker provided the connection that made possible the lucrative deals, became her own connection eventually, the man she trusted implicitly and exclusively to handle her trading.

"This place is like a family," old pro Barney had told her the day of that first tour. "We rely on one another, and we take care of our own."

Barney's integrity was his greatest asset, and the integrity of those he dealt with was their most important quality in his mind. Letting Barney down hurt her almost as much as it hurt him.

"Ellen, you must have known what the man was doing—you had to know before any of the rest of us. Why didn't you blow the whistle right away— and get out?"

Why didn't she? What he was doing was wrong, but he was so powerful, and so important. Everyone looked up to him. . . .

1984

Life had been good to her. A job with a Wall Street firm at a starting salary that seemed shockingly high to those who didn't have Harvard MBAs, a growing circle of friends who laughed when it was suggested they were the prototype of the surely fictional yuppie, that stuffy, self-centered, greedy young person focused on personal success. Certainly her friends were ambitious and competitive, but they were also intelligent, well-educated, thoughtful people who contributed a great deal to society.

Young people on Wall Street were starting at salaries higher than their fathers made after twenty years, but then it was a young person's business, requiring energy and stamina. Ellen's hours were long, and after working hours the right kind of social life was a requirement of the profession. One never knew whom one might meet at a reception, what important contact might be made over cocktails. The better one's social life, the more important the potential clients, and the more success, the more money.

Ellen dressed carefully for the cocktail party that would change her life, but no more carefully than she prepared for any party where she might make business contacts. It was important for a young woman in her position to look successful but not too rich, which meant wearing Escada rather than Armani, Louis Feraud rather than Chanel. Tonight's dress was the requisite black, a simple crepe from Carolyne Roehm. Her bright hair was tamed into a mass at the nape of her neck, held by a flat black bow.

She turned from the tall mirror behind the bedroom door and called to her roommate, "Carey, do
you think the bow is a bit too cute?"

Carey Steele surveyed her carefully. "No, I think
it's a good touch. You look awfully sophisticated
for your age, and you know how you intimidate
people at times. The bow is a good idea."

Ellen relied on Carey's judgment in these matters. The two of them had little in common, but
Carey was easygoing and pleasant to live with, and
the flair for style that made her a rising star in the
tough New York retail market was a real asset in a
roommate. As a buyer for one of the top stores, she
was also able to alert Ellen to the designer sales that
kept her image sufficiently ahead of her income.

"You look just right, Ellen. Maybe you'll meet an
exciting man."

"The only exciting man I want to meet," Ellen
replied, "is Walter Lasker."

"You're kidding—he's really going to be there? I
thought he never stopped working long enough to
enjoy himself."

Walter Lasker was at the height of his fame—a
genius who always knew when a stock would rise
or fall, when to buy and when to sell. He made a
million dollars a day, some said. A workaholic who
often spoke on several phones at once, who rarely
slept, who stood at a special high desk because he
had too much energy to sit down. Young investment bankers and brokers fought to meet him,
fawned over him, begged to be noticed by him;
those he tapped could aspire to success beyond
their wildest dreams.

Ellen didn't dream; she acted. She had prepared for this evening carefully, but it was only the first step in a campaign to bring her work to the great man's attention. It was ironic that for once she had apparently underestimated herself, for the meeting was far different from what she had expected.

The room was crowded, and the crowd was thickest around Walter Lasker, so Ellen waited until he appeared to be moving toward the door before she moved into his path and, smiling, introduced herself.

"Ellen Brandon Stanwood. It's an honor to meet you, sir."

His pale eyes surveyed her calmly, then he nodded. "Yes, Donald Kornblatt tells me you're one of his brightest young brokers. Don't look so surprised—I rarely forget a name or a face."

For once she was flustered. "I'm flattered you've even heard my name."

He smiled and handed her a card. "Come see me tomorrow morning. Seven o'clock in my office. We'll talk about your future."

As he moved away she stood stunned, clutching the card in her hand. There were whispers around her and envious looks from those in the group who had overheard the brief conversation.

"Wow, you just hit the jackpot, Ellen," the young man standing next to her said. "He's going to offer you a job with him."

"Do you really think so? He knows almost nothing about me, and he scarcely spoke to me."

"Listen, the man doesn't make small talk. If he

wants to talk to you, he thinks you can do something for him. Bottom line. That's the kind of man he is."

She was up before five o'clock the next morning, trying on outfits, shaking Carey awake to get her advice. She hesitated over pulling her hair back under a bow but decided that Walter Lasker would not be intimidated by her and she might as well look like what she was—an aggressive, ambitious Wall Street broker.

Neither was she intimidated by the man or his surroundings. In the pale creamy cocoon of the large office overlooking the city, she sat watching him work the phones. He spoke easily and confidently, unconcerned that she was listening to the conversations that would play a role in shaping his day once the market opened.

"Well, are you interested in joining me?" was his first question to her, and her response was a cool, "Of course. If we can come to terms."

He laughed. "E. B., I heard you were tough. And good. Understand one thing—I'm not making any statements for feminism. I expect you to be as good as a man, and I'll treat you the same as I would any man. I don't want to hear any discussion about the fact that the person I've chosen to work with me is a woman."

"Agreed," she answered. "I've never gotten anywhere yet on the basis of my sex, and I have no interest in trying. I'll help younger women if I can simply because I think the new crop of women MBAs has a lot to offer, but I'll only help those who are good."

"One last thing. I've had you checked out thoroughly, and haven't found anything negative, but I need to be certain. I can't have anyone with me who has any skeletons in the closet, anything in his or her background that could reflect badly on me."

"There's nothing," she said. "I'm as honest as you are."

Things moved fast after that; time seemed to speed up, and her busy life became even busier. She was able to crowd more into her day by paying others to take care of the tasks that cut into work and important social activities. Using a hired car and driver gave her time to and from the office to complete paperwork. Soon she had left the cramped apartment she shared with Carey to move into her own elegant condominium. It would have been fun to decorate it herself, but too time-consuming. She hired it done, and the results were lovely. The one thing she refused to give in to the interior designer on was the question of art.

"I will not have you buying art for me. I will particularly not have paintings on my walls that are chosen to match the decor. You will leave the walls bare until I can take the time to choose what I like. Period."

So her beautifully furnished condo featured simple white walls with only a few fabric hangings. The irony was that people admired the look, and the combination of tradition and minimalism soon became all the rage with her designer's clients.

Simply being included in Walter Lasker's small group of intimates made her name and her income. Within a year after her first project with the great man, she was making close to $1 million a year in fees and projected to make far more. In a time of big titles and bigger incomes for risk takers, she was suddenly a senior vice-president of a prestigious firm at an incredibly early age and already in demand as a mentor for young women interested in the fast track in nontraditional fields.

It had been her father who first expressed some uneasiness about her situation. "I don't like that man," he said. "There's something about him that I just don't trust."

"Dad," she said, laughing, "you're just not used to the New York personality. This is a man who works so hard and whose mind is so active that he averages four hours of sleep a night—and you know you've always recommended hard work as the road to success."

Her father had shaken his head. "No, there's just something about the man. . . ." And this was three full years before anyone else saw anything wrong.

1987

She knew now beyond question that her father had been right in his suspicions. For several months she, too, had known but had done nothing. At first she simply thought she'd misunderstood what was going on; the whispers of insider trading could not touch this brilliant man. There had to be a mistake, she told herself.

From the beginning she had been puzzled by his ability to make brilliant decisions based on data available to everyone and on his own intuition. Working with the same facts, she herself could not reach the conclusions that came so easily to him. Like some kind of mystic, he would reach out from his aerie high above the street and pick the stocks that would make tomorrow's gains.

As she became more experienced herself, the doubt began to creep into her mind. She knew she was very good at this business, but she couldn't imagine making so few mistakes and pulling off so many coups. But as his confidence in her grew, he became more open with her, until that day when she sat in his office waiting to speak to him.

When he hung up the phone his eyes glittered with excitement."Quick, E. B., North Hill Industries. Buy."

"But why?" she asked. "They're dead in the water right now—the supercomputer business is slowing, and they haven't diversified sufficiently to develop a secure base."

"They've made a breakthrough in artificial intelligence. It will be announced next week. The stock is at a record low, so we can pick up a big block of it legitimately just on the basis of price-earnings ratio."

"But how do you know this? Who told you?"

"Don't ask silly questions, E. B. Just get on the phone and get busy."

Insider trading. The dreaded words echoed in her mind. He had a source inside the company. "Walter, I can't make a buy on the basis of insider information, you know that. Can you assure me that's not what this is?"

"E. B., don't pretend to be naive. It doesn't suit you. You know perfectly well this is a business based on information, and none of us would be worth a damn if we didn't have our sources. Of course I got a tip from a friend inside, and he'll make some money on it as well. It's only fair."

"But it's against the law—if you get caught . . ."

"I won't. Nor will you." He turned away and picked up a telephone, effectively dismissing her.

For several nights she scarcely slept, trying to decide what she should do. If she left her job, she would have to explain why, but to report her mentor to the SEC? To tear him down . . . how could she do that? Not only that—careful questioning made it clear that her associates knew the truth and were perfectly comfortable with it.

"E. B.," one of them said to her, "you can play it any way you like. But this is a tough market, and everyone needs some kind of an edge. You're lucky—you're smarter than the rest of us, and maybe you're not in a hurry. But you'll find most of us need that edge to make it, and it doesn't hurt anyone."

She didn't argue, but she knew that even if this was the way everyone else on Wall Street did business, she couldn't bring herself to use an advantage gained in this way. She explained to Walter Lasker that she was just not comfortable with it and would have to excuse herself from transactions based on this type of information.

Lasker stared at her coolly. "Perhaps I made a

mistake in bringing you on, E. B. I don't like people around me who think they're more moral than the rest of us. What gives you the right to judge Wall Street?"

"I'm not pretending to be more moral, Walter, and I'm not judging anyone. I simply have very strong personal feelings about the way I work. And I don't feel right about it. Look, you know I'm performing better than almost anyone else in this office. I'll continue to work at that level. Just bear with me on this, please?"

Lasker agreed, but she knew her position in the firm had been damaged. She was no longer included in the intimate discussions in the great man's office, and she noticed a sudden coolness from her co-workers. But the worst part of it was the growing discomfort she felt about the way Lasker and Company did business and the knowledge that if they really were breaking the law, her silence made her as guilty as the rest of them.

Then the investigations started; the rumors flew. A friend in the media confirmed it; there would be a crackdown on insider trading at the highest levels. She knew she had to go to the SEC right away.

She decided to tell Greg Marinelli what she was planning to do. She had been seeing Greg, a well-known entertainment lawyer, for several months between his trips to the West Coast and her late nights at the office. Greg was the first man who wasn't intimidated by her success. Although they hadn't talked in terms of a permanent relationship, there was a certain seriousness involved that made it important to her that he know and understand what she was planning to do. His reaction shocked her.

"Don't be silly, Ellen. You simply can't do that. You can't get involved."

She stood at the window of his penthouse, looking over the beautiful city below. "I've made a decision," she said firmly. "I haven't done it, but I've condoned it, and I can't live with that any longer. They may never catch up with Walter, and that would make me feel even worse, seeing others destroyed while he sits up there smugly looking down at the fools who play by the rules. I know it will be hard, but I am involved, and I have to take some responsibility for what's happened."

He moved to her side and grasped her shoulders. "Ellen, don't do this. You haven't done anything wrong, and if you go to the SEC over this, you'll destroy your career—your future. I can't let you do it."

She stared at their reflections in the darkening window, his handsome face gazing over her shoulder.

"We make a good couple, Ellen. We can have a wonderful future. Let's not spoil it."

But she refused to give in, and he refused to understand.

She accepted a measure of the blame because of her delay in reporting what she knew; she'd realized she would be censured and perhaps face a heavy fine. But the upheaval created by her actions, the careers destroyed by her testimony, the damage to her own career from which she knew she could never recover—it was all so much harder than she had expected. When it was over she found herself truly alone, with no future.

Oh, yes, she was vindicated to a degree. A slap on the wrist, an expression of gratitude for her honesty in coming forward. Walter Lasker went to prison, but Ellen Brandon Stanwood was locked in a prison of pain and regret, a prison with bars no less strong because they were invisible.

Now she was torn between wishing her father were alive to comfort her and to give her advice, and relief that he'd never known of her failure. If only she'd listened, but New York was so exciting and her own success so heady.

It was only last spring that she'd been featured in *Vogue* magazine as one of the "Women to Watch" in New York. Her long and hectic day was described in detail: the early rising and streamlined beauty routine, the limousine ride to the office while completing early phone calls and paperwork, the business day spent at top speed with brief interludes for supervised fitness routines and care for her signature tawny hair or her nails. The article described in detail the small dinner parties in her new Manhattan co-op; skirted tables in the library for twelve to twenty special friends, flowers and produce chosen especially for her, candlelight gleaming on the Georgian silver, the best vintages from her growing wine cellar.

She shook her head and leaned back against the

airplane seat. They should write about her day now, she thought. She woke up early in Carey Steele's guest room. Carey was one of her few remaining friends—the rest seemed to have disappeared. Most of them had been, after all, business associates. Carey seemed uncomfortable with her—maybe a bit formal—but she had helped and she hadn't openly judged her.

Her toilette today had consisted of a quick shower and a comb through her hair; breakfast of a cup of instant coffee and dry toast. She had glanced only briefly at her reflection in narrow twill slacks and a heavy cashmere pullover before pulling on the creamy leather jacket and dragging her suitcases to a cab heading for Newark Airport to catch a crowded and less-than-comfortable flight west. How strange it had seemed to walk by the passengers in first class; they didn't seem to notice her standing in the aisle. When she rode up front everyone had noticed—and admired her. The flight attendants had hovered, and her fellow passengers stared openly. Could it be that without the power, without the prestige—and the money—she was invisible? Could it be that she was no longer beautiful?

A tear of self-pity tried to squeeze under her closed lids, but she fought it back. I will not feel sorry for myself, she thought. I'm just tired and discouraged. I will treat this trip to Montana as a vacation and a chance to sort out my life. I don't have to *stay* there. After all, I did it once and I can do it again. And *I will*. But for the first time in her life, she felt a small grain of doubt. How could she possibly do it over again, and where?

The sound of the engines changed, and she felt the first indications that the plane was beginning its descent. For most of the trip she had resolutely kept her eyes closed, refusing to eat the artificial-looking breakfast and studiously avoiding contact with her seatmates. She had forgotten how small and cramped the seats were in the rear cabin.

She would be arriving in Billings soon. It was a shame she hadn't had a chance to find out more about the city, since she planned to spend as much time as possible there, away from the ranch. Not that she didn't appreciate her uncle's offer to let her stay there while she was deciding what to do with her life, but a real, working ranch was not her kind of place. She had always shuddered at the thought of vacationing on a dude ranch; she had often joked that horses seemed to her to be little more than an inferior form of transportation and were smelly, not very bright animals to boot. She would be particularly nice to her uncle, and particularly grateful, but would make it clear that the city was more to her taste.

She had not seen John Brandon, her mother's brother, since she was a small child. It was he who had coined the nickname "Brandy" for her when he visited the family in Connecticut one Christmas.

"That little girl has hair just the color of a good old brandy, sis," he had commented. "She's going to be something when she grows into that hair and those green eyes! You're going to have all the boys hangin' round here." From that day until she was a teenager everyone knew her as Brandy, but by the time she was sixteen she had convinced most people to call her Ellen instead, which seemed to her more dignified. The "E. B." nickname, which pleased her with its masculine, businesslike impression had been coined once she hit Wall Street. She had needed to cultivate that kind of image to hold her own in the powerful world into which she had moved.

The FASTEN YOUR SEAT BELTS sign was on now, but Ellen still could see little through the cloud cover. She wondered whether she would recognize the uncle she hadn't seen since she was a small child. John Brandon had been the misfit in his New England family. Why he had insisted on attending college in Montana, no one knew. He had returned east only for brief visits, and those had stopped twenty years ago. She knew he was a rancher in Montana, apparently successful, but little else about him and remembered only that he had always seemed very old. Her mother had told her it was a trick of memory; his hair had gone gray by the time he was thirty, and to a small child gray hair means old.

It seemed strange to her that he had kept up with her career in New York, but when his letter arrived she could only believe someone was watching over her. Her eyes had misted with tears as she read:

Dear Brandy,

   It has been a long time since I've seen you, and I'm sorry I didn't keep in touch with you after your mom and dad died. We're pretty removed from your kind of civilization out here, and I'm afraid I just let time slip by. I was pretty cut up about your mom—

she was my only sister, and I surely do miss her.

It seems to me with all that's been going on back there you might be looking for a place to get away to for a while, and since I'm your only kin, I feel kind of responsible for seeing you're taken care of. Your dad always figured you could take care of yourself just fine, but I figure we all need a hand now and then when things get tough.

I'd be pleased to have you come out to the ranch and stay. It's different from what you're used to, but Montana grows on you, and I think it would be good for you to try something new. Consider it another challenge, if you will. Of course it's also a chance for me to get to know you and make up for all the years I just couldn't take the time away from here to get back east.

Please call and let me know when you can get here. Just pack up and come on right now, if you like. You can leave a message with Hattie, my housekeeper, if I'm not around, and I'll just pick you up in Billings. Bring plenty of casual clothes, because we don't dress up a lot out here. You can always pick up some jeans for riding when you get here.

I can't wait to see you, honey, and show you why I just never did want to leave this place. Maybe you'll feel the same way.

Love,
Your uncle, John Brandon

She had accepted immediately, grabbing at the unexpected chance to escape. The co-op had been sold along with most of the furnishings, and the remainder of her things were put in storage. There didn't seem to be much point in telling anyone she was leaving. Her friends wouldn't be giving her a going-away party, she thought bitterly. She briefly considered telling Greg Marinelli, but she hadn't been ready to face him yet. With a surge of excitement she had decided to make the break clean. It would be a completely new start, with no old friends, no old lovers, no reminders of what had been or what might have been.

Would Greg care? she wondered. Perhaps briefly, before he jetted off on another trip to Hollywood, or London, or Tokyo. A successful entertainment lawyer had plenty of opportunities to meet women, and she had often wondered just how faithful Greg would have been in a serious relationship. He had tried several times in the past few months to reach her, but she'd decided their connection, too, was better cut completely; it was too much a reminder of her past.

As the plane slipped below the clouds at last, she could see only brown hills and a few trees. They seemed to be landing on a flat plateau far from any civilization. She looked inquiringly at the man seated next to her.

"I know." He smiled. "You're wondering where Billings is. We're landing on what they call the rimrock, above town. You could see Billings from the other side of the plane, but it's always startling to someone new. I gather this is your first trip?"

"I've never been in this part of the country," she replied uneasily, "but somehow I expected it to look different. I thought there were more mountains."

"You're thinking about western Montana. It's spectacular country. One of the greatest sights I know is flying over the mountains of western Montana on a sunny fall day. Nothing like it. But this is the east— we're at the edge of the plains right here."

As the 727 sped to a landing, it seemed to be inches from the edge of the rimrock, and she could see the brown hills slipping by. Whatever her uncle saw in this part of the state, it certainly wasn't the scenic beauty.

The airport terminal was small but modern, and it was not until she reached the baggage claim area that she began to notice the people around her. Men in boots and Stetson hats worn even with their western-cut suits, reminded her at first glance of her Texas friends. But there was something different here; the boots were worn, the topstitched jackets more serviceable than well cut, and the women's clothes had a small-town look about them. As she pointed out her Louis Vuitton luggage to the skycap she realized people were staring at her, and as she passed a small group of people waiting near the exit door she overheard:

"They doing another movie here?"

"Naw, not that I heard of."

The rest of the conversation was lost to her.

On the ride down into Billings she checked her uncle's note once again. He said he was in a meeting at the Northern Hotel and asked her to take the hotel shuttle there.

For fifteen minutes she watched and waited for a sight of downtown Billings. From the airport she had seen enough of the town to know that she would not find here the high-rise buildings of the big cities, but she had seen many smaller cities with revitalized downtown cores that were extremely livable and had developed excellent cultural facilities.

When the van pulled up in front of the hotel entrance and she saw only the drab facades of an older city center, with a very few new buildings, she began to wonder if perhaps she should have checked further before making the trip. She ignored the men who tipped their hats as she entered the building and wondered fleetingly why the older woman leaving the hotel had smiled and said hello. She was used to ignoring overfriendly men, but perhaps these people thought she looked like someone they knew.

The lobby was small but comfortable, and she sank gratefully onto a chair to wait for her uncle. The long flight had been more tiring than usual. She closed her eyes briefly but looked up when she heard her name.

"Miss Stanwood?" She smiled at the young desk clerk who stood looking down at her. "Your uncle asked us to watch for you. He'll be down in a few minutes. Can I get you a cup of coffee while you wait?"

"How nice of you. How much is it?"

The young woman waved her purse aside. "It's on us, Miss Stanwood. We promised Mr. Brandon we'd take care of you, and I wouldn't want to let him down."

As she sat drinking her coffee and watching the passersby, Ellen began to wonder just how many people had been told she was coming. Almost everyone who passed nodded or said hello.

A loud voice interrupted her thoughts. "Brandy— Brandy, honey. Sorry I'm late, but the governor just really wanted to get this stuff done before he went back to Helena." A tall, heavyset, white-haired man with weathered features pulled her from her chair and gave her a hug. "Don't look so startled, honey. Don't you even recognize your uncle? I knew you the minute I laid eyes on that hair. My gosh, it's good to see you." He beamed down at her.

She felt her eyes fill with tears. "Uncle John," she said shakily, "it's wonderful to see you, and really kind of you to invite me. I was feeling pretty depressed when I got your first letter."

He hugged her again briefly. "That's what relatives are for, Brandy. I just hope you'll be glad you came."

She felt her own doubts rise to the surface as she recalled the discouraging sights during the ride into town, the obvious isolation of even this community—the biggest city in the state—and the prospect of being totally out of touch with the world she knew.

"We'd better take off right away," her uncle said. "I've got some work to finish up before supper, and it'll take us a couple of hours to get there."

Her heart sank; she was to be even farther from civilization than she imagined. "Two hours?" she asked in disbelief.

"Well," her uncle replied with a grin, "that's if I push the ol' gas pedal through the floor and don't meet any state troopers. Conservative folks usually figure around two and a half."

It was with a sense of resignation and the beginnings of despair that she watched her luggage being placed in the back of a dusty pickup truck and covered with an old tarp. She climbed up to the high bench seat and tried to smile, but she kept visualizing the scratches and nicks that each bump in the road would probably add to her lovely bags, which were scraping across the dirty truck bed as they turned the first corner and headed for Highway 94, her uncle talking nonstop.

By the time they reached the highway, she had begun to resign herself to being called "Brandy" again. After all, she had seriously considered a new name. As annoying to her as this one had been, it at least was familiar.

he old International Harvester pickup jolted along the four-lane interstate. Ellen felt numbed by the utter foreignness of her surroundings, different not only from what she was accustomed to, but from all of her expectations.

She found the landscape oddly disturbing. Billings and the small towns that followed shocked her, not in the way she feared the slums of the East, but in their desolation—the feeling that they had been lost somewhere along the way and had no relevance to today's world. And the vegetation was so sparse.

Mostly she noticed the lack of color—everything seemed the same dull gray brown. As they passed by little towns and lone houses, the green squares of manicured lawns stood out in harsh contrast with the brownness that seemed to be everywhere and to permeate everything.

The dust eddied and whirled, sometimes picking up enough energy to form what her uncle called a "dust devil." There were rocks everywhere, grow-

ing up out of the fields and heaped by the roadside. If a rock was big enough and had the right
shape, it would be doing duty as a fence pole,
wrapped with barbed wire as if it were another
piece of wood.

She found herself exhilarated yet horrified by
this strange brown land, by its immensity and
emptiness. And as if the land weren't enough—
stretching out forever—the sky was infinite. There
were no mountains, or hills, or trees on the horizon that could limit it. She felt surrounded by sky.
Not only was it above her and lapping at the horizon, but she felt that if she looked down at the
ground just right, she would see it lapping at the
roadside.

They'd been on the road the better part of an
hour. Since they'd reached the interstate Uncle
John hadn`t said much; he didn't seem to think
she needed to be entertained, and she was grateful.
She didn't want to deal with the questions she'd
been afraid he would ask. She didn't have answers
ready, and she didn't feel like probing the pain
inside herself to find them just yet.

The truck lumbered off the interstate at a dusty
little town called Custer, where her uncle pulled
into a gas station. The endless dust tasted thick on
her tongue. The windows were rolled down
because there was no air-conditioning in the old
truck.

"Real men don't need air-conditioning," said a
glum voice in the back of her mind. Looking at the
accumulation of grit on the dashboard, she decided that it might be less dusty outside, and perhaps

the meager offerings of this place might include a drinking fountain. She opened the door and climbed down stiffly.

The dust was still bad, but the sunshine and warm, dry air felt good. Uncle John was talking and laughing with several men in the garage. Not for the first time that day did Ellen feel that she was conspicuously overdressed. She didn't feel up to being sociable and was hoping to crawl back into the truck unnoticed when Uncle John's booming voice called to her.

"Brandy!"

The thought flashed through her mind that if she didn't respond to this childhood nickname, she could kill two birds with one stone. Uncle John would learn not to call her that and she could avoid meeting the old men who were staring at her curiously. But her innate good manners—and her realization that she was probably stuck with the nickname for the time being—won out. Steeling herself for the worst, she walked over to the group.

"Brandy, I want you to meet some ol' friends of mine. This here's Mike Jaraczewski, his partner Marty Pajaczek, and their loyal customer, Pat Quinn."

"Loyal customer! Hell! He hasn't bought a thing from us in years. Gramps, you know that Pat hangs around here for all the free pop, free cigarettes, and charmin' company."

"Hell," the short man countered, "I earn ever'thin' I git, managing this place for free while you two go gallivantin' all around town! Someone's gotta work around here."

They all laughed and shook her hand in turn, each wiping a grimy paw on his jeans before reaching out to her. All wore the same dirty Levi's, belted not around the waist but rather low on their hips in what appeared to be the local style.

They asked her about New York City. Was it really that big? Was this her first glimpse of "God's country"? What did she think of Montana so far? Loaded questions, all of them. They seemed to take it for granted that the only reason she was here was because she had "come to her senses," realized that the "big city" wasn't the place for a smart "gal" to be. She certainly couldn't tell them that the only reason she'd come to this windy, dust-laden, barren, unpopulated land was that she'd messed up her life so badly that the city she loved, the life she loved, was probably lost to her forever.

She looked at the men laughing and joking, asking her questions, not waiting for answers. They were all about Uncle John's age or a few years older. Their faces were heavily lined, their hands gnarled and dirty. She suspected that a fingernail brush would meet its ultimate challenge here. Was this what life in "God's country" did to a man? They all looked scoured by the dust and weather. Uncle John didn't show it quite so much, but then perhaps he was a few years younger than the rest, or maybe life had been a little kinder to him. It seemed odd that men who appeared to be his elders called him "Gramps."

She noticed he was watching her; he obviously sensed her distaste for his friends. Everyone was so damn friendly out here! She wasn't used to it, and her discomfort made her want to withdraw even more. She could not imagine ever changing so much that she could be openly friendly with strangers.

"Gramps" announced that it was time to move on. She shook three dirty hands good-bye, felt several strong claps across her shoulders, smiled weakly, and hurried back to the protection of the truck.

The interstate had had a few rough spots, but the gravel road on which they now traveled made her realize she had judged it too harshly. Her uncle dodged the potholes at fifty miles per hour, banked the left-hand turns by crossing to the side of the road, and occasionally slowed down for a jarring experience he described as "washboard." These were narrow ruts that ran across the road in groups of what Ellen estimated to be about seventy-five or a hundred, maybe a thousand at times.

He noticed her nervousness on the turns and smiled. "Brandy, relax. With the dust that gets kicked up you can see an oncoming vehicle for miles."

But there hadn't been any oncoming vehicles for what seemed like hours. Were there no people?

She glanced at her uncle. Perhaps she should have been friendlier to those men; she didn't like to think of herself as a snob. Until now the thought hadn`t really crossed her mind.

"Tell me about ranching," she said to fill the silence that now struck her as too long.

"That's a pretty tall order. What do you want to know?"

"I don't know," she said. "I'm embarrassed to admit I know almost nothing about it, not even what questions to ask. Although I'm certainly well aware that farmers are having serious financial problems, and that the family farm is becoming a life-style of the past."

Her uncle was silent for a moment. "In a sense that's true. Like anything else, farming and ranching must adapt to the changes in technology as well as to the changes in demand. I've tried to do that. Fortunately, I've been around a long time. I was able to acquire plenty of acreage at a good price, years ago. Enough land to support plenty of head of cattle.

"Basically, I have two herds. One herd I use just for beef production. The other herd, considerably smaller, I use for breeding. Artificial insemination has revolutionized ranching. It's amazing what can be done these days, and what's within our grasp. It's important to breed for the most efficient type of cattle possible."

Ellen realized she had asked a question that required an answer much bigger than her interest in the topic. She struggled silently for another comment.

"It must be a lot of work to keep track of all those animals—do you really keep records on all of them?" she finally asked.

"Thank God for computers!" her uncle replied, nodding. "We know which cows are the best mothers, which ones bear the most calves, which calves are likely to be the best bulls, which should be steers. Every single head has its own personal file. Between documenting everything and feeding the beasts, we have more than enough to keep us busy all year long."

She'd had no idea that there could be that much involved in taking care of a few potential steaks. Obviously genuine ranching was much more complex than that portrayed by television ranchers like the Cartwrights of "Bonanza."

"Do you do all this yourself?"

"No, I have a manager, Jake Milburn, who's my right arm. I don't know what I'd do without that boy. He enjoys tracking all this stuff on the computer. He manages the feeding, the haying, everything. I've put in a lot of long hours over the years, and it's nice to be able to afford someone like Jake so I can do something besides work now and then. He's a strange duck, but he sure knows his job."

Thankful for the chance to change the subject, she asked, "What's strange about him?"

"Oh, nothing really, I suppose. He's just different. Kind of quiet and more withdrawn than we're used to. Most folks here just 'are'—it's hard to explain. But I suppose it's that they seem to be part of the scenery, part of the land. Jake always seems to be on the outside looking in."

"Do you have other employees?"

"Yep. I have a chief cook and bottle washer, Hattie. Been here for years. Used to be she'd come and cook only during the summers when things were jumpin', but like I said, I'm getting older and spoiled—it's nice to have someone takin' care of the house and garden and such full-time.

"Then I have three other men who help. Jake pretty much tells them what needs to be done. Duke and Tom are both married. Their wives work in Mosby, they run a little cafe. Joe's single, probably always will be. He's new, a hard worker, but I think he's pretty much a drifter. You'll meet 'em all tonight. During the summer Hattie cooks dinner for all of us. She likes to feed a crowd."

They drove on in silence. Ellen stuck her hand outside the window and let it play with the cool air currents, then caught herself being childlike and immediately withdrew the errant hand.

Uncle John slowed the truck enough to make a sharp turn onto another gravel road. "We're almost there," he announced.

Originally she had imagined a huge old farmhouse surrounded by trees, or perhaps a large log home. Now she was painfully aware that no matter what form the ranch house took, it would not be surrounded by—or built of—trees. There were some trees along the river that they had been following until recently, but those not obviously planted for windbreaks were sparse and scrubby.

"Well, here we are," her uncle said, and she steeled herself for the worst.

The truck slowed for one last turn and followed a dirt road down a narrow draw. They turned a corner around a hill, and there it sat.

Definitely not "Dallas," she thought ruefully. The sprawling ranch house was faced with grimy white aluminum siding and trimmed with the most disgusting color of salmon pink she had ever seen. There had been some attempts at creating decorative flower beds in the front yard, which was more dirt than grass. The flower beds were marked by two big circles of rocks, painted alternately red, white, and blue; the red and blue rocks had a strange metallic gleam to them. In the center of the rock circles were wooden wagon wheels painted white and standing upright. The flowers hadn't done too well; there were some straggly daisylike things that seemed to have survived despite an obvious lack of care.

As the truck swung around to a side door, however, she noticed a vegetable garden out back—it reminded her of one that her parents had when she was little—that obviously had rated much better care, a clear demonstration of priorities. There was a barn beyond the garden that apparently had been painted the traditional red around 1950. On the other side of the garden, opposite the barn, were two trailers, double wide, she later learned. This was where Duke and Tom lived with their wives, Uncle John pointed out. The cabin where Jake lived was beyond a trailer and screened by a stack of hay bales.

She stepped down from the truck and stood blinking, trying to adjust her mental picture to the reality of a modern working ranch.

This was to be her home for the next few months. She couldn't repress a shudder.

Hattie was the first member of the Rocking B family she met. Short, plump, and weathered, with hair a suspicious jet black, Hattie greeted her at the door with a pleasant smile but a critical eye. She was the first person Ellen had encountered in the West who didn't seem overly friendly.

From the minute the two women were introduced, Ellen knew she was on trial.

"Well, let's show you around and get you settled. You can meet everyone else at supper."

As she followed Hattie on a quick tour of the house, she was pleasantly surprised to find it totally different from the garish, tasteless exterior. The furnishings were shabby but comfortable, and the few paintings and prints appeared to be good quality. It was far different from her own tastes, clearly a man's home, but one in which she found herself surprisingly at ease.

Hattie opened the door to a bedroom at the back of the house. "Here's your room. You'll have lots of privacy here and your own bath. There's extra towels in the linen closet down the hall. If you have any questions, be sure and ask either me or Gramps. I'll leave you here. You'll probably want to shower and take a quick nap before dinner."

Her tone was brusque, but Ellen was too tired to be concerned. A warm shower was the first and only thing on her mind at the moment. She tried to sound as friendly as possible. "Yes, thanks, that's exactly what I need."

Ellen methodically and dazedly unpacked her suitcase, then took a shower. The hot water and soap seemed to wash away her exhaustion as well as the grit accumulated from the trek from Billings. She leaned back under the shower head and let herself—body and soul—become immersed. She let her mind go blank. "Hydrotherapy," a friend in college had called it. Nothing like a good hot shower to provide an easy escape from the world, for at least a few minutes.

She dried her hair, pulled it back, and changed into clean slacks and a silk shirt. The shower had washed away the weariness she'd felt when Hattie had suggested a nap. Now, restless and filled with curiosity, she began to explore her new surroundings.

Her room was modestly furnished and decorated. It certainly wasn't what she was accustomed to, but it was comfortable as a temporary retreat. The wide open spaces and lack of nearby neighbors allowed for the luxury of a big picture window at the east end of the room. Ellen opened the curtains and was struck by the view. The harsh brown rolling hills extended forever under that immense blue sky, hard and featureless as the land. The room had been arranged so that the window was the focal point; she could even lie in her bed and look out in the mornings. She shuddered at the idea and quickly pulled the curtains closed.

By the window stood a big rocking chair. It was an ugly chair by anyone's standards, coated with so many layers of dark varnish that the original wood was invisible. But it had wide armrests and a thick green cushion, and it was actually extremely comfortable. It would be a good place for reading, she thought to herself.

All the furniture in the room appeared to have been bought secondhand after hard use—the wood cried out for a good stripping, sanding, and varnishing. Only the clean white of the walls and the big window kept the room from looking like a cheap, old hotel room. The bed was double-size, and the linens looked crisp and new, probably purchased especially for her. A beautiful handmade quilt with bright colors in a pattern of interlocking rings hung over the bed. She had seen that pattern somewhere before—what was it called? It had a name she thought she ought to know somehow.

A large mirror hung above the dresser, and by tilting it back and standing away from it she could get a good full-length view of herself. Even in this casual outfit she felt a little overdressed for her surroundings. "Well," she said to her reflection, "at least you won't have to worry about looking like the locals. Thank God." She shook her head and headed out to explore the rest.

It was a long, rambling ranch-style house. The guest room—Ellen's bedroom—was at the far end, isolated from the main living areas. The walls of the long hallway that led from her room to the living room were covered with framed photographs in a gallery of Brandon family and friends. Cheap drugstore frames bordered nameless faces—weathered, wrinkled, Montana faces. There was her uncle's wedding picture. Brandy couldn't remember ever meeting her aunt Anne. She did remember her mother telling her, in a rare moment of confidence, that Anne had died a few years after the wedding and John had never totally gotten over her. Killed, like her parents, in a tragic auto accident.

She rarely let herself think about the accident or her parents. She missed her father most of all, and the memory of losing him was still painful. She had never been very close to her mother, and now and then she felt guilty that she felt so little sense of loss. Snap out of it! she commanded herself. Nothing could bring her parents back, and there was no point in dwelling on the past.

As she turned away to forge ahead with her exploration, she glanced at the opposite wall and gasped. There was a wedding portrait of her parents. In the black-and-white photograph her father looked as distinguished in his youth as he had in middle age with a successful career and a successful daughter. Even then her mother looked the part of a typical wife, mother, and homemaker, seeming to blend into the background beside her husband. The dutiful wife, Brandy thought, and felt a twinge of annoyance.

Too many memories here. She had enough problems without dwelling on the past. She walked briskly down the hall to the living room.

Here, too, the furnishings were designed with comfort in mind, and other than a disturbing view from a picture window of the gardens ringed with the gaudy metallic blue and red rocks, and the enormous fireplace of soot-blackened stone in the wall facing it, the room was pretty nondescript.

Something about the fireplace caught Ellen's eye. It apparently served a dual purpose, for there was a room on the other side that she could see through the open back of the grate. Curious, she pushed open the door that stood ajar and peered into the room.

Now this was more like it. It must be Uncle John's study, she thought. The big stone fireplace looked so much more inviting on this side of the wall. This was a man's room. Bookcases lined most of the walls, and an old Charles Russell print hung over the wet bar. In one corner a personal computer had been installed next to the gray metal filing cabinets. Another of the big windows faced the ubiquitous prairie, the view unobstructed by dusty driveways and dingy flower gardens. There was a big writing table at the window with an old oak office chair padded with time-darkened red leather. This obviously was where her uncle spent most of his time. Ellen inhaled the room's atmosphere: old leather, a little tobacco, and dusty books. Certainly not anything like the offices she had occupied on Wall Street, but strangely familiar and comforting.

Her thoughts were shattered by the clang of a

fiercely shaken cowbell. "Come on," Hattie yelled, "soup's on!" With a grimace Ellen made her way toward the sound of the dinner bell.

She was surprised to find the dining room empty and hear voices echoing from the back of the house. She stood staring around her, however, transfixed by the absolute ugliness. The room was dominated by a huge round oak table squatting on massive legs, its wild grain darkened by age and years of waxing. What a monstrosity, she thought—the only thing she'd ever seen that was uglier was the sideboard. It was a close contest, but the huge unwieldy piece against the wall was definitely the winner.

"Brandy?" The sound of her uncle's voice behind her made her jump. "Oh, there you are. Get settled all right?"

"Yes, thanks, Uncle John. I heard the dinner bell and . . ." She gestured at the dining room.

"Awful, isn't it." Her uncle laughed. "You don't have to be polite. Nobody likes this room, so we eat in the kitchen. This place is too cold in the winter unless you've got a lot of bodies in here, and it's hotter than blazes in the summer. And the dining room `suite,' as they used to call it, was a gift from Anne's grandmother. She must have ordered it from a Sears catalog about nineteen aught something. Thought she was doing us a favor giving it to us, and true, we did need furniture, so we laughed about the old thing and didn't have the heart to tell her how much we disliked it.

"These days we're not too formal around here anyway, so we use this room for Christmas dinners and parties when we can open up the table and hide the old thing with some decorations. Ought to get rid of it, I guess, but every time I look at it I think of Anne and the jokes we made about it. I still get a chuckle out of them."

The others were waiting for them in the eating area attached to the kitchen, gathering around a big scrubbed pine table. After the oppressive air of the dining room, anything would have looked good to Ellen, but the kitchen really was a pleasant surprise. The yellow-and-orange gingham curtains and the bright place mats gave a cheery air to the large, functional room.

Clearly this was Hattie's domain; the woman's touches absent in the rest of the house were everywhere here, from the gay pot holders hanging on the big electric stove to the fruit-shaped magnets on the refrigerator. Against one wall was an enormous old wood-burning stove, its black surfaces and shiny chromed doors looking as if they received a daily polishing.

"It roasts the best turkey in the world, and it keeps this place warm in the winter," came a gruff comment. Hattie seemed to have eyes in the back of her head.

"Sometimes Hattie actually cooks a Sunday chicken in there, or an apple pie. 'Course, it's been a while, Hattie," a deep voice drawled. Its owner appeared beside Ellen and was introduced as Duke. Then she was introduced to the rest of the crew, including Duke's and Tom's wives, Patsy and Bobbie, and Jake.

It was at this point that Ellen finally took a deep

breath and resigned herself to answering to the name "Brandy." She was too tired of explaining. After all, she thought, she had given some consideration to a name change. Not this one, but she appeared to be stuck with it for the time being.

Brandy wasn't surprised by the questions about the "big city" and "How do you like God's country?" from this bunch. She had realized by now that people didn't really care to hear the answers; they were just making a point.

When the initial assault of questions had subsided, Ellen relaxed on her chair and let the conversation wash over her, grateful for the respite. The rest of the group were discussing the day's happenings and local gossip while Hattie clattered around the big kitchen.

The cafe where Patsy and Bobbie worked apparently served as a clearinghouse for news concerning the neighbors. And it was obvious from the excitement in Patsy's high-pitched, nasal voice that the bad news was what she particularly enjoyed. When Tom mentioned that he'd heard the Smiths were planning on taking a Caribbean cruise at Christmas, Patsy snorted and shook her head.

"Them folks is all talk. You'd believe anything, Tom."

Tom retreated into silence and remained mute for the rest of the evening.

Duke kept right on in his slow drawl, oblivious of the reactions of his listeners. He regaled them with a full description of the Smiths' new tractor, which actually seemed to interest her uncle and Jake.

Brandy tried not to glance at her watch too obviously, but she had rarely been this bored. The other women were keeping up their inane chatter at their end of the table, but Brandy was more interested in analyzing the men and their conversations.

Tom was sandy-haired with hazel eyes, slight of build, and well muscled. His faded coloring and quiet manner combined to make him seem almost invisible. Probably protective coloration designed to keep his sharp-tongued wife from noticing him, she thought.

Duke was big and affable, slightly overweight and sloppy in a pair of baggy Levi's and an old checked shirt. A worn, grayed undershirt showed through the gap left by missing buttons. He laughed at his own jokes a great deal, providing his audience with startling flashes of gold. Brandy had never seen so many gold crowns in one mouth.

Bobbie, Duke's wife, had mousy brown hair framing a pale face with listless gray eyes; she looked like a female counterpart to Tom.

But the person who intrigued Brandy was Jake Milburn, the ranch manager. When her uncle had described him as "a strange duck," she had assumed his appearance was strange, but nothing was further from the truth. She had never encountered a man with so much raw animal magnetism, yet he seemed completely unaware of her. He rarely entered the conversation but nodded and smiled to indicate his interest.

His face, neck, and forearms were browned by the weather, and the strong muscles of his shoulders and chest were apparent even under the denim shirt he wore—denim that almost matched the intense blue of his eyes. There were flecks of gray in his wavy dark hair and sun wrinkles at the corners of his eyes, but the strong, chiseled face was clearly that of a man in his prime.

She realized she was staring at him when his gaze turned to meet hers, and the piercing gaze brought a hot blush to her cheeks. She found herself smiling self-consciously and looked away. She was annoyed with herself, particularly because she felt not only a repulsion at his raw maleness, but also an odd and compelling attraction.

Hattie called, "Okay, gang, come and get it," and Bobbie jumped up and scurried in to help. The others halted their conversation. Suddenly Brandy had a feeling she was being watched.

Across the table, Joe, the other hired hand, was leering at her openly. When she returned his gaze, his crooked smile broadened and his eyes rested on her breasts for a moment, then returned to her face to complete an obvious appraisal.

She was furious; this sallow, unpleasant-looking man had practically undressed her with his eyes, publicly. She felt dirty—but no one else seemed even to have noticed.

Platters and bowls of food suddenly were slammed down on the table in front of her, and her heart sank. Overcooked canned vegetables, mounds of fried potatoes, and a whole platter of Wonder bread greeted her dismayed look. This can't be real, she thought; people don't really eat like this.

She was hungry but could identify nothing edible with the possible exception of some green beans, and they were definitely marginal. She could not imagine forcing down the gelatin with fruit cocktail or the commercially baked white bread. Surely there must have been a problem in the kitchen tonight.

The fragrance of cooking beef reminded her that Montana beef was supposed to be among the best, but it had been so long since she'd had red meat that she didn't think her stomach would know how to deal with it. Five years ago she had eliminated red meat from her diet and since then had relied on beans, fish, and occasionally chicken for protein.

She began a distracted reply to Bobbie's question about the weather in New York but was halted in midsentence as Hattie dropped a gigantic T-bone steak on her dinner plate with an audible plop. It was obviously on the rare side of medium, still sizzling from the grill and dripping with red juices.

"Actually," she began nervously, "I was just planning on eating some of the vegetables here on the table. I don't eat red meat." Everyone turned to look at her; the silence was deafening. She rushed to fill the silence with an explanation. "It's really not good for you." The words were out of her mouth before she could stop them.

"Just vegetables!" Hattie barked. "Girl, this is Montana's finest. Meat doesn't get any better than this."

"But, you see, I don't eat red meat," Brandy repeated.

An uncomfortable silence settled over the table.

She knew she didn't dare explain to them how unhealthful this type of high-fat, cholesterol-laden meat was, but they ought to respect her right to refuse to poison her system with it.

"Brandy, give it a try. I think you'll like it." Uncle John's voice was gentle but firm. His look told her there was no room for argument. She proceeded to cut the slab into bite-size chunks.

As she forced herself to eat, the others at the table accompanied her with loud conversation, lip smacking, and occasional belches. They ate with elbows on the table, talked with mouths open and grease glistening on their chins. Even the women burped daintily between their giggles.

Jake Milburn ate quietly, apparently ignoring her, but when she caught the flash of his blue eyes she had the feeling he was laughing at her. Her cheeks burned as she poked at the reddish meat and now and then reluctantly ate a small piece under Hattie's unrelenting gaze.

Brandy could scarcely keep herself from getting sick.

*B*y the time she excused herself and returned to her room, she was exhausted, irritable, and slightly nauseated. She could almost feel the reaction of her stomach when the heavy food hit it.

She kicked off her shoes and sat dejectedly on the edge of the bed. I'm not going to be able to take this, she thought. She lay back and closed her eyes for a minute.

What was wrong with these people? They acted as if there were something odd about her, as if she weren't normal . . . she, of all people. She'd always been a perfectly normal, well-adjusted.

Her eyelids began to droop. She was suddenly so tired. Was someone calling her? A faint voice she could barely hear. . . .

"Brandy? . . . Brandy Stanwood, will you please come here right now!"

Her mother's steps clicked closer down the long hallway, but Brandy scrunched her eleven-year-old body deeper into the big leather chair and continued to read.

"Brandy, I told you to go outside and get some fresh air." Her mother stood in the study doorway, hands on her hips, her pale face disapproving. "You've been shut up in here all morning, and it's a beautiful day. Now go outside and play—I saw Tommy and Pam heading down to the park, and I'm sure they'd love to see you."

"Mmm. Probably." She continued to turn the pages slowly, absorbed in the story. Her mother reached down and grabbed the book, snapping it shut.

"You lost my place," Brandy wailed. "I was just getting to the best part."

"Out. I want you dressed and outside in five minutes, young lady, and no more sass."

Brandy sighed. She stood up and pulled her robe around her and marched with head high, anger in every step, to her room.

Five minutes later she stood at the back door, heavy hair held back with a headband, wearing denim shorts and a loose sweatshirt.

"May I go now?"

"Yes." Her mother smiled. "Be back by five, please."

"Where's Dad? Is he going to the office?"

"Don't even think about it. It's Saturday afternoon and you should be out playing. So scoot."

Brandy sauntered around the side of the house, looked carefully back toward the kitchen, and ran quickly around the side of the detached garage. She peeked out; her mother hadn't seen her. She made her way through the tall grass along the side yard fence to the back of the garage and from there ran toward the house to the huge oak tree that shaded the breakfast room. She climbed quickly into its branches and settled herself in the juncture of a huge limb and the broad trunk.

The perfect observation point. From here, screened by the heavy foliage, she could see the garage and driveway perfectly, but she was invisible. From under the loose sweatshirt she pulled a heavy book and looked at it with satisfaction. *The Power and the Dream* by William Manchester. Such a good book—so much better than fiction; fiction was so pointless, after all. Who cared about silly stories when there was so much to learn?

She had read for around a half hour when a noise below caught her attention. Peering through the leaves, she spotted her father, briefcase in hand, walking toward the garage.

"Dad. Psst, Dad. Wait up." She shinned quickly down from her perch, book in hand. "I've been waiting for you—are we going to the office now?"

"Sure, kitten. You going to bring something to read?"

"No, I'd rather help you today. Can I work on the books for you again?"

The two of them walked arm in arm to the garage. As Brandy's father backed the car out, she turned and looked toward the house. Her mother stood in the kitchen doorway, staring after them.

Brandy gave her a brief wave and a smile of victory before turning back to her father, but he didn't seem to notice the figure in the doorway.

I'm going to be just like him when I grow up. I wish I was grown up now so no one could tell me what to do. I hate people telling me what to do. When I'm grown up I'll never ever have to listen to anyone again. I'll do exactly what I want all the time.

She smiled happily, imagining that wonderful time when she would be in complete control of her life. Life wasn't too bad now, actually, but it would get better—she knew it would.

As an adult, Brandy had learned the hard truth and was learning more unpleasant lessons every day. That miserable first dinner at the ranch set the stage for the evenings that followed. By her third day she began to dread dinnertime. Her uncle, Hattie, and Jake were the only ones who chewed their food with their mouths closed. Brandy would avoid looking at people as they ate, trying to keep her stomach from rebelling. The talk always revolved around the boring details of ranch life or the personal trials and tribulations of people she didn't know and whom, after hearing from Patsy and Bobbie the most personal details of their lives, she didn't care to know. Unfortunately it seemed that they were all related to one another, and soon she felt she knew the dirty secrets of every family in eastern Montana.

At first Brandy tried to steer the conversation away from tractors and local gossip. Thinking that clothes would be a safe topic to engage the women, she spoke up on her third night. "That's a pretty blouse you're wearing, Patsy. The color looks good on you." Patsy eyed her suspiciously, and Brandy became acutely aware of her own casual sueded silk blouse.

"Yeah," Patsy replied, "I got it at that place next door to the diner—the Town and Country. Of course, they ain't a big fancy department store. Selection i'n't great, but it's all real nice stuff. You wouldn't find anything *you'd* wear there." Turning to Bobbie, she added, "You wouldn't believe who I saw in Town and Country yesterday. Mary Harris's boy. Selling shoes. He's the first one in that family to get and hold a respectable job. Lila, the store manager, says he's doing real good, but you know those Harrises. Remember when . . ."

Brandy sighed and gave up for the evening.

The next night, since clothes didn't work with the women, she thought she might try state politics with the men to see if that would get them off the ongoing subjects of tractors and cattle. She brought up an article she had read in the *Billings Gazette* about the shocking behavior of a municipal court judge in the town of Wolf Point.

"How can he get away with that?" she said, honestly curious. "Granted, he isn't breaking laws, but disparaging people's parents, threatening to jail everyone on staff when he gets angry, letting drunk drivers off. How does he manage to get elected year after year? He's obviously crazy!"

Bobbie burst in, "I don't see where you can talk about folks here. It don't sound to me like your New York politicians are so lily white."

Duke's laughter immediately broke the tension. "Brandy, you got a lot to learn. The judge's family's been here since before Montana gained state-hood. If he's telling some fool in the court that he's going to get a big fine because the judge remembers the guy's father in the same courtroom twenty years ago for the same offense, no one's going to argue. Chances are, half the town agrees with the judge."

"You know, I knew his niece years ago. . . ."

Brandy couldn't believe her ears; it was Uncle John joining in the regaling of the local folk history. Did everything boil down to who was related to whom? Whatever happened to world events? Brandy felt she was being engulfed by a provincialism so narrow she could scarcely breathe.

One night she finally stumbled on a topic that had nothing to do with tractors or local gossip. Tom commented in passing that Saturday night he was planning on settling down into his easy chair with a good book.

Brandy's heart jumped. A kindred spirit, she thought. She supposed she had judged Tom too harshly when she'd decided that he had little to contribute.

"Tom," she began in a confidential tone, "I love to read, too. What have you read lately?"

Unfortunately it turned out Tom lived and breathed Louis L'Amour and Zane Grey. He'd read hundreds of books in the genre. He began to tell her about not just the most recent, but all of his favorite books, which appeared to Brandy to be variations on the same plot. No one had ever asked him about his books before, and Tom was so grateful to have an eager listener that he failed to notice that Brandy's eyes had glazed over in the first five minutes of his answer and that she was nodding and murmuring, "Mmm-hmm," to her mashed potatoes.

Brandy hadn't had time over the past few years to read even good fiction. Her single-minded pursuit of success allowed her little time to read for pleasure. She tried to be polite and listen patiently as Tom described some of his particular favorites. Brandy realized that he was as interested in the lives of the nonexistent people in these books as the others were in the dull and virtually nonexistent lives of the Rocking B's neighbors.

As this thought occurred to her she happened to look up at Jake sitting across the table. He had said little to her in the days since her arrival. He'd smile and nod politely, but he rarely spoke. At first she thought he was shy and tongue-tied, uncomfortable in the presence of a beautiful woman. Now she realized that he was simply observing her. There he sat, smug amusement dancing in his blue eyes, as she was being relentlessly anesthetized by Tom's ramblings. He was really enjoying himself watching her struggle. She felt herself flush with anger.

She excused herself from the table and carried her dishes out to the kitchen. As she turned to retreat to her room, she found Jake standing beside her.

"Give it time," he said. His voice was gentle and his eyes were dancing. "Don't try so hard."

Brandy would have been calmed by the voice alone, but the dancing eyes and the sheer power of his maleness left her feeling oddly off balance.

"I beg your pardon?" she said.

"Don't work so hard. They'll let you in soon enough."

The nerve of this man, assuming she felt left out, taking it upon himself to give her unwanted advice.

"Thanks. But I can take care of myself. Even if you do find my behavior so amusing." She stormed out of the room.

Angry as his meddling made her, she subconsciously tried to follow his advice in the following weeks. She bit her tongue often, didn't jump into or begin conversations. Still, try as she might she just couldn't fit in, and to be honest, she didn't want to. The problem was trying to get along with everyone without having to fit in.

She had spent too many years asserting herself in a world dominated by powerful men. She knew that often it would have been better for her to keep her mouth shut, especially when Tom's wife, Patsy, would voice an opinion designed to irritate her. Usually these remarks had something to do with easterners being overeducated, snobbish, and appallingly helpless when stranded "out here where books and knowin' the right people aren't goin' to do you a lick of good."

Occasionally Brandy would respond with a remark about cowboys surviving in Manhattan, but her responses seemed only to fan the flames rather than squelch the attacks. Unfortunately there seemed to be an almost daily supply of stories about people from out of state who had misjudged the elements or the wildlife. Sometimes Patsy's stories weren't current, but the point was clear enough: she didn`t like easterners, particularly Brandy.

The worst of these attacks started at dinner during Brandy's second week. It was the end of the tourist season for Glacier National Park in Montana's northwestern corner. Three girls from Connecticut had been backpacking in a restricted area in the park, having blatantly defied the warnings of the park rangers. They had refused to seriously consider the very real threat posed by grizzly bears. The grizzly is an extremely dangerous and unpredictable animal with a keen sense of smell. The girls hadn't been careful about keeping food away from their tent, and a bear attacked and mauled them. One was killed.

Patsy seized on this tragic story as an example of why "them people from back east jus' don't belong out here." She managed to bring it up several times, each time making the same negative comments with great relish until Brandy could hardly contain herself. On the fourth day of ghoulish rehashing she decided it was best to confront Patsy openly.

"Patsy, I'm from the East, and I feel that your continual references to this story are directed at me. Does my presence here bother you that much?"

She had committed the mistake of underestimating her enemy. She had expected the mousy-looking creature to crumble at the first sign of confrontation; instead the pale eyes flashed with antagonism.

"Yeah, as a matter of fact. You know yer uncle is looked up to by folks 'round here. He don't need a trashy no-'count big-city crook hangin' 'round lookin' for handouts."

The words left Brandy breathless. She'd been working so hard to forget. No reference had been made to what had happened to her. She'd almost convinced herself that no one knew. She bit back her tears and fled to her room.

She'd gotten off to a disastrous start, and through no fault of her own! Tom and Duke simply ignored her most of the time. The women picked at her. In spite of her resolve her temper flared repeatedly, but she couldn't seem to handle the confrontations. Joe stared at her with a contemptuous sneer. The sneer was probably the result of a scar that pulled at his upper lip, but his eyes were humorless, and Brandy suspected that scar or no, the sneer would have been there nonetheless.

The truth was that Brandy was learning things about herself that she had never before known and was ill equipped to deal with. When her long slide to ruin had begun, she would find herself staring at her reflection in the mirror. Was this the face of a woman who could be so blind, so stupid? For months she had turned a blind eye toward the corruption around her, rationalizing it away. That was a side of herself that she didn't like.

Now to add to the problems she faced, she was becoming extremely emotional. In these last weeks she continually felt herself a hairbreadth away from tears. Never in her life had her emotions been so close to the surface, so difficult to control.

During the stress-filled days of her testimony before the SEC and in the busy months afterward, when she'd focused on clearing up her affairs in New York, she had been able to close her mind to the growing turmoil inside her, but now suddenly it kept rising to the surface; she kept having to force it down, and the effort exhausted her. What was it? Guilt? Probably. She felt like a criminal even though she had done nothing wrong. Resentment and frustration? Oh, yes, definitely that. All her plans, her future—perhaps she was crying for the death of her dreams. Brandy fought to hang on every time Patsy made a caustic remark about her fancy clothes or even when Tom expressed his surprise that she had never heard of famous authors like his favorites—the kind normal people read. Alternately Brandy wanted to lash out in anger or burst into tears.

At least Hattie remained polite, if distant. She refused Brandy access to her domain in the kitchen but was never openly rude. Brandy's uncle, of course, had been good to her, but he wasn`t around enough to do much good. He was the only one who would make an effort to speak to her at dinner while the rest of the conversation revolved around local gossip and the work of the ranch. She marveled at the fact that her uncle always managed to keep his own personal sense of dignity and yet be obviously comfortable around these people.

She wished she were more like him, comfortable with anyone, anywhere, and above all comfortable with himself.

The ranch manager, Jake, was different. As her uncle had described him on her first day, he really did seem to be on the outside looking in. Other than that one night at dinner, he only spoke when spoken to, rarely even glanced at Brandy; this was probably his way of expressing disapproval of the "New York crook." He was the classic Marlboro man—ruggedly handsome, silent, undoubtedly a male chauvinist of the macho variety. Nice to look at in a rough sort of way, but nothing she'd really want to take home. She wondered what he thought of her now. Did he realize how hard she was working to adapt in this strange place? Did he have even a glimmer of appreciation for what she was going through? She pictured him in her mind's eye for a moment, smiling at her from across the dinner table. Well, really, only his eyes smiled. His face could have been cut in stone. Honestly, she thought, why did she care what that stupid cowboy thought of her?

Why was she here? There was nothing here for her. No friends or people she'd even consider for friends. And the prospects for romance were even dimmer. There was a limited supply of national news, and a quality newspaper was unheard of in this state. She was going through withdrawal, and she knew it. The worst thing of all was that there was no one in the world she could turn to. No friends left in New York. None here.

She was lying on the bed still fully dressed when a knock on her door roused her from her reverie.

"Can I come in?" Her uncle poked his silvery head inside.

"Sure." She sniffed and sat up.

"I overheard that exchange in there. You okay?"

"Fine. I'm not going to let someone like that get to me," Brandy replied.

"Good. I didn't think you would."

Brandy's heart sank. Patsy's taunting did get to her, and she was hoping her uncle would jump to her defense. John Brandon simply stood in the doorway, looking at her.

"Brandy, I know they haven't made it easy for you. If I come down on them, they'll treat you better, but they'll never respect you. You have to show them what you're made of. I'm sorry, but you have to prove yourself to them, and I can't do it for you. If you decide to stay in Montana, you're going to have to make it with the natives on your own. Folks know a little bit about your troubles back east. My good name can't erase that."

Brandy bit her lip. She sat on the edge of the bed, trying to hold herself together.

She had no idea how long she sat there. It was dark outside when she finally moved. Her uncle had left long ago. It was then that she finally let the tears come.

T he next few weeks passed in a blur. Brandy found
herself sleeping late in the mornings and yawning uncontrollably soon after their five-thirty
suppers. She ate little of the heavy meals but had
the feeling she was growing fatter every day, blowing up slowly until her arms and legs were heavy
and her mind dulled. During the days she read
voraciously, escaping into any novel she could
find in her uncle's library

John Brandon reassured her. "You've been going
on sheer nerve for too long, hon. You need this
period for your body to catch up on rest and do
some healing. Pretty soon you'll be ready to get on
with things, but no point in rushing it."

She spent most of her time in her uncle's study-
office, a big comfortable paneled room with soft,
shabby leather chairs to curl up on while he worked
at the desk or conferred with the ranch manager.
The comfort of the old brown chair with its plaid
blanket, the murmur of her uncle's voice on the
telephone, the rustling of paper, all brought back

fleeting memories that she could not quite identify. One day it came to her as she heard him ordering feed and found herself wondering what the feed grain market was doing. It was like being back in her father's office on Saturday mornings, the same comfortable male presence, the same background voices and sounds. But she was no longer involved; this time she was an observer, and for now it felt strangely satisfying.

John Brandon knew she was getting back to normal when he heard loud voices in the kitchen one morning and found Hattie shaking a pudgy finger at Brandy while Jake sat watching in amusement.

"Young lady, you'll eat what we got in this house, and I ain't buying no fancy New York food for anybody. We eat good here, and if you're too picky to appreciate it, then you can just go somewhere else."

"Uncle John," Brandy pleaded, "will you tell this woman I cannot eat oatmeal and eggs and bacon and potatoes and God knows what-all for breakfast in the morning when I haven't got a blasted thing to do all day. I simply told her I'd just like a piece of melon and some dry toast."

"Hey, calm down, you two. Brandy, you have to understand things are different here. We've got plenty of fruit canned for winter—Hattie works her fingers to the bone canning—and we've got plenty of apples if you want something fresh. We don't see the need for things like California melons out of season. And Hattie, just say so calmly and don't yell." Hattie turned back to her stove but continued to mutter under her breath.

Brandy's cheeks reddened. She could see the ranch manager smiling—laughing at her, of course. What a smug, annoying man! Hattie banged a plate down in front of her, but she ignored it and concentrated on her coffee. She needed exercise so badly, and despite the featurelessness of the area, when she tried to run she found no level ground anywhere and had to be satisfied with brisk walks in the crisp fall air

Perhaps she was coming to life again; she certainly was beginning to feel irritable and trapped. She thought with horror of what it would be like to spend a lifetime here, with no escape

Jake asked, "Are you feeling up to ridin' yet, Brandy?"

She looked blank for a minute. "Oh—you mean riding a *horse*? I don't ride."

"Well, then Jake will have to teach you," her uncle volunteered. "He has some time now that we're pretty well set for winter, and you ought to get out before the snow really hits."

She knew Jake was laughing at the idea of watching her make a fool of herself on a horse. But the two of them were insistent, and she did need some exercise. She'd always been athletic, so perhaps it wouldn't be so bad.

Dressed in a stiff pair of jeans her uncle had apparently purchased for her on a trip into town, she stood awkwardly watching as Jake saddled an enormous black animal that turned to glare at her as she approached.

"Isn't that kind of a big horse for a beginner?" she asked.

Jake laughed. "Size isn't the important thing, Brandy. Sheba here is a nice gentle mare. Hattie's four-year-old granddaughter always pesters me to set her up on Sheba's back and lead her around the yard so she can tell everyone she rode the *big* horse."

Well, she thought, if a four-year-old can do it . . .

By lunchtime she had learned it was not that easy. Gritting her teeth and pretending she wasn't miserably uncomfortable was exhausting, and when Sheba looked back at her and then turned around despite Brandy's frantic yanking on the reins, she knew it was time to give up

"Sheba's got the right idea. I think it's time to head for the barn." She sat stiffly, knowing she looked foolish, and she decided that her first lesson would be her last. As she slid to the ground and turned to head back to the house, Jake grabbed her arm. "Wait a minute," he said. "You can't just park a horse like you do a car. We still have work to do. Horses don't feed and care for themselves, you know."

She couldn't believe the backbreaking work involved simply in putting a horse away. Although she suspected that pitching fresh hay, carrying slopping pails of water, and brushing down the odorous animals was more than a person would normally be expected to do.

Jake removed Sheba's bridle and placed a halter over her head, then attached two ropes to the halter and secured her between two posts so she could not move her head too far. He spoke gently to the horse and patted her frequently. From his pocket he pulled large chunks of carrot, which he fed to Sheba in total disregard of the enormous teeth; Brandy shuddered at the thought of putting her fingers near that mouth. But horse and cowboy both seemed to know exactly where the carrot ended and the hard, callused palm began. Silently Jake offered the carrot to Brandy, his eyes dancing

She looked at him in shock. "Me? Oh, no. You feed her. I'm too fond of my fingers."

"She's a gentle horse—don't let her size fool you. Here, give her a piece."

Brandy looked closely at the horse's mouth; it looked awfully wet. She'll drool on my hand, she thought. I'm going to be sick. But she steeled herself and cautiously held her arm out stiffly, eyes closed, her hand at least two feet from Sheba's mouth. Jake took her hand and moved it directly under the horse's nose, and she screwed her eyes tighter shut. This will be over in a minute, she told herself, and she felt a sudden soft, velvety brushing against her hand as the big animal sniffed her palm and accepted the treat from her.

"See?" Jake said. "Sheba's a real lady. You thought she'd slobber on your hand, didn't you?"

Brandy colored. "Sorry, Sheba, my mistake." She laughed nervously. It wasn't so bad, she thought, but she still wasn't convinced she wanted to get close to this creature.

Next Jake showed her how to brush the horse down. She was amazed at the dust that rose from Sheba's flanks. This task didn't seem so bad, just boring, and she attacked it with vigor, since Sheba was tied fast to the posts and could not reach her.

She began to have reservations, however, when the brushing approached the creature's hooves. They looked very hard.

"Just keep talking and patting her," Jake said. "Let her know where you are at all times, and let her know you're very calm."

"But I'm not calm." Brandy tried to keep her voice even. "What if she attacks me with her feet?"

"Hooves. They're hooves, not feet. And be alert, but don't worry. She's been through this a million times, and she's not likely to get annoyed with you unless you startle her. Don't do anything unexpected, and she'll let you carry on.

"Here," he said, "let me show you how to clean her hooves." He had a nasty-looking wooden-handled metal pick in his hand, and she backed away so he couldn't hand it to her. As she watched him picking at the horse's hooves with the sharp instrument, she suddenly was acutely aware of the smell of the straw and manure around her. Sheba had lifted her tail and done an absolutely disgusting thing. The smell was overpowering. Brandy didn't want to appear weak-stomached in front of this man, so she swallowed hard and breathed shallowly through her mouth so the odor wouldn't be so noticeable. She watched Jake work, trying not to think of all the filth those hooves had stepped in the course of a day. She wasn't sure if she could eat ever again.

"Next," Jake added cheerfully, "we'll work on her teeth." Brandy decided it was time to get some fresh air.

She was very quiet at lunch, freshly showered

and changed but still smelling the lingering odor of horse and the mess she had stepped in, ruining her good Nike athletic shoes. Jake hadn't been sympathetic. "You need some boots," was all he'd said.

She tried not to eat the split pea soup and bacon sandwiches placed in front of her, but the warmth of the soup was soothing, and she suddenly felt ravenous. Jake and her uncle were discussing a run over to Roundup that afternoon to pick up some supplies. They invited her to join them, but the thought of sitting next to Jake's muscular, male-smelling body made her feel queasy. He was so raw, somehow; there was something to be said for the veneer of civilization that separated men from animals. And of course, she preferred a man who had at least enough education to hold an intelligent conversation.

She spent the afternoon mentally drafting a letter to Greg in New York. She was beginning to realize she had been wrong to close that chapter in her life. He really was a fascinating person, she thought. And such a considerate—and talented— lover.

What a difference between Greg and the men she had seen out here. He had approached her with finesse, wooed her with charm, and made certain that when they were together, the harsh and seamy aspects of human existence never touched them. They came together in a world of perfumed linens, of languorous mornings high above the city, of winter fireplaces that reflected the flames of their own passion. If that passion was controlled and kept in check, it simply added to the excitement when their bodies finally touched.

But she knew she could not contact Greg yet. He had always found her competitiveness exciting— had said that part of her appeal for him was her independence, the fact that she never came to him in need, but always in strength. She could only go back to Greg if—*when*, she corrected herself—she was on her feet again. How horrified he would be at her present situation, at this place! She closed her eyes and tried unsuccessfully to forget her memories and her longings.

The men returned from their errands as Hattie was putting supper on the table, and they joined in a great deal of laughing and whispering with Hattie's granddaughter, who was spending the day with her. The little girl could hardly sit still at the supper table. "Guess what?" she said. "I know something you don't know, and it's about a present! A really neat present!" She giggled at Brandy and kicked the table leg.

"Now you just hush and don't spoil people's surprises." Uncle John winked at her and threw her into another fit of giggling. "Susie here helped us unload the truck, didn't you, Suze? But she peeked in the packages."

"Brandy will get her present after supper," he assured the little girl. Brandy had a sudden suspicion that the present was not one she would appreciate. She remembered with mounting horror Jake telling her that the little girl loved riding more than anything.

When they had finished their coffee, John Brandon left the room and returned with a large box. Susie bounced excitedly beside Brandy. As she opened the box, Brandy's heart sank. I can't stand it, she thought. My body aches so badly already that I can barely move, and I was right—they've bought me cowboy boots. She looked around the room at the expectant faces. "Well, I'm stunned," she said shakily. "I can't wait to try them on!"

She looked down at her feet and wondered if there was any way, without moaning in pain, she could possibly lift even one foot to put on the ugly boots with their uncomfortable-looking pointed toes. It appeared that her personal trainer had missed some muscles in her regular workouts, and she knew exactly where each one was. The others were watching her expectantly. Gritting her teeth, she carefully slipped one foot, then the other, into the awkward boots. Slowly rising, she donned what she hoped was more a smile than a grimace and said, "Gosh, they fit perfectly. I'm . . . uh . . . overwhelmed."

It was not easy getting up the next morning. But Jake seemed not to notice her discomfort and informed her at breakfast that Sheba was saddled and waiting for some exercise. Neither he nor her uncle would give in to her arguments.

"Exercise is the best thing for you, hon—got to loosen up those sore muscles," her uncle said cheerfully. So, sighing helplessly, she finally pulled on the horrible boots and followed Jake awkwardly to the barn. She could feel an extra chill in the air; snow should soon be on the way, and perhaps an end to Sheba's exercise. She secretly wished that this horse would need to hibernate.

She was not a good student. But in the weeks that followed both Jake and her uncle pretended not to notice and simply assumed she would be ready to ride several mornings a week. The lessons continued on a regular basis until they became an unpleasant but regular part of her life, one of those forms of exercise in which the best part was stopping. Her young and well-disciplined body had stopped hurting after the first few days, but she was certain the tension in her shoulders would return for the rest of her life every time someone mentioned the word *horse*. How surprised Greg would be if she told him on her return to New York that she missed her morning rides. No chance of that, she thought grimly

In the beginning they had stayed close to the house and barn, but when it was clear she could stay on the horse and give her some sort of guidance, they began exploring the farther reaches of the ranch, and she found herself checking fences with Jake as they followed the property line at the base of the hills to the west. She learned little about Jake on their outings, despite her growing curiosity. He really was very different from the others she had met in Montana: quiet and self-assured and, despite his classic cowboy look, surprisingly literate. She caught him out one day in an allusion that only a very well read man would understand.

"Well," he responded to her questioning, "I spend a lot of time by myself, and I've always been a compulsive reader—read everything I get my hands on. Books are better company than people sometimes."

"Did you go to college?" she asked. He seemed not to hear her and spurred his big bay horse ahead to a rise.

"Look here," he called. "Here's something that will make you wonder what century you're in."

As she drew her horse beside him, she could see in the brown valley ahead a herd of grazing animals, dark, rough-looking beasts with huge heads. She gazed in awe. "Why, those are buffalo, aren't they? I thought the buffalo were wiped out years ago."

"The wild buffalo almost were, but there's been quite a comeback," he said. "This is one of several captive herds, though. Ed Schroeder raises them mostly for enjoyment and for experimentation. You'll find a number of places where you can buy buffalo meat, and people have experimented a bit with what they call a `beefalo' hybrid. Next time we get into town I'll buy you a buffalo burger.

"The plains aren't the same as they were a century ago, but from here it looks as if it could be the 1880s. You almost expect to see Indians stalking the buffalo from behind those rocks over there."

"Have you studied Montana history?" she asked.

"A bit," was his terse reply, and the brief moment of communication was lost as he wheeled his horse and headed back along the fence line. Exasperated, she clumsily pulled at the reins and turned Sheba to follow. Why was he so irritating? Every time she tried to have a pleasant conversation with him—or ask a question—he turned into a sullen boor. And he was really such an attractive-looking man. She had come to realize, observing him working with her uncle, that he must be far better educated and certainly more intelligent than he seemed. Today's ranching was clearly far more complex than the herding, branding, and trail drives of the Old West. She had come to suspect that much of the crude behavior and illiterate-sounding conversation was purposeful—a means of defining the male role in a very old-fashioned way.

7

As Brandy's energy increased, the monotony of ranch life became a daily problem. She could not help in the kitchen, since she and Hattie had achieved only a polite standoff and Hattie had made it clear that no one was welcome to touch the equipment in her domain. On her day off she sent Roseann, a young Native American girl, to cook for them, but the girl was too shy to speak to Brandy and became very disturbed if Brandy touched anything. It seemed clear that Hattie had warned her not to let Brandy near the kitchen.

Brandy offered to help her uncle, but he informed her kindly but firmly that running the ranch was not for novices, and unless she would like to assist with clerical work and bookkeeping, there was little she could do to help. Since she had no interest or experience in either area, she decided to look elsewhere.

Short trips into Mosby, Roundup, and other nearby towns convinced her that there was nothing suitable for her there, and although Billings was much larger, she had not returned since she'd arrived.

When her uncle informed her they were invited to a political reception in Billings, she was delighted.

"You need to meet some of these folks, Brandy," he said. "You might enjoy working on a campaign, and everyone from the governor on down should be at this fund-raiser."

"I'd love a chance to meet some people," she said, "but I don't know the first thing about politics."

"You're a real smart girl, and I think you've learned some hard lessons that could be a big help to you—and the folks around you—in a campaign. There's a real temptation to fudge on the rules when the tough times come in politics, and I know you wouldn't be tempted."

Brandy was startled at her uncle's comments. This was the first time he had even alluded to her problems, and she knew he was telling her he trusted and believed in her.

She reached over and squeezed his hand. "Thanks for believing in me. It means a lot."

He smiled and closed the conversation with a nod. "You'd better think about what you're going to wear into Billings Friday, because I want to show off my pretty niece to all those political hot-shots and their nosy wives."

That was indeed a problem. Her wardrobe had been supplemented by jeans, boots, and sweaters, but she sensed that her dress clothes were subtly wrong. Perhaps she should go into town and buy something in polyester knit, she thought to herself. Some of these women dressed as if they'd been frozen in time twenty years ago, and maybe she ought to fit in. Laughing at herself, she pulled clothing from her closet and studied the possibilities. Something nice, but not too nice; something appropriate to the West, but not outrageously western. Something dressy, but not elegant. It was hard having no one to call to compare notes with. Perhaps she would meet some friendly and more sophisticated women at this event. Surely there must be some fairly well traveled and educated people in Billings. She found to her surprise that she missed her women friends as much as the contact with appealing men. If only Carey Steele, with her discerning eye, were here. She'd know immediately what would be exactly right for an evening with a bunch of plains politicians.

By Friday afternoon Brandy had decided on and discarded several outfits, finally settling on a long chamois suede skirt with a green silk shirt that matched her eyes, joined with a silver-studded belt and sparked by the addition of silver bracelets and hoop earrings, and silver-trimmed dress boots. Her hair hung loose in a tawny cloud, much longer than she was used to since she had no access to a good hairdresser.

As she entered the living room, her uncle whistled appreciatively, but she could not help looking at Jake, who stood by the door, for his reaction. He said nothing, but she felt an electricity when their eyes met that startled her. She turned away quickly and concentrated on donning her long crystal fox coat. "I'm all set," she said brightly. "Jake, are you going to this event with us?"

"No," her uncle replied for him. "Jake's got some

things to do in Billings, though, so he'll be riding in to town with us. I had the Buick washed so we can ride in style tonight." Brandy forbore to mention that she, for one, had no intention of making a two-hour trip to Billings in the old pickup truck anyway; she had checked with Duke earlier to be certain Uncle John was planning to take the car.

The drive to Billings seemed long. Jake was a mute presence next to her, and she chattered nervously to her uncle to fill the silence, trying to ignore the growing feeling of tension between her and the dark, masculine figure beside her. When they finally pulled up in front of the hotel, she was glad to step out into the cold night air.

The hotel lobby was crowded, but John Brandon seemed to know everyone. She was introduced to ranchers, legislators, businessmen, and lawyers, along with their wives. They all looked very much alike to her. She learned that the guest of honor was a U.S. senator, who turned out to be the big, friendly outdoorsman who winked at her and told her uncle she was a "real fine-looking gal." She was not shocked by the time a pleasant, weathered man nodded to her and introduced himself as the governor. It was abundantly clear that even politically Montana was very different from anything she had imagined.

The women did not seem particularly friendly. They were generally well dressed in conservative silk or wool, but she did not see one woman with a real sense of style. They all seemed bland and inhibited, and she looked in vain for someone with whom she could find something in common.

She was in the ladies' room when she overheard a snatch of conversation that she realized uncomfortably must be about her:

"Well, she seems to get along with the *men* just fine, but you can tell she thinks she's too good for us."

"Humph. At least *we're* not criminals."

"What about those clothes? She must think she's in Hollywood or something."

"Well, you have to remember these people are easterners. John has fit in pretty well, but he still isn't a native, and his relatives just aren't ever going to fit in here."

Brandy remained, face burning, in the stall until she was certain the group had left the room. She studied her reflection carefully. The outfit that had so offended them looked fine to her. Were they jealous, or was it just not possible for her to fit into any group in this strange place?

"There you are—we've been looking for you." Her uncle caught her arm as she was pushing blindly through the crowd. "Here's the man I particularly wanted you to meet—Howie Morrison. Howie, my niece, Brandy—Ellen Stanwood."

"Glad to meet you, Brandy. Jake Milburn's been telling me you're turning into a pretty good rider. We'll make you a Montanan yet."

She studied the lean, graying man suspiciously but decided he was not teasing her. Could Jake really have complimented her?

"Howie's our state senator," John said, "but we're working on promoting him."

Morrison laughed. "Some promotion! You want

me to run for Congress just so you can get me out of town. Can you imagine, Brandy, your uncle and his cronies are trying to convince me I should move to Washington."

"It sounds like a great idea to me," she said. "You'd like it there, I'm sure. I've always thought it would be fun to live in the capital for a few years myself." Howie Morrison looked as if he'd fit into the Washington scene quite well. Unlike many of the other elected officials, he was dressed in a well-cut dark suit, and his pepper-and-salt hair appeared to have been recently styled. And his English was correct and unaccented.

"If you want to live in Washington, why don't you help me get elected and join us there," Howie suggested.

As he spoke a short, dark-haired woman took his arm. "Before you invite people to Washington," she said, "you'd better consult me."

Brandy recognized the voice as one she had overheard in the ladies' room, and she blushed unwittingly. She smiled grimly at the woman. "Don't worry, I have no intention of getting into politics at this point. I haven't the slightest idea how a campaign works, and I'm not inclined to learn."

"Don't be so quick to dismiss the idea," Howie said. "We'll talk about it again later. In the meantime, this is my wife and keeper, Eila. She tries to make me think she's watching me like a hawk, but the truth is she's so busy running her gallery that I have to schedule lunch with her three weeks ahead."

"Stop that, Howie." The woman laughed. "He likes to pretend I neglect him, but he knows it's not true."

"Eila runs the gallery just down the street here, specializing in contemporary western art," John Brandon said. "And Howie's a lawyer when he's not busy over in Helena, making the world safe for democracy."

The conversation continued in a light vein, and Brandy felt comfortable for the first time that evening. Even Eila seemed pleasant, although Brandy wasn't about to trust her.

As the two of them made their final farewells and walked outside, Uncle John suddenly clapped her on the back and said, "Well, you did just as well as I figured you would, Brandy. The women probably hated you, and the men couldn't quite figure you, but by God they were all impressed."

"But most of them didn't like me, Uncle John. What's so good about that?"

"You showed them you were a lady, and smart, and tough. You've got plenty of time to show them you're somebody they can like."

Perhaps not, she thought. She had been at the ranch for almost two months, and she could not see any point in staying much longer. She would have to begin planning for the future soon.

As they drove out of town, a few flakes of snow falling around them, she realized they were returning to the ranch without Jake.

"Where's Jake?" she asked. "Isn't he coming back with us?"

"Don't you worry about Jake," her uncle said

with a half smile. "That man can take care of himself. He's got some personal business in town, and he'll be back Monday."

She felt a rush of anger, followed by horror. She was jealous! Jealous of a dull, unfriendly cowboy who was probably shacked up with some cheap Billings waitress for the weekend. Or perhaps he was on a binge. She had heard several veiled hints about Jake's disappearances, and Joe had come right out and said it:

"That Milburn's a weird guy, but don't tell me I don't know what the man does when he disappears for a few days ever' now and then. He gets tanked up enough to let loose, and then he comes back to work until he has to let loose again."

Could it be true? Brandy cautioned herself that getting interested in a man like that was ridiculous, even if he wasn't a drunk. She would concentrate on planning her future. But on the long ride home she could not imagine what her future might be.

I t was November, and the darkness of the northern winter was becoming a habit. It was a surprise to learn that winter here was not a steady thing. On this particular day, the air carried freedom in it. That was the only way Brandy could think of it. It wasn't a soft wind that blew against her face. It was strong and insistent. But it wasn't one of those cold, wet Atlantic winds, either, that sent you back to your dwelling begging for mercy.

She couldn`t remember ever feeling so full of life. Snow had fallen last week, and the weather had put a stop to riding. Brandy had assumed that the snow would be with them until May. But then the day before yesterday something strange had happened. This wind had come.

Everyone had called it a chinook. She never would have believed it if she hadn't seen it with her own eyes. Thursday morning she had gotten up for breakfast and spent most of the morning lounging in the study, paging through an old Louis L'Amour novel. At eleven she went into the kitchen to get another cup of coffee and checked the thermometer outside the kitchen window. It read twenty degrees Fahrenheit. At one o'clock when she went back into the kitchen for lunch she noticed that the house had gotten appreciably warmer, and outside, the cloud-covered skies stood in marked contrast with the obviously shrinking snowdrifts. The temperature was now forty-eight degrees.

"It's a chinook," Hattie said. "Warm dry winds that come and go all winter long. Keeps the snowdrifts in check."

So there was no excuse to get out of riding today. Although Brandy still wasn't sold on it as a great sport, she and Jake had been taking little Susie out as often as possible. Susie enjoyed it; it was some sort of exercise for Brandy, and it gave her a chance to get to know this quiet cowboy.

He wasn't as macho as he had seemed. With Susie his patience seemed infinite. Now and then he would ask Brandy questions about life in New York or about her childhood, and when he did he listened intently to her answers, watching her with his kind blue eyes.

Brandy was subconsciously aware that she was attracted to Jake, but she went to great lengths not to admit it to herself. She didn't want another man in her life. Greg would be a tough act to follow sexually. The last thing she needed was a bumbling, tongue-tied cowpoke. She remembered the old westerns on TV, where the cowboy only kissed his horse. The image seemed to fit Jake perfectly.

On this particular Saturday, Brandy and Susie

found Jake in the cow barn, caring for a sick calf he'd brought in from the pasture. The little animal looked up at them with frightened eyes, shivering uncontrollably.

"Is the baby cow going to be okay?" Susie asked Jake. "He looks awful sick, Jake."

"He'll be okay, Susie. The doctor came to see him and gave him a shot. He just needs some rest now."

Susie shuddered at the thought of a shot, but she was satisfied. "Will he be okay if you go riding with us?"

"No, I think he needs some company, honey. You and Brandy go ahead without me." He stood up and motioned to the barnyard. "I saddled Sheba and Lance for you, Brandy, but I really shouldn't go. This is one of the calves from the experimental herd, and he's a pretty valuable little fellow."

He could see her hesitation. "Go ahead—it'll do you both good. Susie's been cooped up for a couple of days now, and both of you could use a break. We don't get a lot of nice days like this, and we have to take advantage of them. You aren't afraid to go on your own, are you?"

The implication that she might not be capable of handling herself was the challenge she needed. "It sounds wonderful," she shot back. "It'll be a pleasant change not to have a baby-sitter tagging along."

As they rode out of the yard Brandy had to smile at the sight of the little girl ahead of her. She was as stubborn as Brandy herself—a determined little thing who believed the world was made just for her. Her chubby body bounced cheerfully on the pony's broad back; her style wasn't exactly classic, but to her it was clearly just fine. So the little legs stuck out straight at times, and her balance was a bit shaky. It's the confidence that counts, Brandy reminded herself. And I hope no one ever destroys that.

"Brandy, let's go see the buffalo, okay?"

"Sure, Susie. Just get the end of your pigtail out of your mouth, please. You'll swallow it."

The little girl laughed gleefully and kicked her pony into an even bouncier gait, her hair still defiantly in her mouth. The trip to see the buffalo— like the nagging about the hair—had become a tradition, and Brandy had to admit she was fascinated with the great beasts as well. True, they didn't do anything terribly interesting, but they were magnificent animals, with an aura of great dignity and the allure of the past.

As she and Susie rode over the hill and looked down to the pasture where the creatures were usually found, Brandy noticed that not only were the beasts nowhere in sight, but there was a large gap in the fence. They continued down the path to the fence. It looked as if the bison had come through the fence to visit the Rocking B.

"Where are they, Brandy?"

"I don't know. It looks like they've come over to visit us. Maybe they're around here somewhere. But I think we better get back and tell Jake. I'm sure Gramps isn't going to be too thrilled that they've knocked down his fence, and Jake's going to have to get a crew out to round them up and repair the damage. Come on—let's head back."

Susie's pony, Lance—short for Lancelot—was known for his even-tempered behavior, but even the most gentle of horses could be spooked into bolting. As they turned around and were riding up the hill, Susie was leading the way. When they reached the crest, they saw that a small group of buffalo had moved into their way and were grazing calmly on the few patches of grass along the path. The larger animals ignored them, but a playful buffalo calf jumped out to greet them, faked a charge, and ran off. Lance leaped in surprise and bolted, tearing across the rough ground with Susie clinging fearfully to his neck, small feet bouncing helplessly against his heaving sides.

It happened so fast that Brandy had no time to think. She simply reacted. She kicked her own mount hard in the sides, snapped the reins, and took off after Susie. Her only thought was to stop the runaway pony.

Time seemed to stand still. The wind, the horse, and the prairie were all one, part of her. Sheba's hoofbeats seemed to echo in her ears. The little girl crying and clinging to the frightened pony's neck was the focus of her attention. She gained quickly on the little horse and was soon beside it. Now what? She wanted to grab the reins to slow the horse, but she wasn't sure she could keep her own balance in the process. She had to do something, though—the ground was rough here, and one stumble could send Susie flying.

Instead of reaching for the reins, Brandy brought Sheba alongside on the right and began turning her horse to the left in a wide circle, keeping Lance on the inside. As the circle tightened, the pony, reassured by the other horse next to it, began to slow down. With the drop in speed, Brandy finally felt comfortable enough to lean over and grab the pony's reins. She slowed both creatures to a halt, slid off the saddle, and gathered the trembling child into her arms.

When the little girl was calm and her tears were wiped away, Brandy lifted her onto Sheba's back, holding her tightly as they rode back to the barnyard. Lance trailed behind on a long lead, his head drooping.

"Look," Susie said. "He's ashamed of himself, isn't he?"

"It wasn't his fault, honey. He was just scared, like you were." Like I was, she thought to herself.

When they reached the barn, Jake and Uncle John were both there to greet them. As Jake helped Susie down, the child chattered excitedly, fully recovered from her trauma.

"Slow down, Susie. You sound like a little chipmunk, the way you're chattering." Jake looked at Brandy for an explanation.

"The buffalo have broken through the fence," she said, catching her breath. "One of the little ones surprised us, and Susie's pony spooked, that's all. She was a real trouper—she hung on and rode like a pro until I was able to slow them down."

"Brandy saved me," insisted the little girl. "I would have been squashed flat if I fell off," she added with satisfaction, and ran off to the house to tell her grandmother about her exciting adventure.

"Kids," her uncle said. "She's already forgotten how scared she was."

"How scared *we* were, you mean. I have to thank Jake for the riding lessons—you may have thought I was a bad pupil all this time, but I guess I absorbed more than I thought."

As she touched his arm and smiled up at him, a shock seemed to run through her body, a charge so strong that she pulled her hand away and stepped back. His face held no expression. Didn't he feel it? she wondered. No, he didn't seem to. For once she had encountered a man who appeared to be immune to her appeal, but she was clearly not immune to him.

Dinner was a celebration that night. Hattie brought out a jug of Gallo Burgundy, and to Brandy it tasted as good somehow as the best French wine from her cellar in New York. The whole Rocking B family saluted Brandy with a toast, Jake and her uncle gazing at her proudly and Hattie hesitating between being grateful and acting suspicious that Brandy had somehow caused the near accident. Tom and Duke slapped her on the back as if she were now one of the guys, and for once Patsy and Bobbie held their tongues. Only Joe made her uncomfortable, staring at her with that knowing look, saying nothing but making it clear what was in his mind.

But the strangest thing was her own feeling—the exhilaration of the ride, the reflected warmth of her uncle's pride in her, and even a certain pleasure at the brief camaraderie she felt with the ranch hands. For the first time since she'd come to this part of the great American desert, Brandy didn't feel alienated or insignificant. For the first time, in the shadow of this vast land, she herself felt somehow larger than life.

B randy now rode with a new enjoyment and a sense
of freedom. It might have been the feeling of
achievement, the pride in herself, that the rescue of Susie had given her; it might have been the
fact that she had overcome her fear. But for some
reason she felt at home in the saddle and was dis-
appointed that there were no more riding lessons.
So she was particularly flattered when Jake asked
her one morning if she'd like to ride along with
him while he checked fences.

"Bundle up and take some heavy gloves. I won't
make you fix the breaks in the fences, but we'll be
out quite a while just checking the perimeter, and
you don't want to get cold."

Brandy had grown used to the ranch habit of
simply grabbing a heavy coat or slicker from the
hooks in the back entryway, although she still
searched for a relatively clean-looking example. It
had been hard at first to adjust to the idea of the
community clothing supply, but after all, she told
herself, it wasn't as if they touched her skin. The

coats seemed just to grow there; she had never bought one herself and hadn't seen evidence of anyone else buying one, but there always seemed to be plenty. Today she chose a heavy tan down jacket to wear over her sweater; Jake apparently had his own blue down vest, which he wore regularly over a series of thick wool shirts.

"Are you sure you won't make me repair the fences?" Brandy teased. "I remember that first ride when you convinced me Sheba had to be totally groomed and bathed and her teeth scraped after a one-hour ride."

He laughed at the memory. "I admit it—I just thought you needed to learn a few things. Guess I overdid. But look at you now—you sit a horse like you were born in the saddle, you do your share around the place, and you can't fool me—you actually enjoy riding, don't you?"

"You're right, and I don't know what made the difference."

"You just loosened up, that's all." The two of them worked comfortably together, saddling the easygoing Sheba and Cherokee, Jake's big bay. The day was clear but chilly, the temperature back at a more normal level after the passing of the warm chinook. The sky, a dull pale gray, held a promise of snow. They rode companionably, easily, following the course of the sluggish river as it paralleled the fence line. The trees along the riverbanks were bare of leaves, many standing in dark puddles and clumps of snow, stark and black against the faded sky.

"Kind of depressing, isn't it?" Jake asked her.

"This time of year can be hard for a person who's not used to it."

"It's hard, I'll admit," she answered. "But I'm beginning to see why people stick it out. There's something challenging about this place, something to be conquered. I know it sounds odd, but in a way, it's the same feeling I found in New York—but don't tell that to anyone back there."

Jake rode quietly beside her for a while before he spoke.

"Brandy, do you realize that's the first time you've ever mentioned New York to me?" He motioned to her to pull up and stopped beside her. His intense blue eyes seemed to soften. They no longer seemed to laugh at her now that she could see the warmth in their depths.

"I think you ought to talk about it, get it off your chest. You don't have to talk to me if you don't want to, but you've got to talk to somebody. I think you're really hurting inside."

"Actually," she said slowly, "I think I'm healing. It's just so hard to explain to people. . . . Maybe it's hard to justify to myself."

"Come on." He swung from his horse and reached up to her. "I've got a blanket here, and the ground looks dry. Haven't got any marshmallows to roast, but I can sure build a fire and we can pretend we're camping out. I brought some coffee so we can warm our insides as well, and if you want to talk, I'm a good listener. If you don't, that's okay, too."

Soon they were sitting before a blazing fire warming themselves with coffee from Jake's thermos. Brandy found herself giggling.

"This is ridiculous," she said, "sitting out in the fields in front of a fire in the middle of the day. I feel like an idiot."

"Hey, don't knock it. At least there's no traffic. At least I don't think. . . ." He leaned over and held his ear against the ground for a moment.

"What in heaven's name are you doing?"

"Old Indian trick—listening for the buffalo herd."

"I think you're faking."

"You don't see any buffalo, do you?"

They laughed together in a new intimacy, the rugged westerner and the New Yorker, now simply two friends in faded jeans and western boots, warming themselves on a cold day in front of a fire on what was once the open prairie. Brandy could scarcely believe it, the bond she felt with this taciturn man who suddenly was smiling and laughing with her. She wasn't sure what the difference was, nor did she dare ask, not wanting to break the spell. This feeling of companionship was so rare in her life, so surprising, that she knew it would disappear if she so much as questioned it.

"Jake, tell me about you. There's got to be more to you than just . . ."

"Just a cowhand? A ranch foreman? A nobody, you mean?"

"No, of course I don't mean . . . I mean . . . You're doing this on purpose, aren't you. You're making me feel awkward so I'll quit asking questions."

He gazed at her in that disconcerting way he had. Suddenly she realized what it was that made her so uncomfortable. He never avoided her eyes—

always looked straight at her without blinking. She wasn't used to that directness.

"You're right, Brandy. I'm doing exactly that. Avoiding your questions. But I promise you, at some point I'll answer them all. I just can't do it right now. Okay? And you've done pretty well yourself, by the way, avoiding questions." He smiled at her, and the corners of those remarkable eyes crinkled into laugh lines.

The mood of easy companionship was broken. Once again Brandy felt the unease his presence created—the physical presence that overwhelmed her with its sheer maleness. And for a while she had felt something else. She changed the subject abruptly with a comment about the cold—she suddenly felt the cold.

Once she had retreated from that dangerous ground, the easy companionship returned. They scattered the remnants of the fire and removed the evidence of their presence, then completed their inspection and returned to the ranch, wrapped in a comfortable silence, protected by the impersonal activity of their work.

Brandy was tired at supper that night, but tired with an easy lassitude, a pleasant weariness that simply reminded her there was a soft bed not far away and perhaps a half hour or so with a good book before she dropped off. The group seemed subdued tonight, she thought. She didn't notice her uncle's inquiring glances, but she did pause now and then for a quick smile at Jake across the table.

✳   ✳   ✳

As the days became shorter life fell into a pleasant, repetitive pattern. Brandy rode when the weather permitted, venturing farther afield now that she was comfortable on horseback. Sometimes Susie rode along when she was left for the day with her grandmother, but more often Brandy rode alone. The special days were those when Jake invited her to accompany him or when her uncle rode out with her and talked about the old days in this part of Montana, the Indian wars, the buffalo herds that once dotted the plains. There was a sweep, a grandeur, about the immensity of this land that she could begin to feel—not always, but every now and then, she had a glimpse of the feeling men like Jake and her uncle must have about the West.

"Uncle John," she asked him one day, "what really made you decide to settle out here? You were an easterner, after all—certainly no one in the family had any connections in the West. What made you do it?"

He thought for a while before answering. "Brandy, I shouldn't tell you this. And if you dare tell anyone . . ." He shook his finger at her. "I mean it—you have to promise. It would ruin me if anyone knew."

What could be so serious? she wondered. A criminal past was out of character for John Brandon; he couldn't have been that different when he was younger. What skeleton could possibly be in his closet? She reined Sheba in and motioned him to stop.

"Uncle John, if you'd rather not tell me . . . I

mean, I don't want to pry, but you know I'd keep a secret. You're family, after all."

"I know. It's just so silly. I didn't know a thing about Montana, and if I had, I'd never have come here. That's right." He nodded in confirmation. "I had no interest in the place at all—intended to work in Boston like the rest of my pals.

"But there was this girl, see . . . now don't you laugh, Brandy. She was coming out here to college at the U, and I was just crazy in love with her, or so I thought. Positively smitten, I was, like some fool sheep. Followed her out here and lost her to some idiot from Great Falls in no time at all. Moped around the campus for a while, but I had too much pride to give up and go home—kind of like you, I guess. So I stayed.

"Well, you know the rest. Montana kind of crept up on me. Next thing you know I'd met Anne, and that was all she wrote. I was a westerner through and through."

They turned and rode quietly for a while, until Brandy again broke the silence.

"Uncle John, tell me about Anne."

"Oh, honey, there's not much to tell. She died so young. Such a beautiful young woman. . . . We had hoped to have a family, but it just didn't happen. I wanted grandkids someday to show around the ranch, but I never even had kids of my own. Well, maybe someday your kids—you think your kids would want to spend their summers on a ranch?"

She blinked back the tears before answering. "My kids will love it, Uncle John. If I ever have kids . . . they'll need a grandfather. But hey, we're getting maudlin. Come on, I'll race you back to the house."

She wheeled Sheba and flew ahead of him to the house, long hair flying unrestrained, rapt in the pleasure of fleeing before the wind.

Her uncle shook his head. Still running, he thought . . . still running.

It was earlier than usual when Brandy woke, but she could hear the comforting murmur of distant voices in the kitchen and the clatter of dishes. It was tempting to luxuriate in bed on a cold November morning, but she had made a place for herself in the Rocking B routine, and the kitchen noises were a siren call to her. Even as deep winter approached, there was plenty of work to do on the ranch, and Brandy was now used to checking in with her uncle each morning for the day's assignments. The work might not seem challenging, but she was beginning to understand the simple satisfaction gained from completing the hard and sometimes mindless chores of life in this rugged country.

There was also the tempting smell of bacon and coffee. She sniffed the air, heard her stomach growl fiercely in response, and slipped out of bed and into jeans and an old sweatshirt.

Uncle John, Jake, and Hattie were in the kitchen, and they greeted her with delight.

"Well! Look who's up!" Uncle John beamed at her.

"Quick! Get the coffee, she looks faint," Jake teased.

"Ugh," she replied, running her fingers through her tangled hair and blinking owlishly.

"Now, you two quiet down," said Hattie, "I told you you were making enough noise to wake the dead."

"Actually," Brandy said guiltily, "I think it was the smell of cooking that woke me. Do you have enough for one more?"

"Well, I'll be! You've finally come to your senses," Hattie said. "You bet, we've got plenty of food. Just fix yourself a place at the table there, and it'll be right up. How do you want your eggs?"

"No, I don't want to overdo it, Hattie." Brandy laughed. "Some fruit and toast will be just fine. I'll take a rain check on the eggs."

The two women grinned at each other in mutual recognition of the empathy that was gradually developing between them. Someday they might even be friends.

Brandy grabbed a plate and utensils and sat down at the table with the men. Hattie would join them in a moment, but she always found some last-minute fussing to do, even after the food had been served.

"So, Jake, you got the list together?"

"Yeah, John. Smith's assured me that they got the part for the tractor, and Duke can install it tomorrow. It shouldn't take too long to pick up the rest. I'll be back before you know it."

"You know," Hattie said, "I could use a few things for the kitchen. We're a little low on some spices, and we sure ought to stock up on flour, sugar, oil, and some other odds and ends. You can buy nice large sizes there in Billings, and it's hard to get the quantity and the prices out here. Do you think you'd have time to just swing by the grocery store?"

Brandy smiled to herself. Hattie had waited to spring this on Jake. Everyone knew of his loathing for shopping and especially his aversion to grocery stores, which he claimed to be overcrowded with people who should have licenses to drive shopping carts. But Hattie, as usual, hit him with the request at the last minute, in front of Uncle John and immediately after Jake had said that this would be a quick trip. John Brandon grinned: he recognized the old trap immediately.

"Looks like she's got you, Jake. Hattie, you got a list?"

"Well, you know, I put one together just before I went to bed last night. I remembered this would be an early morning since Jake was going to town. And it just hit me. All those things we're going to be needing before you know it, and you won't want to make the trip again for a couple of months once the weather gets real bad."

Jake looked from one to another in good-natured exasperation. "You sure you two didn't plan this together? You win, Hattie. Give me the list. But it's gonna cost you. I expect a truly wonderful dinner tonight, and a chocolate cake with your chocolate sour cream frosting."

Brandy spoke up. "Jake, let me go with you.

While you're running all those other errands, I can do the grocery shopping. I haven't been to Billings much. It'd be a nice break."

"You sure? It's a long drive, you know. Not much in the way of scenery. But I'd sure enjoy the company," he added hastily.

Brandy gave her face a quick wash, combed her hair, and grabbed a bag. Jake was waiting in the pickup truck with the engine running, so they would at least have some heat in the cab for the start of their drive. It was a crisp, cold morning, and the frost had to be scraped from the windows. The sun was just rising, and the predawn gray of the sky was beginning to be tinged with a faint blue. There wasn't a cloud in sight. Brandy took a deep breath; the air carried the scent of a wood fire. It smelled so wonderful. She grinned at Jake as she climbed onto the passenger seat.

On the drive to Billings they chatted idly and listened to the radio. Sometimes when a really rousing song came on they would jokingly sing along. Brandy was amazed at how this quiet man had opened up now that they had gotten to know each other. As they drove into Billings, she grew quiet. She couldn't remember another time in her life when she'd simply enjoyed herself without thought for tomorrow. During her high school and college days, she had spent most of her free time studying. In her professional career she had spent most of her free time—and there hadn't been much of that with the hours she worked— making social contacts that would help her business. Even the jokes and laughter in her life had been related to her work or the state of the economy or something political. To joke and laugh simply from sheer happiness, to sing poorly and enjoy it, was something she had never done before.

"Brandy? Are you listening?" Jake's voice broke into her thoughts. "I said I'd drop you off here at the store. You'll need at least forty-five minutes for the groceries alone. Hattie always lists alternatives if you can't find exactly what she wants, but just remember, she's a lot fussier than you'd think possible. So choose wisely. Some things, like the thread and stuff, you can get at the five-and-ten next door. I'll go over to the John Deere dealership and maybe try to fit in another of these errands. Be back in a little over an hour. Meet you in the little cafe across the street. You can just leave the groceries here and we'll pick them up when I get back."

As she jumped down from the truck he said, "Remember, Hattie is fussier than you can imagine. Stick to the brand name on the list unless they're out of it. Then go for the alternate, if she's mentioned it. Otherwise, make your decision very carefully and be prepared to defend it to the death."

She grinned back at him. "Jake, I think I can handle this. We women understand each other."

He shrugged and shook his head. She closed the door firmly and he drove off.

A half hour into her assigned task, Brandy was beginning to understand why Jake hated grocery shopping so much. There seemed to be a conspiracy not to have either Hattie's first- or second-choice items. And Brandy had not really stopped to think about the size of the list. She had never been in a store quite like this, either. Almost everything was sold in bulk. It didn't take too long for her to fill one cart so high that she had to anchor it by a checkout stand and start on a second. Hattie was a good cook, there was no question about it. But Brandy was truly amazed at the variety and quantity of ingredients that her cooking required. She was also amazed at the cost of the goods. The prices were reasonable, but the large quantities made the final bill appalling to someone who had lived alone all of her adult life and was used to paying for the expensive foods she needed for entertaining along with her monthly bills. She was relieved that Uncle John had given her an envelope fat with cash. The store offered charge privileges to the ranchers, but John Brandon preferred to buy food for the ranch on a cash basis. In just under an hour she emerged from the store reeling from the immensity of what she'd previously regarded as a simple task.

At the five-and-dime she made the purchases Hattie requested without any further stress and then was happy to buy a paper and wait for Jake over a cup of coffee in the cafe.

He showed up ten minutes later. "Well, did you survive?" The look on his face was positively smug, and Brandy wondered for a fleeting instant if she had been set up to volunteer for the dreaded mission.

"Oh, it was no problem at all. I don't see why it bothers you so much."

"Liar. You look five years older."

Brandy couldn't keep from smiling. "Why did you let me blunder into that all by myself? You just wait, Mr. Milburn, I'll get even. Older, huh? Now I know where the gray at your temples comes from."

"It's true," he said as he stirred the cup of coffee the waitress placed in front of him. "I bet you did such a good job she'll never trust me with that task again."

They drank their coffee, split an order of toast, and read the paper in companionable silence.

"Well," Jake said, "let's get the groceries. You ready for a few more errands?"

"Sure, I'll wait in the truck."

She didn't, of course. They went into several stores together to fill requests for members of the ranch family. Duke needed a boot repaired. Uncle John needed some computer paper. There was a record that Patsy had asked them to look for, and Tom had a list of three books, all westerns. In each place they had to look at all the merchandise and comment on it. Jake was well known most places; he chatted politely with each proprietor and satisfied their curiosity by introducing Brandy and explaining who she was. It was close to two o'clock when they got under way.

"Jake, that really was a nice change from the routine."

"Think you'll volunteer to shop again?"

"Probably not, but I'll tag along to keep you company."

"Forget it, I'd rather suffer alone if you're not

planning to pull your own weight."

She could tell he was joking; his blue eyes twinkled. And she was pleased that he seemed to enjoy her company. He really was a nice person, not someone for her to be interested in romantically, but certainly he could be a good friend if he were not so reticent and secretive about his past and his life outside the ranch. Every time she started to feel she knew him, she hit a topic he refused to discuss.

They hadn't been out of Billings long when Jake asked suddenly, "Would you like to learn a little about Montana history?"

Brandy immediately thought of the Lewis and Clark trail and the incredibly large book that Tom had loaned to her titled *Sacajawea*. She didn't want to hurt Jake's feelings by saying no, so she offered a noncommittal, "Sure," and hoped he would take the hint.

"Good. I think this will give you a feeling for Montana history you can't get anywhere else. It would be a shame to miss it. It's so powerful."

This comment was made with such a somber tone that Brandy immediately took interest. They turned away from the interstate and began to follow signs to the Custer Battlefield National Monument. The sky was still cloudless, but Brandy felt a heaviness in the air, as if they were driving into a storm. A sense of darkness and foreboding enveloped her as Jake pulled the truck to a stop, and she looked over the harsh landscape.

When they got out the first thing Brandy noticed was the wind. It whipped her hair about and stung her cheeks with its bitter chill. They walked over to the visitor's center. It was closed and silent; no one else was around. As they stood looking across the battlefield, Jake began to describe the Battle of the Little Bighorn.

Brandy was profoundly affected by the horror of that bloody fight more than a century before. This vast land was beginning to be settled. People from the East were beginning to break the ground with iron plows, and barbed-wire fences were beginning to define boundaries where no natural boundaries had ever existed.

June 25, 1876. It was a hot day. The sun would have been high and proud in the sky, making a gradual descent toward the west, not slinking just above the horizon, as it did now on a late November afternoon. In spite of today's bracing cold she could imagine how those soldiers felt in their wool uniforms, choking in the dust as they rode in formation into battle, eager for the conflict, anxious, probably scared. The Indian warriors would have less clothing, less protection, but possibly more courage; they were from a different culture and armed with the strength of their convictions. They were fighting for a land they loved, not a land they longed to exploit. They were fighting for their very existence; the fate of the land and the Indians was inextricably linked. In her mind she could hear the thundering hooves of thousands of horses, the cries and screams. She could feel the hate and anger spawned by the need for one to live with the land and the need for the other to live on the land.

The fenced-in enclosure on the crest of the hill marked the location of the infamous last stand. In desperation, Custer and the remnants of his command had shot their horses to use as breastworks—shelters to afford some protection as they waged battle. Afterward forty-two soldiers were counted behind a barricade of thirty-seven dead horses.

Was it worth it? she wondered. Even though it seemed a significant victory for the Indians, they lost virtually everything. Custer's last stand served only to fuel the hatred and anger against them. What about the whites? They had gained a land and in just over a hundred years had destroyed so much of it. Brandy shook her head in a burst of anger and sorrow.

"This is a terrible place, Jake. It was all so pointless. We should be ashamed. It's like that book about this place—the one by Mills. The same awful feeling."

"You mean *Days of Darkness*?" Jake asked quietly.

"Yes. Awful book. Why do people dwell on such terrible things?"

"To try to understand them, I guess," he replied.

"I'll never understand," she said. "All that killing, and for what?"

But she knew what they were fighting for. It was this land.

She looked north and east from the hill. The prairie stretched out before her. It wasn't too difficult to imagine what it looked like before Custer. Compared with the gentler terrain of the eastern United States, this land was a challenge. A man's country.

Yes, a man's country, offering little beauty to a woman's eye. A harsh land that had caused brutality and pain and still could hurt. She understood why Jake had brought her here, but she could not accept it, nor could she thank him. A place where this kind of thing could happen, and could poison the atmosphere so completely that she could feel it a century later, was not a place for her.

Montana was a challenge, and her months here had been good for her. But she would be haunted by this place forever.

Brandy lay in bed looking out the big picture window, watching the sky. It was early on the morning of Christmas Eve. She couldn't remember the last time she'd seen the sun rise. She knew that she had never really paid any attention to it before. In New York she preferred to put in her extra hours at the office at night, though occasionally she would drag herself in to work before dawn. But she never took time to notice what was going on in the world around her.

The sky was so beautiful. No one had ever mentioned the thin band of green that was the first shade of color to break free of the dark night sky. After the green, yellow began to brighten the whole sky, pushing the darkness away. Then orange and red streaks climbed up from the black horizon. The sun emerged then, fiery, looking angry at first. As its redness gradually faded, the blue crept down around it. Finally the sky was its intense Montana blue, too deep to be believed.

What a change the last few weeks had made in

her life. It was as if she had awakened fully for the first time and everything around her seemed brighter and more intense than ever before. From irritability, her nerve endings had grown to sensitivity; the very touch of things gave her intense pleasure.

Her own new openness seemed to have helped the others to accept her, and she found herself a part of the close-knit group as the Rocking B prepared for the Christmas season. Even Hattie, so protective of her domain, had tried some of her suggestions and took pride in her "newfangled recipes."

"You boys need to watch the way you eat," she astounded them by announcing one Sunday. "We're cutting out some of this fried stuff and eating more wholesome food." A rebellion was averted when the hands were convinced that she really wasn't going to make them change their eating habits that much, and they weren't going to be deprived of their steak.

Brandy laughed to herself at the memory of their outrage. She savored the view of the sky for a few more minutes, luxuriating in the warm down comforter. She was too awake now to consider going back to sleep. She sighed and climbed out of the bed, pulled on her fuzzy robe and slippers, and padded down the hall to find a cup of coffee

Christmas. She had mixed emotions—missing her parents during the holidays as always, missing New York, but surprisingly glad to be here. She knew that was why she had awakened so early. She was excited about Christmas.

A big party was planned for tonight. People from nearby ranches were coming, plus Howie and his wife, Eila. Brandy frowned to herself. She enjoyed Howie—he showed little of the "good ol' boy" attitude so common here. She enjoyed conversing with him, matching her wits against his. But his wife, Eila, was another story. It was clear from their first meeting in Billings that Eila had no use for Brandy or any woman of "her type." Well, maybe Eila would keep herself busy chatting with all the ranch wives.

Brandy was going to enjoy herself.

In the kitchen Hattie was kneading bread dough and ordering Roseann about. She smiled at Brandy with uncharacteristic warmth. "Well! You're up early. Come have a cup of coffee, I've got cinnamon rolls in the oven. They'll be out in a few minutes."

Brandy smiled warmly in response and helped herself to the dark brew. She sat at the table, watching the two women work and enjoying the wonderful odors of Christmas baking. She didn't feel the least bit guilty not offering to help—she knew by now when to stay out of the way. She was content to sit quietly with her thoughts.

She hadn't done much shopping for this Christmas. It would be her poorest on record. She didn't have any spare cash to speak of, but in spite of that, or maybe because of it, in many ways it would be the best in a long time.

For gifts she had either baked something or found a special possession of her own to give away. Susie was getting her bright purple beret and matching scarf. The little girl had been coveting the set for weeks. Brandy had managed to sneak into the kitchen a few days before and bake several loaves of cranberry bread, now wrapped and well hidden in the big freezer in the basement. Patsy and Bobbie and their husbands would receive these. Joe, too; although she still found him repugnant, she could not leave him out. Perhaps her mistrust was unjustified—she'd try to withhold judgment.

Hattie was special. Brandy knew that finally they had attained a truce. She respected the older woman and understood now that Hattie's reserve was not hostile, only cautious. Hattie's present would be two strands of beads, one silver and the other red, and matching earrings. Hattie lived in polyester and wore little makeup, but she was very particular about her hair—dyed black and carefully coiffed. Underneath the gruff exterior Hattie allowed herself to indulge in a little womanly vanity.

Uncle John was going to receive an old collection of pictures of her mother. Although the siblings had drifted apart over the years, John had a keen interest in his sister's life. He asked Brandy about her mother often.

Jake's had been the most difficult. She knew that a loaf of cranberry bread would probably be enough for him, but she wanted to do something more. She was surprised at the closeness that had developed between them, a gentle and tentative friendship that grew despite all the things they left unsaid. Perhaps it was the respect they showed for each other's privacy that made it so comfortable.

The right gift for Jake would be special, but not too personal, she thought.

He continued to puzzle her with his knowledge of the world, the sophistication that sometimes showed through the surface simplicity. He was well read, certainly, and she noticed that when they were deeply engrossed in a conversation, his broad western accent was not so pronounced. After noticing this phenomenon several times, Brandy asked him about it. He grinned, shrugged off her questions, and told her she was "listenin' better, that's all."

He was open in talking about his childhood in Texas. She now knew everything about his first horse, a major player in his life. She knew that both his parents had passed away several years ago and that he still kept in touch with his aunts, uncles, and cousins. But Jake never talked about himself beyond age eighteen. The last fifteen years of his life were locked carefully behind a screen of "Oh, not much, just hung out, did the usual things." But what the usual things were, she could not discover. Brandy became convinced that he too had something in his past from which he had run away.

She had tried to find out a little about him from the others. Hattie and Bobbie were very tight-lipped. Brandy figured that they probably knew nothing and were seriously frustrated by Jake's mystique. They both could quote the family trees for at least three generations of everyone else in the county.

Her uncle merely replied that "Jake doesn't put much stock in his background" and "he's the best damn foreman in the state. The Rocking B would be lost without him."

As an avenue of final resort, she casually dropped a question to Patsy one day. The response she received made her angry at herself for prying and at Patsy for being Patsy.

"Well, I don' know where he come from," she'd drawled, "or why he's here, for that matter. He always acts like he's too good for the rest of us. But at least no one else here has to slink off for a week or so every three or four months an' go on a bender."

She cast a sidelong look at Brandy. "I pity the gal that gits involved with him. At least my man knows how to handle his liquor."

The next few weeks Brandy was alternately angry with herself for prying and watching to see if Jake drank more beer than anyone else at local get-togethers. He didn't, but he did become more quiet and thoughtful while the other men became louder and more quarrelsome.

Eventually she decided to quit worrying about his past, which was none of her business, and simply enjoy the present, which was getting better every day.

She had decided on two Christmas presents for Jake. She would give him a loaf of cranberry bread along with the others. In private, away from prying eyes, she would present him with a favorite book of poems by John Donne. Brandy had enjoyed poetry when life was not too busy. She had kept this book with her through the years, always thinking that when things slowed down she would read it through again.

Jake had come into the study one stormy after-noon a week before and had noticed her reading it. "It's been a long time since I've read Donne. I'd like to sit down with him myself again someday."

She was going to ask when a cowboy would have time to read Donne, but her uncle burst into the room, mumbling about the futures market, and the moment was lost.

Brandy spent the rest of the morning helping around the house. At one o'clock she took a hot bubble bath, washed her long, thick hair and arranged it in a French braid, and donned her nicest French silk lingerie and silk hose. It felt good to have the touch of silk against her body again; she had forgotten how sensuous it felt.

At three o'clock she was ready. She wore an olive-green silk dress and a creamy scarf with a design of orange-red poinsettias. She looked sleek and rich. The extra pounds gained from Hattie's cooking had been converted into muscle from the riding. Looking at herself in the mirror, she knew she looked better now than she ever had in her life. As she walked into the study to find her uncle, she heard a low whistle of appreciation. She turned and saw Jake looking at her. The intensity in his eyes took her breath away. His gaze swept over her, and her skin tingled.

"You sure do look pretty, Miss Stanwood. Makes a man appreciate the East," he teased.

She cocked an appraising eye at him. Clean-shaven, smelling vaguely of sandalwood soap, he wore a gray suit with a white shirt and a teal-colored striped tie. The contrast with his tanned, weathered face made him look much more rugged than his flannel shirts and jeans jacket ever did. The teal in his tie was reflected in his eyes. She'd always thought of him as a very masculine and attractive man, but until this moment she had never realized how spectacularly handsome he really was.

"Thank you. Ya don' look so bad yerself, Mr. Milburn," she mimicked.

He smiled slowly in response.

Brandy was mystified. Somehow this man was subtly different from her riding companion. Perhaps it was the suit—clearly tailor-made. He wore what looked suspiciously like Italian leather shoes, too. Before today she would have bet her soul that he wore his old riding boots in the shower, to bed, everywhere.

Maybe that's what he does on those benders Patsy referred to, she thought. He doesn't drink himself into a stupor, he shops.

"Well. There you two young people are. My, oh my, Brandy, if you don't look special! You'll knock 'em dead in that outfit." Her uncle was dressed in a western-cut suit, string tie, and his Sunday boots, gray hair moistened and brushed back carefully. Brandy had never seen him in a glum mood, but she had no idea that he could be so ebullient. She smiled and gave him a big hug.

"Merry Christmas, Uncle John."

"Well, Jake, you're looking mighty professional tonight. Glad you decided to stick around. Merry Christmas!" The men shook hands. Separated by years only, John Brandon and Jake Milburn were two of a kind. Men of the West, open and honest, possessing genuine self-confidence. They would never play the games that others accepted without question. Their success would be gained in their own ways and be measured by their own standards.

When the doorbell rang, John Brandon held his arm for Brandy to slide hers through, and the three of them went to greet the first guests.

The party was going well. The food was delicious, the guests were mingling happily. The large table in the dining room had been cleared off, and now the men were gathering around it and arguing about what would be the best way to move it and where it should be moved to. Apparently there was going to be dancing. Several musicians had emerged from the group—a guitar player, a fiddler, a harmonica player, and a vocalist. Known as the Musselshell Quartet, this group of ranchers had formed years ago, and Brandy was witnessing a Christmas tradition. She watched in amusement as the men argued and groaned about the weight of the table, how it was getting heavier each year.

Howie came up behind her and dropped a hand on her shoulder.

"Young lady, I'd like a word with you."

She turned and smiled and followed him into the study, surprised to see her uncle already seated on the leather couch with his feet on the coffee table and a glass of whiskey in his hand.

"Would you like a drink, love?" John Brandon asked, getting up and making his way over to the liquor cabinet.

She looked from one to the other, wondering what they had cooked up. "From the looks of it, I'm going to need one," she said.

"Wise choice, my girl. John, I think she's the right one." Howie grinned.

"All right, you two, out with it."

A meaningful look passed between the two men. It was not lost on Brandy, but she had no idea what they had in mind. Her uncle handed her a drink and motioned her to the big leather chair.

"Brandy, you're a smart lady. You've been a big success in the business world and dealt with some mighty powerful people. I've got a proposal for you, a real challenge, but something I think you're up to. In fact, something I think you'll excel in." Howie gave her a steady look.

"I've been in the state legislature for ten years now," he continued, "and it's time I moved on. I'm going to run for Congress now that the seat's open. I want you to manage my campaign."

Brandy held her breath. She didn't want to say the wrong thing. This could be a chance of a lifetime. If she did this well, it would be a big stepping-stone back to New York. Howard Morrison was offering her a resurrection.

She let the breath out slowly, then took a sip of her whiskey, mulling over the possibilities and the pitfalls. She had an uncanny business sense; she'd proven that over and over again. Managing a campaign would probably be like managing any business, only the pace would be much faster because the life of a campaign was limited, so there would be no time for long-term development.

She knew that she could be an asset to any business venture. But she also knew that she could be its greatest handicap. Through her own fault, she had soiled her reputation—what would the press do with her past? As public as the scandal in New York had been, the press wouldn't have to go too far to drag her through the mud here in Montana.

"Sir, you must know my background. With all due respect, are you sure you've thought this through completely? My reputation hardly rivals that of Snow White's, and I could be a great liability."

"Brandy, this is politics. You're not going to find Snow White anywhere in sight. You're young, and young people are entitled to some mistakes. You may have made a big one, but it's not big enough to bury either you or me. I need business savvy. I need someone who has a lot of energy and who can think fast and make good decisions. I think your assets far outweigh your liabilities in this situation."

John Brandon cleared his throat. "Brandy, I think you would do well to consider this. I think it'll be a good thing for both of you."

Brandy smiled. Her old corporate armor hid the excitement and turmoil she felt. "Howie, I will seriously consider it, but I don't know the first thing about political campaigns. I don't even know where to go for advice."

"Don't worry," Howie said. "There's plenty of training for campaign managers. We can send you back to Washington for a short course, and you'd come back here and hit the ground running. I know you can do it."

"Thank you." She shook his hand. "I will think about it. I'm not going to make a decision tonight. Would the end of the week be soon enough?"

Howie grinned. He knew he had her interest. "Sure thing."

She glanced at her uncle, who was looking very pleased with himself. Brandy felt a shiver of anticipation; she knew it was time to go back into the real world again, and this might be an opportunity. Certainly she had never thought of politics as a career, and she really wasn't ready to subject herself to the press again—but she would think about it.

She excused herself and wandered back to the party. The dancing had started. Jake was dancing with one of the rancher's wives as the others gathered around watching. They were doing one of those complicated country-western dances. She had never seen this side of Jake; he was full of surprises. She watched for a few moments and then caught herself wondering if he would dance with her. She felt a twinge of jealousy. She tried to push the feeling away, but it continued to nag at her. The music ended, and people clapped and cheered. Jake bowed to his partner, made a joke about being thirsty, and wound his way off the dance floor.

"There you are," he said as he came up to Brandy. "I've hardly seen you all night." He glanced toward the study. "What do those two have up their sleeves?"

He steered her toward the bar as she explained Howie's proposal.

"Sounds like a good opportunity," he said. "Are you considering it?"

"Sure I'm considering it. It's too good an opportunity not to look at."

"Then what's holding you back?"

She looked at him sharply. "You mean you knew nothing of this?"

"Why should I?"

"You're my uncle's confidant, you're his right arm. He must have said something to you."

"You know," he said, "your uncle is good at keeping his own counsel when he wants to. If you were a heifer, I'm sure he would have said something to me. But you're his niece." He grinned down at her. "There's a difference."

She gave him an angry look, but his smile melted her anger. She found herself grinning back. "I suppose so," she replied, "but you must know my past. Don't you think that'd be enough to ruin any campaign?"

"Could. But you've got a lot of other things going for you that'd offset that. You can't let that one mistake stop you from going on with your life, you know."

She looked at him again, this time with new eyes. She didn't see Roy Rogers anymore. The Marlboro man image was gone, too. This man before her was a real find. He was a true friend, and one who just happened to be incredibly attractive

She smiled up at him. "Let's dance," she said.

The evening flew by. They didn't dance with each other exclusively, but they spent as much time on the dance floor as possible. Brandy couldn't remember the last time she'd had so much fun. People began to leave, saying it was the best party ever, threatening to do it all over again next year. Finally the band packed up. Brandy stood on the front porch with her uncle and Jake, shaking hands, wishing everyone a Merry Christmas. The night was cold and she was shivering, but it didn't seem to matter.

After the last guest drove off, John Brandon said, "Well, kids, let's go have one more nightcap." They trooped back to the study, threw another log on the fire, and slowly sipped their drinks. They talked about the people who had shown up. John Brandon and Jake told some stories of past Christmas parties. They joked and laughed until they cried.

Finally John Brandon said, "Well, I'm going to hit the hay. Don't anybody even think of waking me up early to open presents. I'm getting too old to ignore a hangover. I've earned the one I'm going to have, so I'll see you all around noon."

Sitting alone in the study, Brandy and Jake looked at each other for a long moment. Jake broke the silence.

"Speaking of presents," he began, "I found something that I think will go just fine with those big green eyes of yours." He walked across the room, picked up his jacket, and fished around in the inside pocket.

"If it's okay with you, I'd like to give this to you now."

He handed her a small box. She unwrapped it carefully. Inside lay an oval brooch of carved Alaska jade set in a fourteen-karat gold rim. The green of the stone was deep and rich, and the gold frame around it was bold with clean, simple lines.

"Thank you. Jake, it's beautiful. I don't know what to say. . ."

"I saw it, and it reminded me of your eyes. That stone was made for you."

She gave him a hug. The electricity between them was tangible. For a moment she thought he was going to kiss her, but he pulled away.

"Well, I must confess, I got a present for you, too. Stay here, I'll be right back." She ran lightly down to her room and pulled out his package from the closet.

"Here you are," she said when she returned to the study, "it's not much. . . ."

She stopped. She knew she shouldn't be apologizing for a present. But would he like it?

"Brandy, this is your own copy." He smiled at her. "Thank you."

As he leaned over to hug her, the sensations welled up inside her. The strength of his arms, his lean, muscled chest; she felt overpowered by her sudden shocking desire for him. He kissed her cheek and murmured her name. He kissed her cheek again, then held her face in his hands and kissed her on the lips. She responded passionately, savoring his kisses as she had savored the sunrise that morning.

He placed a hand on each of her shoulders and held her a little away from him. His eyes searched her face.

"Maybe I'd best be going."

"No, please," she heard herself say. "I don't want that."

"What do you want?" His voice was a hoarse whisper.

"I'm almost afraid to want anything, but I'd like you to stay."

He stood up, leaned over her for a moment, and caressed her cheek. Then, without a word, he scooped her into his arms and carried her to her bedroom.

The moonlight poured in through the picture window. There was no need for a lamp. She stood in front of him, her eyes locked on his. He kissed her on the lips gently, then their mutual passion welled up again. His tongue was insistent, exploring her mouth as she trembled with pleasure. His hands roamed expertly over her body until they found the zipper on the back of her silk dress and in one clean motion slid it to the floor. She reached out for him, fingers hesitating, then moving rapidly over the buttons of his shirt, caressing as she bared his chest. Soon they both stood naked in the moonlight. She shivered, not from the cold, but because she had never felt this exhilarated and alive before. The stillness between them raged with their unsated passion. He led her to the bed, gently pulling her under the soft down comforter, his hard-muscled body providing a delicious contrast against her burning skin.

She wanted him right then. Every nerve in her body was screaming for satisfaction. He ignored her whispered moans and began to explore her body with his mouth. His tongue teased at each nipple in turn and then glided down to her navel. He gently kissed the insides of her thighs and she arched toward him, but he continued to her feet and she felt his soft breath at her toes. She moaned again and his mouth came up to meet hers; she could stand it no longer, she thought, and with a cry she arched upward to meet his now searching body.

They moved as one, rapidly and with cries of joy, to the sweet culmination of their passion, then lay spent, hands touching lightly, as their bodies cooled. She wanted to touch every inch of him, to keep the feel of his hard body and tender hands in her memory forever. This was the way a man and a woman were meant to come together.

She woke late the next morning, well rested and happy. Jake had left sometime before dawn. The house was silent. She stretched and nuzzled the pillow that still carried his scent. Her loins stirred at the memory provoked by the smell of him.

She'd never felt so complete. She felt fully alive, possibly for the first time in her life. Discovering this feeling was worth the exile she'd undertaken in this vast and barren land. Brandy sat up in bed, drew her knees under her chin, and watched the sun glistening on the snow on the prairie. It too seemed alive and bursting with joy.

The next week was filled with wonderful surprises. She and Jake stole as much time alone together as they could. They were greedy for each other's company. Brandy had always prided herself on her ability to stay in control and somewhat detached in her relationships with men. Certainly with Greg she'd always maintained her control.

It was totally different with Jake. She didn't feel out of control, but she did feel as if she were on a journey in uncharted lands. The quiet wintertime pace of the ranch, coupled with the stormy afternoons that followed Christmas, provided Brandy and Jake with precious times together. There were lazy afternoons when they lay in each other's arms and talked for hours, and he would listen attentively to her as she told him about her life, growing up in New England, working and fighting her way to the top on Wall Street. He would ask questions, not idle ones to pass the time, and while she answered he would stroke her body and lightly trace with his fingers the pendant he had given her as it lay between her breasts.

One evening their hands accidentally touched at the dinner table while she was passing him a plate. The electricity from that unexpected touch shot through her body like a lightning bolt. Their eyes met, hers longing for the intensity of his caress, his dancing mischievously. After dinner they thought of some excuse to leave the others and strolled over to his cabin, where they made love in the dim glow of a kerosene lamp while a fire roared in the potbellied stove.

On Thursday afternoon while Brandy was in the ranch house alone, a blizzard came up. Her uncle was in town getting some supplies, and Hattie was off visiting her daughter. Brandy looked out the kitchen window, thinking that it was a perfect waste of an afternoon. She knew that beyond the white blanket was the cabin where Jake was inadvertently cloistered, but the blowing snow hid all landmarks and she knew she could never find her way there. She sighed, thinking sometimes life just wasn't fair. The wind screamed eerily, and she shivered. Her aching for Jake was almost unbearable. As she started to leave the kitchen the back door burst open, and in a rush of wind and snow and fierce cold, Jake came in.

"Are you crazy?" Brandy cried. She was delighted to see him but shocked that he would risk losing his way in the blinding snowstorm.

He slammed the door against the wind and grinned. "Well, shucks, ma'am," he drawled, "that's no way to greet a man come to rescue a helpless li'l lady such as yourself from this here dangerous storm."

"What if you'd lost your way?" She was trying to be stern, but she could feel her face breaking into a silly grin.

"You probably never noticed that wire that runs from the eaves of this house out to my cabin," he said.

She had, but she hadn't given it much thought.

Jake continued, "I've got a rope that I can throw over it, and by pulling the rope along, I can figure the general direction to the house."

He came forward and put his arms around her. "Besides," he murmured, pressing his warm lips against the nape of her neck, "I didn't see any point in you wasting away in this big house all by yourself when there's a glorious storm outside."

New Year's Eve day dawned cold and bright. Promise was in the air—the promise of spring and perhaps a new direction. During these past few days, Brandy, for the first time in her life, had let her heart rule. How strange that the problems she had foreseen in a relationship with a man like Jake now seemed insignificant. The tenderness between them was more important to her than any practical considerations her head tried to place in front of her.

At some point she and Jake would have to deal with the differences in their backgrounds and lifestyles, but now was not the time. Now she knew only that he was a sensitive, caring person who made her feel more of a woman than she had ever felt before. They could work out the details of a long-term relationship later. She was eager for the challenges ahead.

She stretched briefly, then tossed back the covers. She didn't want to waste any of the day in bed. She got up, showered, and dressed in her jeans, favorite flannel shirt, and boots. A quick brush through her hair and a dab of lipstick, and she hurried to join the others for breakfast. Jake would tease her for over-sleeping, smiling at their shared secret of late nights spent whispering and holding each other until the early dawn broke over them. She decided that after breakfast they would go for a ride together.

Her stomach did a little flip when she walked into the kitchen and saw Joe at the table, looking particularly smug. His narrow eyes were gleaming with some malicious secret. She had never felt comfortable around Joe. But Hattie was bustling around the kitchen with her air of no-nonsense normality. She and Brandy exchanged pleasantries. Wasn't the weather grand? Christmas had been wonderful. Brandy wondered why Jake was so late to breakfast, but he would probably be in soon.

She helped herself to some orange juice and toast and found a banana that looked fresh. Hattie shot her a concerned look that said without words, that isn't enough to keep a girl healthy. Brandy returned the look with a smile and sat down across the table from Joe, trying to put as much distance between them as possible. He had a way of infring-ing on her sense of personal space. She would look up to find him staring at her. When she turned and met his gaze, he would let his eyes wander over her body in a calculating way, every thought apparent on his face. No one else seemed to notice it, so she tried to ignore him; the others paid little attention to him, why should she? A loner, they said.

Where was Jake? Maybe she should have gone to wake him up. Although she and Jake assumed the others in the household suspected their new relationship, neither was ready to acknowledge it openly. They were jealous of what little privacy they had.

Hattie ambled out of the kitchen, leaving Brandy alone with Joe. She concentrated on her toast.

"Well," he said, "if you're waiting for Jake, you got a long wait ahead."

"Excuse me?"

"I said if you're counting on Jake, you ain't gonna have a good day." He laughed at his own words.

She was startled but said nothing.

"He does it every time," he whispered. "Finds hisself some pretty gal, has a good time, and then just disappears. Sometimes for weeks, but at least for a couple of days. I'd've of thought you'd have more sense than that, being such a smart East Coast gal. Humph! Getting caught up with a no-'count who calls hisself a foreman, but don't do next to nothing." He shook his head in mock disgust.

What was the joke? Surely he wasn't serious. Jake would have said something to her if he was leaving, she was sure of it. She rose abruptly and left the table without responding. She could feel his gaze on her retreating back as she grabbed a heavy jacket from the back entry and slammed out into the yard.

The wind was cold and bracing. She leaned into it as she made her way over to Jake's small cabin. He had simply slept in; perhaps a calf was sick. She had checked in the barn on her way to the cabin, but there was no sign of him. Cherokee was in his stall, so he wasn't out working somewhere. Her heart sank as she came around the front of the cabin and saw that his jeep was gone. Maybe he'd had to run an early morning errand. That was it. Come on, Brandy, she said to herself, you're being ridiculous to worry. Uncle John will know where he is.

But John Brandon didn't reassure her. His face clouded, and he was silent for moment. "Didn't, uh, didn't Jake say anything to you?" She was more startled by her uncle's apparent speechlessness than she would have been at anything he might have said. He was peering at her now as if trying to read her face. "Honey, I guess you'll just have to talk to Jake about it when he gets back. I figured he'd told you he was planning this trip."

"You mean you know where he is and you won't tell me?" she asked.

"Brandy," he said, "I don't have any idea where he is. He said he had to take off for a while, but I don't know where he went, and what he does or doesn't tell you is between you two. I don't push Jake for information myself—I respect his privacy.

"Jake's the best ranch manager around. I put up with his absence now and then, and the rest of the time he gives me a hundred and fifty percent of his effort. But he's got his own life, and I don't pry. He'll be back."

"Did he say how long he'll be gone?" she asked. Perhaps this was a sudden day trip, something that had come up—he'd be back so soon, he hadn't thought to tell her.

"Three weeks, he said."

Three weeks. With those words her hopes were dashed completely. There was no way she could continue to delude herself. He had made a fool of her.

She remembered his silence when she'd talked about New Year's. He had simply smiled and squeezed her hand when she'd rattled on—so foolishly, it turned out. She had simply assumed—and he hadn't even bothered to tell her the truth. Now she recalled in a new light the incident two days ago when she had opened the door into her uncle's study, not knowing anyone was in the room. Jake had stood with his broad back to her, talking softly into the telephone.

"Look, I said I'd make it," she'd heard. "Don't worry—I'll be there." She had cleared her throat to let him know she was there, and he had signaled her to wait—he was just about finished with the call.

"What was that about?" she had asked.

"Nothing important. Just somebody nagging me about a project." And his lips, and his hands . . . had made her forget.

Until now, when the scene replayed itself in her mind, over and over, so she could examine every nuance and dissect each word—every painful, heart-stabbing word. Every word that clearly indicated he had planned all along to leave her at the end of the week with no warning and no explanation.

She could feel the hot tears well up in her eyes. Her uncle had been shoveling a path up the walk, clearing the night's soft dusting of snow. He turned back to his task, and she ran to the barn. Her thoughts were churning in confusion; how could Jake have fooled her so? How could he be so different from the man she thought she saw?

Everything that had seemed so clear was now so obviously wrong.

Joe had been telling her the truth, that was clear. After leading her on, letting her think he cared, Jake had simply turned and left without a word.

She saddled Sheba, working clumsily with tear-clouded eyes, and rode out through the gate and toward the hills. She rode hard, not noticing the cold and the gathering clouds. It was only when she felt her fingers stiffening and burning with the cold that she turned and galloped back to the barn. Once again her life was in turmoil, and the promise of better things to come had disintegrated in an instant, leaving the bleak landscape and a lonely silence.

Once she might have searched harder for an explanation. Once she had been confident that no man would prefer another woman, would leave her if he had a choice. But the growing up she had done in the past year had taught her that things were not so simple, and that Ellen Stanwood did not always win—or indeed, survive the battle. With sharpened senses, with newly healed pride and sensitive nerve endings, she felt her expectations were different and her attitude, if not as optimistic, far more realistic about human behavior.

Once again she had been abandoned. Once again she had allowed herself to rely on another person for her happiness—only briefly this time, but she had teetered on the edge of the trap. And just as she was beginning to hope, just as she was about to step out over the abyss, the truth was slammed home again. But this time she was not going to drift, to doubt. This time she was going to bounce to her feet, accept the hard lesson, and get on with her life.

She would not be fooled by love. The search for love was the key to a woman's failure, and realization that the search was futile was the final chapter in her year of hard lessons—the eternal Cinderella searches vainly for Prince Charming instead of taking charge of her own future. And her own Prince Charming? Her happily-ever-after? Oh, he came riding on a horse all right. He galloped into her life and swept her off her feet all right. And then he galloped out.

Just passing through. From now on her feet would be firmly planted.

As she rubbed Sheba down, she dried her tears and made a pledge: it would take time, but she would forget Jake and her humiliation, and she would show them all. She would once again make it to the top through her own skill. This past week had been only a brief break in her recovery.

New Year's Eve was a dismal affair. She went with her uncle to a private party at the Elks Lodge in Roundup. When she and Jake had talked about it, she had laughed at the idea of New Year's Eve with the Elks; now, through her swollen eyes, it seemed a depressing and very unfunny place. She tried to be cheerful but eventually settled for having a little too much to drink. She made a sincere effort to be civil and not to offend any of her new friends. She spent the evening wishing desperately to be alone.

On New Year's Day she sat alone in the study.

Outside, tiny snowflakes swirled up in little clouds that Montanans called a "ground blizzard." The fire was burning merrily in the fireplace in marked contrast with her black mood and aching head.

She wished she could talk to someone, but that would simply underscore her weakness and show her vulnerability, and besides, whom would she talk to? There was a tacit understanding that she didn't really want anyone at the ranch to intrude on her personal life, so no one spoke to her about Jake or mentioned him around her. But when they thought she wasn't listening they made comments to each other.

"Must've been the Christmas party got him started. Funny, you don't hardly ever see him drunk. You'd think he could control it better than that. Guess he's one of them binge drinkers, takes off when he's under pressure and just gets falling-down drunk."

It was Patsy who replied, "Yeah, and we all know what kind of pressure was on him."

Brandy could hear Joe and Patsy snickering together and was certain they meant her to hear. Hattie, Tom, and Bobbie were much more circumspect, but they too were convinced that Jake had a drinking problem. John Brandon had not spoken about Jake to his niece since the morning the ranch manager had disappeared. There were a few times that first week that she thought he was going to bring up the subject, but she managed to change the direction of the conversation and keep it rolling away from the painful topic.

How could she have fallen for someone like

that? She shook her head ruefully. A few months in Montana had apparently damaged her judgment. But she was back to normal now and armed against the appeal of any unsuitable man, no matter how sexually attractive. Perhaps it was because she was vulnerable that he created such an electricity in her. Electricity that strong was dangerous; a woman could get a terrible shock.

Even passion should be under control, she reminded herself. Self-control is what differentiates us from animals. Animal pleasure—lust—is a poor basis for a lasting relationship between a man and a woman, and all the things she and Jake had seemed to have in common were—in the light of day— merely imaginary outgrowths of that unbridled passion. Jake was exactly what he had seemed from the start, a handsome cowboy, a little quieter than the rest, maybe a little better read, but nothing more.

Brandy had been thinking a lot about Greg. He had his faults, but he was her kind of person, leading her kind of life. He didn't take off on benders, and he didn't live on some godforsaken tundra. He understood perfectly the life-style she wanted.

It was time to get her life together and get out of here. She had looked at all the options, considered them step by step, and she had her plan in place. In no time at all she would be able to return to the East. A tiny bit of luck, some hard work, clever planning, and the obvious popularity of Howard Morrison would be her ticket.

She uncapped her old Cross pen and, smiling grimly, began to write. "Dear Greg, I realize it's been a long time . . ."

With a determined effort Brandy pulled herself out of the lethargy created by the bleakness around her and began to look ahead. Writing the letter to Greg had been a good first step. In reopening the door to their relationship, she had opened the door to her recovery. She reread the letter carefully several times before sealing it. It held just the right tone—a slightly rueful note, but not apologetic, a hint of humor, her old strength. She nodded with satisfaction.

Now to move on, and away from the cocoon of the Rocking B. The others were beginning to get on her nerves; most of the household had become edgy and restless with what they called cabin fever. But Brandy had no intention of letting herself be trapped for the winter in this prison. There was a better choice out there, and she was going after it. Winter in Billings wouldn't be much more attractive, but if she played it right and got lucky, one winter—just one—and she could say good-bye to this godforsaken country forever.

Washington. It would be very different from New York, but exciting and challenging, and she was ready for a new challenge. A position of power with a congressman, even a congressman from a small state, could provide rapid entry to a new and respected career. Howard Morrison could very well win the election if he put together a good campaign, and as campaign manager she would be in a position to play an influential role after the election.

The carved jade pendant that had for a short time burned against her breast with the heat of passion now lay cold and buried at the back of a drawer, where she would not have to look at it and be reminded of what she thought it had signified. Her uncle never mentioned its absence, although she was sure he had noticed. She had never discussed Jake with him, and he did not try to bring up the subject himself. Brandy admired him for that—he knew she was a very private person, and he always respected that privacy. Emotions, mawkish sentimentality, the rubbish of relationships—all of these should remain as carefully screened as a person's garbage; they had no place in public view.

As had always been her habit in business, she began mapping out a strategy to achieve her short- and long-term goals. The campaign manager's job had been offered to her, but there were clearly barriers to be surmounted, not least of which was to allay the very obvious suspicions of Howie's wife, Eila. The tight-lipped, narrowed-eyed glances she had caught told Brandy that unless she could convince Eila she was a friend—and uninterested in

Howie—she could not possibly keep the job without destructive conflict.

Eila was the kind of woman Brandy usually enjoyed, intelligent and creative, far more open to the rest of the world than many Montanans she had met. Her art gallery appeared to be as important to Eila as Brandy's career had always been to her, and Brandy was sure this capable woman was the equal of any of the gallery owners she had met in the East. Although it featured western art, as did many local galleries, it included some very unusual contemporary pieces.

Brandy had visited the gallery in Billings several times to look at the work of a particular local artist, a Native American man who painted dark, expressive abstracts hinting at the bloody past of his tribe, full of anguish over the bleakness of the landscape and their wasted lives. He was becoming recognized enough that his work was priced above Brandy's current resources, but she meant to begin collecting his paintings as soon as she could afford it and had thought several times that if only Eila were friendlier, she would ask her about the possibility of buying one particular oil on monthly payments.

This would, she decided, be a good starting point for an assault on Eila's antagonism. In her New York days Brandy would have laughed at the thought of putting so much effort into such a small project, but she knew that her future—and her escape—depended on each small step that would take her to Washington and back to life.

It took Brandy a few days to map out a plan of attack, but the following Monday she was ready.

Eila was sitting at her desk near the gallery window when the dusty Buick drove up. She frowned as Brandy emerged. Brandy waved cheerfully, slung her large leather bag across her shoulder, and picked her way through the melting snow at curbside.

"Good morning," Brandy called. "I decided to celebrate the chinook with a drive into town today. I figure by the time I get ready to go back tonight, all the snow will be melted and even I can make it easily."

"Yes, I'm sure that's true. Was there something in particular you wanted to see?" Eila asked coolly. She folded her arms in a gesture that Brandy knew was not welcoming.

Brandy continued to smile brightly, however, and proceeded with her plan. "I'm here for a couple of reasons," she said as she moved toward the back of the gallery and the paintings that interested her. "The first is that I absolutely can't get enough of Thomas Littlehorse's work, and I had to come in and see it again." She smiled ruefully at Eila. "I'm sure you know I can't afford it right now, but when I have the money I'm going to buy that painting."

Eila gave her an odd look. She brushed her dark curls off her forehead and inspected Brandy for a moment. "Do you really understand Thomas's work?" she asked.

They both looked at the painting in front of them, a small but powerful oil in which the bulk of a mesa seemed to loom through swirls of dust or snow, and a lone figure, dwarfed by the mesa behind it, appeared to lift its arms in supplication or despair—but never resignation. Somehow it seemed clear that the figure was fighting against the forces of nature that were so cruel. Brandy tried to describe to the older woman how she felt about the painting, but it was difficult to express in words.

"I know I can never completely understand the way a man like Thomas Littlehorse thinks," she concluded. "But when I look at this painting I can feel his pain, and as crazy as this sounds, I feel the pain of this picture relates to me. If there is any way I can buy the painting, I want to have it. And that's one reason I'm here today. It says something to me directly, and even though you and I don't know each other very well, I have to believe you understand because everything in this gallery says you do."

She had not meant to expose herself so completely, but now that she had said it, she knew it was right. Eila looked stunned, but she was nodding. A bridge had been created between them, a small and fragile one, but something to build on.

She challenged Eila with a look. "My second reason for being here is that you and I need to get to know each other. Our lives are going to cross soon, and I don't want you for an enemy. So I'd like to buy you lunch and talk about whether there is any way I can buy this painting, and find out what I have to do to convince you I'd like to be friends."

Eila thought briefly, then nodded. "You're right," she said. "We ought to talk. Besides, I'm always interested in a new customer. If you want to buy,

I'll figure out a way to sell. And I'm hungry."

The little restaurant down the street was crowded, but Eila seemed to be well known by both the customers and the help, and they were seated almost immediately at a table away from the crowd. Their silence was awkward at first as both tried to decide where a conversation should start, and they gratefully ordered a bottle of wine at the waiter's suggestion, hoping a glass or two would break the ice.

After desultory small talk, Brandy decided to approach the subject head on. She announced to Eila that she had decided to accept Howie's offer to be his campaign manager, with the hope that it would lead to a return to the East Coast.

"I'll be blunt, Eila. I know you don't trust me, and maybe you never will. But I have no personal interest in your husband at all, and will do everything I can to make that clear. I have no interest in *any* man here in Montana," she emphasized with a painful catch in her throat. "I do have a relationship with a man in New York, and I've decided I want to go back to him. Running this campaign seems like a good way to get started back to the life I really want."

"Are you sure you really want it? I can't help but think that your reaction to Thomas Littlehorse's work means something more than an appreciation of art. Don't you think you've changed since you've been here?"

Brandy looked at the dark-haired woman in surprise. She was impressed that Eila had taken that much interest in her months in Montana. "I guess

I thought so for a while," she said. "But I was wrong. I think Thomas Littlehorse's work says something universal—it's not something I appreciate only because of Montana."

Eila shook her head. "I don't agree, but we won't argue about it. Let me start by saying I'm sorry I haven't been friendlier to you. I really haven't given you a chance, and I'm willing to do that. I guess it's because Howie's career is so important to him, and I was concerned that you weren't the type to take it seriously. I'm willing to take your word for it, okay? The campaign job is fine with me. Just don't let Howie down." She waited for Brandy's affirming nod, then continued. "Now, let's talk about how I can help you own your painting—because you've convinced me it ought to be yours—and how you can help me and Thomas.

"Thomas is becoming well known regionally, and he's had a show in Dallas recently. But he hasn't yet hit the New York market, and I'm trying to get him a start there. If you can give us some ideas of people to contact, or any introductions to gallery owners, it would help a lot. And I know we could work out some kind of time-payment plan on the painting." She laughed at Brandy's delight. "Don't worry," she added, "you'll pay for it. I plan to have my husband deduct it from your salary."

As they lingered over their lunch and giggled over a second bottle of wine and more personal conversation, Brandy mentally thanked Thomas Littlehorse. The young artist not only had added something to her life with his work, but it looked as if he had brought her a friend.

It became a long and happy lunch, and the two women returned to the gallery only long enough to place a red "Sold" sticker on the painting before driving to the Morrisons' house for dinner and a discussion with Howie of the upcoming campaign and Brandy's role in it. She called her uncle to tell him she would be spending the night with the Morrisons, and they settled down to an extended analysis of the political situation, alternative strategies, and, most important, raising the money. Brandy felt handicapped by her lack of political experience, but both Howie and Eila assured her that her expertise in the business world would pay off in the job.

"As I mentioned before," Howie said, "there's a campaign management school next month in Washington we can send you to. It's a week long—just enough to give you the technical stuff you need, and time for you to meet the people in the national party who count, particularly those who hold the purse strings."

"Aha," Eila said. "You want to get back east, and fate is sending you there in no time at all. You can spend some time with your friend Greg, and compare him with Montana men."

Brandy blushed, remembering her lunchtime confession to Eila about her fling with Jake and her hurt that he'd turned out to be just another Montana cowboy after all. "I'm sure the comparison will be interesting," she said. "But right now I'm more interested in the job, and Howie is going to be the number one man in my life, like it or not." She and Eila shared a smile; today the two of them had achieved a total understanding. Howie was a man who deserved their support, and with Eila at his side and Brandy behind them, he could go a long way.

How far? she wondered. Could this one job be the means to success even greater than she had achieved—or even imagined—before? Personal wealth seemed unimportant now, but power— power was a stronger elixir today. She knew that it was power that meant everything to her, the control over her life and the forces around her. Like the figure in the painting, she would fight the elements. And she would win.

With Brandy's decision to move to Billings, the gloom of winter became less noticeable. There were cold days still—unpleasantly cold, in fact—when the temperature dropped below zero and the wind chill made the outdoor air unbearable. But there were more important things to think about than the weather, and Brandy had to admit that New York wasn't exactly balmy in winter, either. Her uncle teased her about getting back east to the kind of winter she was used to, but she just smiled.

John Brandon was obviously pleased at her choice to start on a new career. His enthusiasm for her move to Billings began to annoy her a bit, in fact. One night after dinner as they sat talking in his study, she jokingly mentioned she thought he was glad to see her go.

"After all, I've been living off you for months, Uncle John. You're probably just itching to get the spare bedroom emptied out."

Her uncle became very serious. "Don't you joke

about that, hon. I'd be happy to have you right here as long as you want. We take family seriously around here. Ask Ed Schroeder, for instance, how his dad got to Montana during the Great Depression. He'll tell you, too—it was when folks in the East some places couldn't even feed their kids, and his dad was sent to live with relatives in Montana because they at least had food. Didn't have much, but they had five kids move in with them, and they welcomed every last one.

"Now, I know you aren't desperate for a meal— half the time you don't eat enough to keep a bird alive anyhow. But I'm here to tell you I'll keep you here as long as you'll stay. You're family, and I care about you."

She held up a hand as if to ward him off. "Okay, okay, I give in. You're a persuasive man, Uncle John, and what you've done for me . . . I can't tell you how much it's meant. But you know I won't stay in Montana permanently."

"Oh, I know you're not ready for that. But I'd like it if you could think of the ranch as sort of a home base. I know this house isn't the kind of place a woman would want to live in, but I've got an idea . . I've been thinking about it a lot. This place is pretty shabby, and even Hattie has been making remarks lately as to how she'd like to see the place looking a little nicer. You've been influencing her some."

Brandy laughed. "Hattie and I are getting along pretty well now that we've agreed to respect each other's tastes. She thinks I'm crazy, but she doesn't make me eat beef at every meal, and a couple of times she's even let me cook something myself. Usually it's when Susie is here to run interference, but it's a start."

"You know that rise about a hundred yards east of the house, overlooking the river?" her uncle asked. "Well, how do you think that would do for a spot to build a new house?"

She stared at him, stunned. "A new house! Why?"

"Because with you here I realize it's silly to keep living like this when I can afford something nicer. I'm pretty involved in politics in this state, and it's ridiculous that I can't have a real nice event out here. Oh, I know everybody loves coming out here for Christmas, and for the picnic on the Fourth, but they'd still come if the place had a little class."

Brandy took his hand. "Uncle John," she said, "you have more class than anyone I know, but you're right. You deserve a nicer place, and wouldn't Hattie love a new kitchen!"

The two of them spent the rest of the evening talking about how a new ranch house should look and how it should be situated. Brandy won the argument that the house should face east toward the rising sun, with windows looking out over the hills rather than down toward the river. "The sunrise is the most magnificent view you have here," she insisted. "Let's showcase it."

Her uncle insisted—and she agreed reluctantly—that the house should be as practical and comfortably casual as the old one, but with better design and with finer materials. They plotted a spacious living room with paneled walls and beamed ceiling, with a huge stone fireplace separating it from a formal dining room. Ground was to be broken in the spring, but many of the decisions would have to be made over the winter months and furniture and materials chosen.

Brandy began to feel the familiar pressure of days that were full enough that her activities had to be prioritized, and that old familiar stress was exciting. Her activities were different, but the pressure was the same and the challenge of getting it all done was still the most enjoyable part of it. She planned to save most weekends to spend with her uncle on the ranch and for rides with Susie, who was not happy at losing her riding companion and new idol. Even Hattie made a few caustic remarks:

"You'd better get out here on the weekends, Brandy. I didn't learn some of your silly eastern ways just to waste the effort, you know. If I'm going to cook this stuff, you're going to be here to eat it."

Brandy had been dreading Jake's return. If she could get away from the ranch and settled in Billings before he came back, it would help, she thought. Away from the setting in which Jake was so appealing, the atmosphere that had clouded her judgment, she could more easily deal with her anger and embarrassment.

She almost made it. On the day Jake returned to the Rocking B she was preparing to clear out most of her clothes and personal things from the ranch house. She'd leave some jeans, her boots, and weekend gear, but everything else would go with her to the small apartment she had found in town. She lugged her bags to the back door where the

Buick was drawn up and sat down at the kitchen table for a last cup of coffee with Hattie while she waited for Duke to carry her luggage out to the car.

The kitchen smelled of baking, spicy and yeasty, and the windows were steamed against the cold air outside. Hattie bustled between the big old stove and the counter, humming as she pulled big pans of rolls from the oven.

It would be hard to tear herself away from the comfort of the ranch kitchen, Brandy realized. She stretched her legs out in front of her and contemplated the worn moccasins on her feet. Should she change to her boots? No, they were even worse looking. Fine for the ranch, but not for town. Maybe she'd pick up a new pair of cowboy boots to wear with slacks; they were so comfortable.

"Well, I guess I have everything, Hattie."

"No matter. You'll be back most weekends anyhow." The housekeeper lifted a huge hot cinnamon roll out of the pan and set it, glistening with melting icing, on a plate.

"Here. Give yourself some energy. The minute you get away from here I know you're going to go right back to your bad eating habits, so you just stoke up now so you don't get so skinny again."

Hattie stood, arms folded and face stern, while Brandy contemplated the cinnamon roll.

Brandy shook her head, teasing. "Oh, Hattie, I just don't think this would be good for me."

Hattie reached out to grab it away from her, and Brandy pulled the plate back.

"Don't you dare! I'd kill for one of your cinnamon rolls, and you know it."

They were both laughing, Brandy's mouth full of hot roll, when she heard her uncle's voice from the hall.

"Here's Jake."

She and Hattie stopped, frozen in the midst of their laughter, as they heard the jeep pull up outside.

Oh, no—I can't deal with this, Brandy thought. She pushed back her chair and grabbed her coat and gloves. "I'd better see if Duke has my bags in the car, Hattie. Have to get going—I promised Eila I'd meet her at the gallery before noon to pick up some kitchen things she's loaning me."

"Go ahead, rush off. You'll come rushing back, though, soon enough." Hattie turned back to her stove. "I'm packing a tray of cinnamon rolls for you anyway, so you don't forget to come home."

Brandy gave her a hug and headed for the door, pulling her coat on as she went. "I already said good-bye to Uncle John, Hattie—see you in a couple of weeks, probably."

Jake was standing by the jeep, talking with Tom and Duke, as she stepped outside. In his heavy sheepskin coat with the collar turned up against the wind, he looked a powerful figure, tanned profile strong in the light as he tipped his head back in laughter. As she opened the car door he turned and saw her, and the lightning crackled between them despite her determination.

I hate him. I won't let him get to me—but I have to get out of here. Smiling grimly, she waved to him as she got into the car and started the engine.

"Brandy—wait." He ran toward her.

Her knuckles tightened on the wheel. But she took a deep breath and kept the smile on her face. "Hello, Jake. I'm surprised to see you back so soon," she said coolly.

He gave her a slightly puzzled look and leaned down to the open car window. "It seems like a very long time to me, Brandy. I'm so glad to see you. I've been looking forward to today constantly. . ."

"Jake, I've got to get going. I'm meeting Eila in town."

"I'll wait for you—how long will you be?" His blue eyes pierced her, but she held on to her smoldering anger and resisted their pull. That's the worst part, she told herself. He knows how appealing he is, and he uses it—draws women into his trap with those eyes. I will not lower myself to the level of his women. Supported by her renewed fury at her own foolishness and her desire to hurt him as he had hurt her, she looked back at him unflinchingly.

"I'm moving into Billings, Jake. I took the job with Howie Morrison, managing his campaign."

"That's wonderful! Hang on a few minutes and I'll come with you—I'll help you carry this stuff and we'll go out and celebrate. I have a surprise for you."

"No thanks, Jake. I think it's best to forget about what happened between us. It was a pleasant interlude, but not something I want to continue."

He looked stunned. "You can't be serious. . . . Brandy, how can you say that? What could have happened in the past three weeks that changed things?"

"What could have happened? Why, nothing happened, Jake. You took off, and it gave me a chance to get back to normal, that's all. We need to keep things in perspective. I admit it's hard to keep one's perspective in this godforsaken place in the winter, but that's no reason to continue something that's not going anywhere."

"Why do you say it's not going anywhere?"

She shook her head. "Oh, Jake, why drag this on? We can't change who and what we are, and obviously we have very different attitudes—but that's not surprising, is it? With our very different backgrounds, I mean?" She pushed down the car door lock and put the big car into gear.

"This is ridiculous, Brandy—you're just not making sense. Come on, we need to go somewhere where we can have a real conversation."

She shook her head, holding back the tears that were growing harder to control. "I guess I was lucky you left when you did," she made herself say lightly. "Things were so dull around here I might have convinced myself I really cared about you. And wouldn't that have been awkward!" She waved him away from the open window. "I'll see you around," she said to his stony face.

As she rolled up the window against the bitter January chill, carefully avoiding his gaze, the tears threatened to spill over. She bit her lip and blinked them away, turning the Buick into the gravel drive and moving as rapidly as possible away from her pain and her temptation. She could taste blood on her lip where she had bitten it.

When she was certain she was well out of sight

of the ranch, she pulled over. She was shaking uncontrollably. Drawing deep, ragged breaths, she tried to calm herself. *I hate him. I know I'm doing the right thing. It was stupid of me ever to get involved with a man like that.* The shaking continued.

"Damn him!" she cried, overwhelmed with rage and despair. "Damn him!"

Eila didn't mention Brandy's *tear-reddened eyes or her pale, set face.* She simply set about helping her in her own calm, reassuring way. She turned the gallery over to an assistant for the remainder of the day so she could help Brandy move her few things into the small apartment and put away the kitchen utensils and dishes she had loaned her.

"Look," she said, standing back from the open cupboards with hands on her jeans-clad hips. "Don't the colors look nice?"

Brandy could not help but smile. The odds and ends of dishes and mixing bowls were a crazy mix of pattern and color, but together they had a cheery, casual sort of devil-may-care look that she had to admit she liked. Mexican pottery joined old blue graniteware and bright Melmac in an appealing mélange.

"You're right. It's too bad I can't keep the cupboard doors open." And she felt better as they went about their work—Eila was so good to have around, so sensible, but so sensitive.

Eila had loaned her enough furniture to supplement the bed, which was Brandy's one major investment, and had sent her off shopping with a complete list of the towels, incidentals, and cleaning supplies she would need, many of which Brandy would never have thought of otherwise. She remembered ruefully the things she had in storage but realized how incongruous her New York furniture would look in this small, boxy apartment, three rooms that would have fit into a third of her expensive Manhattan space. But the rooms were light and airy, and she felt good about being here; all in all, her new surroundings were looking very satisfactory.

She was surprised at how simple she wanted her environment to be. Perhaps, she thought, I'm trying to simplify my life because things have become so complicated. But somehow she knew she would always prefer this open, sparse look. Even back in the East, her life—and her environment—would remain uncluttered.

After all, she had started a trend in the East with her bare white walls; this was only the culmination of that trend—Montana minimalism, one might call it. And although the furniture was old and mismatched, it was all simple and functional, and she had added dhurrie rugs and cheerful cushions in the living room and bedroom for those touches of color she liked to have around her.

But the focus of the living room, and indeed the center of the entire apartment, was the painting by Thomas Littlehorse. It dominated the tiny living room with its power and seemed to reach into the other rooms with its presence. Brandy knew the other walls of the apartment must remain bare and white. Somehow she felt it would be wrong to allow anything to compete with or distract from this one strong image that inspired her.

Each time she studied the painting she found some new meaning in it, sometimes contradictory meanings. The lone figure seemed to her to represent so many different strengths and longings; to her it represented all of mankind in its varied needs and calls for strength from a higher power.

What was it that made her feel so strongly about this painting? she wondered. When Eila had introduced her to Thomas, she'd felt the same strange pull in his keen black eyes. She'd mentioned to Eila her feelings about the painting and about Thomas himself, but it seemed foolish to attach too much significance to her impressions. She would simply enjoy it and keep her superstitions to herself.

Eila had surprised her that first night in the apartment by returning after dinner and delivering the painting with a bottle of wine and two glasses.

"You've made a payment on it," she said. "We're talking to the gallery you suggested in New York, and it was a good lead—they're going to take some of Thomas's work on consignment. But if you miss a payment, you're in deep trouble," she threatened with mock seriousness. "The wine is for your housewarming, and I'm here to celebrate it with you."

They toasted the painting, the apartment, the future. They seemed to have been friends forever. Brandy knew Eila didn't always agree with her—

she was quite open about it—but even their arguments were enjoyable, and both had the same kind of determination in support of Howie. Brandy grew to respect him even more as she worked with him. He was a strong, honest legislator who seemed really to care about his constituents and felt he had a real vocation to serve them. The campaign was a necessary part of the job, and he played the part well. But she soon found that he preferred what he considered real work to the games of the campaign.

In the early stages, managing a campaign turned out to a large extent to be managing her candidate's time and competing with his legislative office for that time. The law firm would manage without him, but his legislative staff fought fiercely for his attention. She was able to schedule an hour of private time with him after the first few weeks to discuss the problem.

"Howie, you're superb at raising money, we have a great campaign finance committee—with my uncle as chairman, we've got it made—and I think I'm starting to get a good organization put together. But I can see already there's going to be a problem with your office staff, and I just don't have the experience to know how to deal with it. We have to work together if we're going to win this thing."

"Be patient, Brandy," he answered. "You'll be leaving for Washington in a few weeks, and they'll give you all the answers at the campaign school. People in Washington assure me they know everything, anyway."

The school was coming up fast, and she worked

long hours to get the campaign organization operating well enough that she could be gone for a week. The primary race did not look too difficult, but she did not believe in leaving anything to chance. The primary election was a marker in the road ahead. If she could reach that point, she would be halfway there. It was a superstitious thing; like some sort of magical ritual, she felt if she did it right, the difficulties in her life would fade away. The need to concentrate on building the perfect campaign was good for her now. She could immerse herself in the job, all attention focused on mastering this new set of skills. At the end of the long day, sleep beckoned and came easily, with only scattered thoughts of Jake to disturb her rest.

She was comfortable with the pattern and the barriers she had set up to avoid contact with Jake. Her new home telephone was unlisted, and Howie's secretary generally answered the telephone for her in her temporary campaign headquarters. Jake had tried repeatedly to reach her, but she had managed to avoid talking to him. It was only because she was concentrating on something else that she absentmindedly picked up the telephone herself one day.

"Brandy?"

She froze in place. She felt as if her heart had stopped. His voice had the physical impact of a blow to her diaphragm, and for a moment she could not breathe.

"Brandy? Are you there?"

"Jake."

"I'm glad I finally caught you. Look, we really need to talk. You know, you owe me an explanation."

"I owe you? I owe you nothing, Jake. I don't want to discuss it. Please just leave me alone—I've had enough problems to deal with this past year, and I don't need you hounding me. Just leave me alone." Her voice sounded calm even to her ears; the shock of hearing his voice unexpectedly had drained all expression from it.

"Brandy, I'm trying to understand," he said, "but this is crazy. I thought I knew you."

"I guess you didn't know me," she replied coolly. "And I certainly didn't know you."

"I thought we were beginning to know each other very well."

"How can you know someone who won't even be honest with you? You weren't honest with me, were you, Jake?" For a brief, crazy moment she felt a twinge of hope. Perhaps there was an explanation. But the feeble spark was quickly extinguished. It flared only for a thoughtless moment before her strength and his voice extinguished it.

"No," he answered slowly, "I admit I wasn't totally honest with you. But I had my reasons, and when the time was right I would have told you. I certainly deserve a chance to explain."

"Sorry, Jake. You may think it's pretty amusing coming from me, but I put a high premium on honesty." She dropped the telephone receiver into its cradle and sat staring at the wall in front of her, willing herself to stop thinking, to catch her

breath, to remember what it was she had been trying to do.

That was the only afternoon she left the office
early, and the last time that winter that she cried.

There were still no signs of spring in Montana the day Brandy left for Washington. The wind was blustery and cold, and the hills remained bare. But Brandy felt spring inside, if not in the air; her step quickened with excitement, and she felt herself smiling at everyone she passed.

How different this trip would be from her last cross-country flight. She felt a tingle of excitement as she thought ahead to her reunion with Greg. One week in Washington and then a glorious weekend in New York at Greg's penthouse, just the two of them. She knew what he meant when he'd whispered that he had special plans for her; she shivered with anticipation.

Gone now were the warm memories of her time with Jake, burned out by anger. They avoided each other when she went to the ranch for weekends and were particularly polite at the dinner table. Her uncle appeared concerned but did not interfere.

Jake had made one last effort to talk to her one Sunday morning as she was returning from an early ride. He'd confronted her as she'd walked out of the barn, and stood, blocking her way.

"Jake, please," she said. "It's cold, and I want to take off my boots and get into a hot shower." She pulled off her hat and pushed the tumbled hair behind her ears. Folding her arms in front of her, she stared up at him coolly, steeling herself against the spark in his blue eyes.

"I know. You don't want to talk about it. I won't bother you anymore . . . for now."

"For now," she said. "And how long is `for now'? A very long time, I hope."

"For now is until you're ready to talk, Brandy. I know you've had a tough time, and I don't want to make it any worse. But we have something unfinished, and you know it."

He stopped her angry words with his hand. "Just listen. We had something very special going, and I think it could be something very long-lasting. I made a mistake in not being totally honest with you in the beginning, but you weren't ready for what I had to tell you."

She pushed away from him angrily, disturbed at his closeness. "Let me by, Jake. I don't want to hear any more."

"You don't have to hear any more right now. I'm willing to wait for a while. But I'm not going to go away."

He stepped back to let her by, and she strode purposefully, hair flying, to the house. It felt good to slam the back door, but it didn't dissipate the image in her mind of the tall, broad-shouldered figure, cool and strong-looking in his comfortable working gear, looking after her calmly, his face showing little evidence of what he was feeling.

"Damn you," she muttered to herself. "You're so cool. And I let my emotions get the best of me again."

Jake had not bothered her since, but he had written her letters—letters that she had stacked unopened on her desk and then one evening tossed into her bag and carried home with her. They rested now in the drawer of the table by the sofa, never totally forgotten, but out of her sight. She hoped by the time she returned they would be out of her mind.

Because now there was Greg, and surely Greg would make her forget.

When she'd finally called to tell Greg the details of her trip, he had seemed thrilled to hear her voice. "Ellen, you idiot, what were you trying to prove by running off? I was frantic trying to track you down. I wanted to explain to you, clear up our misunderstanding. I hope you got my letter."

"It's all right, Greg, we can talk about it later."

"You know I was just concerned about you, don't you—that I didn't want you to go through all that? I was only thinking about you, and you can be so blasted stubborn. Darling, you know I'd have stuck by you if you'd asked."

"It's all right, Greg." She laughed. "I'm fine now—everything's fine now—and I'm excited about seeing you." He really was pleased to hear from her, that was clear; whether he'd have stuck by her was a question that, fortunately, didn't have to be answered. She was back to normal now and could renew a relationship with Greg based on equality, not need. And that, she knew, was the only kind of relationship worth having. With Greg she would never have to worry about being hurt, because she would never lose control.

Once she'd convinced him she was only coming for a brief visit, not returning home for good, he began mapping out their days.

"Well, I'm not very happy that you'll only be here for a weekend, but it's better than nothing, and it's a perfect time for you to be here. Friday night is the Hospital Fund Ball, and everyone we know will be there."

Brandy still was not certain she was ready to face her former friends and associates, but Greg had brushed off her objections and rattled off a list of important New Yorkers who were anxious to see her again. They probably were curious about what had happened to her, she mused. Hoping that she was poor, or miserable, or shockingly aged. She'd show them.

Most of her time on the flight she spent looking over materials from previous campaign schools. She knew she would be starting with less experience than the other students, and just as she had always done in business, she was working to give herself an edge.

When they landed at National Airport, a brief glance outside showed her that winter was still in force here as well. A gray, drizzly day was her welcome. A skycap gathered her luggage and led her to the cab line. The hotel where the school was being held was not far from the airport, in Virginia rather than the District of Columbia, either so the students wouldn't be tempted by the sights and activities of the capital or, more likely, because many of the northern Virginia hotels were older and less expensive. She hoped they were not too inexpensive; a week of little sleep on an uncomfortable mattress would not help her excel at the campaign school.

She arrived in time for the opening reception, and after unpacking her bags and carefully hanging the special dresses she had brought for her New York weekend, she changed into a simple suede skirt and shirt and found her way to the hospitality suite. Although she thought she had been careful to dress simply—she had been warned that campaign operatives were not known for their elegance—she realized when she entered the room that she had not dressed down far enough. The others were in casual slacks or collegiate-looking sweaters and skirts.

Her innate sense of style and striking appearance made a sharp contrast to the crowd around her. Most of her fellow students were surprisingly young, and many seemed to be acquainted already. They seemed to speak in a special code, reminding one another of campaigns and candidates of the past in terms she could scarcely understand. Terms like "GOTV," "targeting," "GRPs," "RNC." For a moment she felt an urge to walk out. Why should she compete with these people in a world she obviously did not understand? But she caught herself, remembering what Howard had told her before she'd left Billings.

"Brandy, you probably won't feel you have much in common with the people you meet this week. You may feel you don't know anything after you've listened to them a while. But just remember that every profession has its special language, and by the time you finish this week, you'll realize you know just as much as they do about running a campaign, if not more. It's like running a business in a lot of ways. You just have to catch up on the terminology."

She smiled to herself. Howard was probably right. After all, what could be more political than the environment she had left behind in New York?

Brandy moved to the nearest group and introduced herself. They were pleasant and seemed curious about her and her campaign. None of them had ever visited Montana, and the unusual nature of political campaigning in a state so large geographically and small in terms of population clearly intrigued them. These people talked about nothing but politics, she discovered. They lived, breathed, and ate politics. When they finished discussing their own campaigns, they started on others they'd heard about. She began to harbor serious doubts that she could ever feel at home in this group.

But there was no time to worry about herself. The school started fast, with instructors throwing information at them at an incredible rate and expecting it back at almost the same pace. By the second day Brandy was certain she'd never survive; one group had already stayed up all night working on an assignment. By the third day she had reversed herself; she thought she might make it.

Her sense of organization helped her more as the others began to wear themselves out with evenings in the bar—talking politics, of course—and all-night working sessions. By Thursday she hadn't made lots of friends, but she was clearly a leader in the class. Political operatives apparently respected power; she could feel their deference.

By the time she had to meet with the Republican party staff, who would decide on the level of importance of Howard's campaign, she felt comfortable. She was glad she had picked up the proper terminology in the past few days. She spoke with confidence of the implications of the survey data, the campaign's strategy, and the targeting of the district's voters. When she left to return to the hotel, she knew Howard Morrison's race would receive top priority—and top funding.

She was flushed with excitement when she rejoined the group at the hotel. They crowded around her excitedly; she was the first to actually approach the party for campaign support, and they all knew how critical the outcome would be.

"We got it," she cried. "Howard's on the A list!" The young people who a week ago had seemed so alien, and so featureless, were suddenly her closest friends. She understood all at once the feeling of camaraderie she had observed among them. We're all in this together, she thought. We'll all have the same experiences. Some will win, and some will lose, but we understand things that no one on the outside can possibly know. And as different as I am from these strange and single-minded people, I will always have a bond with them.

These people were now friends and resources—contacts she could call on for help over the next few months. She had a network again.

On the final day of the school, it was as if she had been initiated into a club. One of the young men was as blunt with her as he had been in his questions for the instructors. "Brandy," he said, "when you walked in that first night I figured somebody had made a big mistake. But you know, we've all decided you ain't so bad after all." He slapped her on the back and joined the others in a cheer for her—an emotional moment in an exhausting week.

Several weeks later the lead trainer called and during the conversation told her that the group had all known who she was. Political operatives were great newspaper readers, and her "secret" had been no secret to them. In her mind that made those in the group even more admirable, for no one had ever alluded to it.

It was hard to refocus her thoughts for the New York weekend. When she boarded the shuttle at National Airport she was still caught up in the political fervor she knew would not interest Greg in the least. She consciously willed herself to think about the weekend and the excitement of seeing Greg again.

Her life was split into separate little pieces, she thought. Her Montana experience, her political self, her New York persona; somehow she'd have to get the pieces all put together into the semblance of a single life. But not now. Right now she was still growing, and changing, and learning.

17

The cab dropped Brandy on Park Avenue in front of Greg's building. She could hardly keep from grinning broadly; even the surliness of the cab driver didn't bother her today. New York! Home! The crowds, the shops, the sounds, the very atmosphere, excited her. This, she told herself, is where I belong.

It almost seemed that her blood was running faster, slowed by the long months at Montana's leisurely pace but now returning to the surge that she needed to keep her going in New York's high-powered world. Washington had been a start, but nothing compared with this.

The doorman buzzed her upstairs, and Greg greeted her at the door with a kiss—and a very dry martini. "You look gorgeous," she cried. "I can't tell you how wonderful everything and everyone looks."

"You've missed me after all. Weren't there any big macho cowboys out there to keep you happy?" He did not seem to notice her startled look but pulled her close to him and tipped her head up to look into her eyes.

"I've missed you, Ellen," he said. "I can't tell you how much. It's wonderful to have you back in my arms."

She studied his lean, handsome face carefully. "Yes," she said, "you are truly the world's sexiest man."

He laughed and pushed her away playfully. "Not right now, sweet. You need to get unpacked and start dressing. We have cocktails at the Whitneys' at seven."

She looked at him questioningly.

"Well, there will be two hundred or so of their closest friends there, too. I worked on a project with Randolph and his people recently, and we hit it off. You'll like him."

Brandy tried to picture her uncle or any of her Montana friends in this environment. How out of place they would be! Strangely enough, Jake was the only one of the Montana group she could imagine fitting in at a New York society party. Something about his manner was almost universally acceptable—but she put Jake out of her mind.

That Friday evening seemed to be surrounded by a golden cloud. It contrasted so sharply with her new life that it hardly seemed real.

Although the sleek green-beaded dress she wore was not new, she could see that it looked different on her now. Perhaps it was the subtle roundness of muscle as the dress slid over her body, or the healthy color of her face. It had been a long time since she'd protected her skin from sun and weather, but strangely enough the result was a glow of health.

Greg was clearly impressed. He studied her carefully. "Is it the hair," he asked, "or something else about you?"

She glanced in the mirror to assess herself, touching the full, tawny cloud of hair lightly. "I have let my hair grow quite a bit," she agreed. "But maybe it's just that I feel so good. I'm so excited to be back."

The evening whirled past. Cocktails with the cream of New York society, then on to one of the season's many charity balls. Greg knew everyone, of course, and she was surprised by the friendliness of the people she knew but had not seen for so long. True, no one begged her to meet them for lunch or tea, but she was relieved to find that she felt completely comfortable and very much at home.

It helped that she and Greg made such a striking couple. Greg was as usual totally at ease, a slight smile on his tanned face, blue eyes sparkling at the women whose hands he squeezed lightly, his white teeth gleaming. He could have been a star as easily as one of his clients, but he was always more interested in power than visibility, and entertainment law had provided him with more than enough opportunities for power and contacts and, of course, money.

There was one brief moment when she was certain she saw some unfriendly stares from a whispering group, but she could hold her head high now. Even the most successful of her Wall Street friends were impressed by her new career in politics. If they only knew, she thought to herself, how mundane political work really was—but they didn't, and she wasn't about to tell them.

The limousine ride home was another wonderful surprise. Greg had stocked the bar with champagne and ordered his driver to take a leisurely cruise around the city while they relaxed in their very private cocoon.

"Well," he asked, "what do you think? Feel good about being back? You certainly were the center of speculation tonight. It was nice to be able to tell people you were with me—you looked spectacular."

She leaned her head against his shoulder and sighed. "I can't tell you how good it feels," she said.

He pulled her to him and teased her lips lightly with his tongue, then kissed her with a growing fervor. "We have a lot to catch up on," he whispered. As he explored her face and shoulders with his lips, he reached over to tap lightly on the glass that separated them from the driver, a signal to return home.

There was a fire burning in the living room fireplace when they returned and yet another bottle of Dom Pérignon chilling in an ebony bucket on the low glass table in front of the fire. The crackling fire seemed incongruous somehow in this modern room with its unsullied expanses of creamy white, but when Brandy looked into the flames and felt Greg's hands on her shoulders, the room around her faded away.

"I had planned for us to sit on the terrace," he said, "but it's a bit cool even with the garden heaters, and I don't want you to get chilled. Everything has to be perfect for my Ellen."

She felt a stirring of impatience as he began their familiar routine of lovemaking, but she pushed it aside and entered eagerly into their slow and measured duet. They sipped champagne as their hands and lips delicately explored, and finally he touched her cheek and whispered, "Now?"

"Yes, now," she replied, and led him into the familiar master bedroom.

Nothing had changed in the huge room overlooking the lights of the city. The draperies were open on the view and the bedcovers turned back neatly. A dim light burned in a corner. Nothing was changed, nor, mechanically, had their lovemaking. Greg knew every nerve ending, every pleasure center in her body, and slowly he reacquainted himself with each of them.

"This is your night, my love," he whispered. "I want to give you the most pleasure a man can give a woman. I want you to have something to remember, so you'll remember where you belong, and so you'll come back to me soon." He smiled to himself as he lowered his body to hers to complete their union. It was a strange smile, but she was beyond analyzing as their bodies joined.

She touched his hair absently as they lay still twined together. She felt at peace with herself— surely she did. If some small thing seemed missing, she didn't let herself think what it was. Briefly she recalled Jake's lovemaking—the sheer joy she had felt at the touch of his body. She shivered slightly as she remembered the abandon, the uncontrolled passion. of their embrace. No, so much easier with Greg . . . comfortable . . . safe.

She woke the next morning to the sound of rain pelting the long window overlooking the terrace. March in New York was no better than usual this year. But, wrapped in a silk robe and enjoying a late breakfast in the library, Brandy scarcely noticed the gusts of rain outside the windows. Milagros, Greg's housekeeper, was delighted to see her.

"Oh, Miss Brandon, it's so nice to have you back. When Mister Gregory told me you had gone I just couldn't believe it. Why, you better go after that pretty lady, I said. You never going to find anybody good as her." Milagros beamed as she poured coffee for the two of them. "You going to be in for dinner, Mister Gregory?"

Greg looked up from the newspaper briefly. "No, you can go ahead after you get the place tidied up. We'll be out most of the day. Still want to go to that art gallery, love?"

"I do," Brandy replied. "I know you don't particularly like western art, but Thomas Littlehorse is unique. Seriously—I can't tell you how impressive this man is. Even someone with your good taste would like his work."

"Hey, don't get snappish, Ellen. I don't mind taking a look at his things. If he's as good as you say, I thought I might suggest to T. J. Three that he join us at the gallery. He has money to burn, and he's wild about western art."

"T. J. Three?"

"Terrence John Cavanaugh the Third, remember? Surely you haven't forgotten the most deadly dull old-money intellectual bore in New York."

"Greg, he's a brilliant man," Brandy protested. "And I'll bet he's got foresight enough to appreciate Thomas's work."

"If you're that sure of this Indian of yours, I'll call T. J. and tell him we've got a real find for him. "I hope there's enough in it for you."

Brandy puzzled over his last comment as he left the room, but she let it pass. How exciting it would be if she could find an important collector who appreciated Thomas. His single one-man show in New York had been well received, but it hadn't generated the big sales he needed to establish his reputation.

And Greg's judgment was correct. He had a wonderful ability to know exactly what a person would be interested in; he seemed to know almost instinctively their weaknesses, their greatest desires.

T. J. was ecstatic over their find. "My God, Ellen, the man is superb. Where ever did you find him? Just look at this—" He gestured at a small but powerful oil on the wall near them. "If this doesn't make you cry, you're not human. And this—the sheer size of the piece is awesome, but the anger—I'd almost be afraid to hang it."

Brandy and T. J. spent an hour studying the work at the gallery and another hour over cocktails, discussing Thomas and the importance of his work. T. J. became uncharacteristically animated as he described to them the excitement of discovering a new artist. "It's truly amazing," he said, "to see technique like Thomas's in an artist who is almost completely unschooled, and who grew up with no exposure to art. There has to be something about that part of the country. I get a glimpse of some of the same feeling, strangely enough, from Jay Mills's writing. And of course he must live quite close to you there, too, I gather."

"Jay Mills? The novelist? Why, I had no idea he lived in eastern Montana. I would think someone that well known would be talked about, and I certainly haven't heard a word about him since I've been there."

"He apparently keeps to himself. Doesn't like a lot of attention. I happen to know his publisher rather well, and he told me that Mills lives out that way. Drives him crazy the way the man avoids the limelight."

Brandy nodded thoughtfully. "You know, it's funny that you say Thomas' work reminds you of Jay Mills' writing. I tried to read that best-seller of his, *Days of Darkness*, a couple of years ago, and I couldn't get through it. I've never been very patient with fiction. But after spending some time in Montana, I ought to try again."

"My dear, with the strong feeling you have for Thomas's work," T. J. admonished her, "you're depriving yourself of an important experience if you don't read Jay Mills."

"I suppose you're right," she agreed. A nudge from Greg interrupted her thought. He was glancing subtly but meaningfully at his watch, and she suddenly realized he had been silent for some time.

T. J. started. "My goodness, you two probably have plans, and I must be at home by seven. Ellen, I'll work with the gallery—I want to buy at least two of the pieces we saw—but I also want to visit the artist in Montana as soon as possible. He sounds like a fascinating man." He leaned over to kiss her cheek. "My dear, you have given me a priceless gift. Thank you. And you, too, Gregory, for thinking of me." He turned and strode out, his portly figure commanding immediate attention as he called for his ageless Rolls-Royce.

Greg smiled at Brandy. "A gift, he says. Your share of the commission on those two paintings he bought will be a tidy sum, and I assume you have an ongoing deal so you'll share in any future sales he makes to T. J. Congratulations. You haven't lost your touch."

She stared at him. "Did you really think—what in heaven's name gave you the idea I was doing this for money? Thomas Littlehorse is a great artist and a friend, not someone I can make money from."

"You're joking. Do you mean we've wasted all this time with that boor and you aren't making a cent from it? What's wrong with you?"

"What's wrong is wrong with *you*," she snapped, "if you think making money is all I care about."

The argument was put on hold through a tense dinner and was still unresolved at bedtime.

"Look, Ellen, you have to understand that I'm confused. A year ago you'd have agreed with me completely. Now suddenly you come back from the Wild West with some crazy nickname and talk about art and ideals. It's hard to adjust." He did look confused as well as contrite, a highly unusual state for Gregory Marinelli, and she could not stay angry with him. Perhaps she *had* changed.

Greg had planned their weekend thoroughly. Reassuring her that it was important for her to renew old contacts, he had scheduled a brunch on Sunday for thirty friends and business associates who he felt might be useful to her in her new career. She protested that she hadn't looked beyond that fall's election, but he was insistent.

"Ellen, you have to get back to normal as fast as you can. I won't bring up yesterday again, but it's not like you not to be planning ahead. But you'll be okay." He smiled. "My tough, gutsy woman will be back in no time. I can see glimpses of her already."

Why did that make her uncomfortable? Brandy wondered. Surely she wanted to complete her recovery? She resolved to enjoy the brunch, however, rather than use it to develop contacts. This weekend was supposed to be for relaxation.

Milagros had outdone herself with the food, and as usual, Greg and his staff—with extra serving people from an agency—made party giving look effortless. Greg appeared not even to notice the arrival of platters of food, the refreshing of the guests' mimosas, the refilling of empty dishes and clearing of soiled china. It was only once during the party that Brandy caught that subtle motion to a waiter that indicated displeasure. How nice to be able to thoroughly enjoy one's own parties; she had almost forgotten the pleasure of having everything taken care of for her.

She was standing in the library talking with a group of Wall Street investment bankers, not totally at ease because she wasn't certain how they felt about her involvement in the Lasker prosecution. She was circling the topics everyone really was thinking about, and glancing covertly at the doorway in hopes that Greg would appear, when she was rescued unexpectedly by a low, husky voice calling her name.

She turned in surprise. A tall woman stood grinning at her, arms spread in welcome. "Julia, I don't believe it!" Brandy rushed to meet her, and the older woman hugged her warmly.

"You look wonderful," Brandy said.

"And you as well. Everyone's been talking about how good you look these days. Everything okay?"

"Oh, Julia, everything is just fine—and I have so much to tell you. I'm so glad Greg asked you. This is his weekend, so I can't just abandon him, but I wish I could spend some time with you now that I'm getting my life in order. You may have some ideas for me, and I'm dying to know what you've been up to."

The older woman nodded. "Let's talk about that. I'm glad you're ready to be friends again."

In the excitement of their reunion, Brandy had forgotten the strain of their last meeting; she flushed at the memory of her behavior.

Julia Butler Lee was a free-lance writer and former reporter who had interviewed Brandy for a magazine article when Brandy was one of the fresh young faces on Wall Street. Although Julia was much older, Brandy had felt immediately comfortable with the casual, outgoing woman, and they had become good friends, meeting regularly for lunch or the theater, talking on the telephone at least weekly.

When Brandy began her meteoric rise, their meetings became fewer and their phone calls rare. Brandy would regularly add Julia's name to her "to call" list and fully intend to at least touch base with her, but somehow even her time on the car phone was taken up with business or business friends.

As the clouds began to appear on the horizon for the big names in the business, Julia called her and insisted on meeting for lunch. It was a rushed meal sandwiched between appointments and did not end well. Julia warned her that her contacts in the media felt the SEC was going to go after key people—big names—on the Street. She told her bluntly that she was convinced Brandy would be hurt by the investigation and urged her to get out.

Brandy was furious—partly because she knew by then what she had to do and was still fighting it—and they did not part friends. Julia had written her a note after Brandy cooperated in the investigation, but Brandy couldn't face her, not after the things she'd said. Her cheeks burned with shame when she thought about the words she had used to lash out at Julia, words propelled by the increasing effort it took to continue her denial. She knew Julia was right. That was the reason for the terrible things she had said, and she realized now that Julia must have understood. Brandy had wanted to apologize at the time, but the words would not come, and she had assumed that it was too late.

Now it looked as if they could be friends again, and it had been so much easier than Brandy had expected. The past was behind them—no need to dig it up. She suddenly realized that Julia was one of the few New York friends she had really missed. She went through the motions with the other guests but spent most of her time with Julia in the library.

After everyone but Julia had left, Greg finally reminded Brandy—a note of slight annoyance in his voice—that she had better get ready to head for the airport.

"Oh, Greg," she said apologetically, "I'm so sorry I've neglected you this afternoon. It's just so good to see Julia again, and we have so much to catch up on."

Julia squeezed Greg's shoulder as she passed him, shrugging into her tan raincoat. "Greg, you've been wonderfully patient with us," she said. "I'll take off now and let you two say your good-byes in peace. By the way, Ellen has invited me to spend some time at her uncle's ranch. I'm thinking of doing a piece on Montana for an outdoor magazine, and she knows how I love to ride." She turned to look at him and added casually, "Why don't you come along? Ellen says there's plenty of room."

Greg laughed and shook his head emphatically. "You're joking, of course. Dirt and discomfort are not my style—nor are cowboys and Indians. I'll wait for Ellen to come back to New York, and I'm willing to bet it will be soon." He looked down at her, eyes full of meaning, and brushed the hair from her face. Brandy felt as if she were surrounded by an enormous soft cocoon. Did she really have the energy to return to Montana and the struggle to start over? But it would only be temporary. Although Greg had not been specific about their future together, she was sure he planned to make the relationship permanent. And that was what she wanted, wasn't it?

18

Brandy had planned to spend the long flight back to Billings working on a rough draft of the campaign plan. The plane was not crowded, so she had a row to herself. But it was hard to concentrate; her thoughts kept intruding, and they were not thoughts about the campaign.

Now that the weekend lay behind her, she felt depressed and let-down somehow. All the excitement of her return to New York had been short-lived, and already she was more confused than ever about the future. It was only now, moving away from it, that it hit her: she had changed even more than she had realized. She had enjoyed her visit, but New York no longer seemed like home to her.

So where was her home? Certainly not in Montana. Perhaps it was just Greg—the arguments they'd had over the weekend.

She laid her head back against the seat and, eyes closed, tried to analyze the things that had bothered her. The incident with T. J. Three, for a start. Greg had assumed she was introducing Thomas

Littlehorse's art to a collector in order to make money. And he was right, of course—a year ago she probably would have.

But a year ago she hadn't known Thomas or his work—she wouldn't have had any reason to care about him as a person. Still, Greg couldn't understand that difference.

And his thinly veiled sarcasm when he talked about the ranch—his annoyance when she tried to explain the strange pull of the prairie. Yet how could she expect him to understand something he'd never experienced? Ah, there was no point in trying to analyze everything, she told herself. New York wasn't perfect, but she still loved it—she just noticed more of the unpleasant details you found in every big city now that she wasn't in such a rush. And Greg . . . well, Greg wasn't perfect, either, any more than she was. But he cared about her, and he represented the life she wanted. Maybe they could work out the differences.

When she returned east permanently she knew it would all be much simpler. She still felt a shiver of excitement at the thought of returning to New York . . . well, Washington first, of course. And Greg was the kind of man she always pictured by her side when she dreamed of her return.

She ordered a glass of mineral water from the flight attendant and pulled out the notes she had taken at the campaign workshop. She was excited about immersing herself in the familiar routine of management. Running a political campaign was clearly more time-consuming than an ordinary full-time job, and that was exactly what she needed in order to eliminate the conflicts that she wasn't ready to deal with. That wide Montana sky outside and the disturbing figures in the barren landscape would not intrude in the familiar world she was going to create around her.

She scarcely noticed the change of planes in Denver, and it seemed to her she had just resettled herself with her papers on the Denver-Billings flight when the note of the engines changed and the pilot announced they were beginning the approach to the Billings airport.

It was almost nine o'clock when they landed, and Brandy expected to take a cab home to a hot bath and some kind of snack—she had skipped what passed for dinner on the plane. As she walked up the ramp and into the gate area, she was trying to remember exactly what she had in the freezer. So she didn't notice a familiar face in the crowd.

"Brandy."

"Eila—what are you doing here?" Brandy hugged her friend warmly, then stepped back and frowned down at her in mock anger.

"You didn't come all the way out here just to meet me, did you?"

"Of course not," Eila said seriously, "I was just driving by and I decided to stop to see if there were any strangers coming into town." Laughing, she picked up Brandy's underseat bag and started down the broad hallway to the baggage area. "Come on, slowpoke, I've got dinner waiting, and Howie will beat us home if we don't hurry."

Brandy retrieved her bag from the carousel and

had started back to join Eila when she suddenly dropped the suitcase. "Eila! I'm such an idiot! I forgot to tell you the most exciting news of the whole trip. "

"Well, don't scare me half to death. Tell me what it is."

"It's Thomas," Brandy said excitedly. "Have you ever heard of Terrence J. Cavanaugh the Third?"

"Of course—who hasn't! He's one of the foremost collectors of western art in this country. Oh, Brandy, don't tell me he's buying one of Thomas's paintings."

Brandy held up two fingers and grinned at her friend. "And more later," she added.

"Oh, my God, I don't believe it." Eila enveloped Brandy in a hug, then held her at arm's length. "Do you realize what this means?"

"Of course I do—that's why I'm so excited," Brandy answered.

"But you never told me you knew Cavanaugh. Why didn't you mention it before?"

"Well, to tell you the truth I didn't know him all that well. You have Greg Marinelli to thank for this one. It was his idea to invite T. J. to see Thomas's work—he doesn't like western art himself, but he figured if Thomas was any good, T. J. would thank him for the opportunity. As he did."

"That was very thoughtful of Greg," Eila said.

"Yes. Well, it certainly turned out well. Let's go—I'm starving."

Howie had not only beaten them to the Morrisons' comfortable home overlooking the city, he had chilled a bottle of champagne and was ready with glasses when they walked in.

"Wow, you really are glad to see me," Brandy said. "Champagne?"

Howie gathered them both close and gave Eila a kiss. "I've got great news to celebrate—not that I'm not glad to see you back, Brandy, but this is important to you, too."

"So, are you going to keep us in suspense forever?"

Howie simply smiled as he peeled the foil from the champagne cork and showed the two of them the label. They nodded appreciatively. Holding a towel around the bottle and using his thumbs in the best wine steward fashion, he popped the cork neatly and poured three glasses of the pale golden liquid. He handed each of them a glass and raised his own in a toast.

"To our new campaign chairman," he said solemnly. "Art Wilson."

Brandy felt a thrill of excitement run through her. This was it . . . this was what they had needed to make this campaign a winner, the last piece in the puzzle.

"Howie, I can't believe it. Art Wilson hasn't been associated with a congressional campaign in twenty years. Uncle John told me that—said Art told him he was fed up with penny-ante campaigns and penny-ante people. Nothing but presidential campaigns were worth his attention, he said."

"Well," Howie said, "he's just changed his mind. Actually said I was the first candidate for Congress he'd seen in twenty years who deserved to be elected."

The three of them could barely contain their

excitement. Rejuvenated by Howie's pleasure and Eila's obvious pride, Brandy forgot the late hour. Art Wilson was indeed a coup for any campaign. The most powerful political figure in the state. He could bring in a flood of money simply by giving his approval to the candidate. Most of the time he restricted his activities to raising huge war chests for the party's presidential candidates, and getting him to agree to chair the campaign committee could make the financial difference between winning and losing the election. With Art Wilson on board, the campaign didn't even need a paid finance director, just a volunteer to collect the checks and coordinate the fund-raising events.

"You need to talk to Art tomorrow, Brandy. I've told him you're managing the campaign, and he wants to meet you. Just remember, he's a little old-fashioned, but he's really a good old guy."

Brandy saw nothing but good times ahead for the Morrison campaign.

Until she met Art Wilson.

She was amused to see that his office was in a sense a western caricature of the Walter Lasker power suite. On the tenth and top floor of a bank building, it overlooked a city somewhat less spectacular than New York, but the view was still impressive by local standards. His office was large, but instead of the cool, understated elegance of a wealthy Wall Street tycoon, it featured oversize leather furniture, low tables scarred by boot heels, a credenza stacked with papers and maps, and the overwhelming odor of old cigar smoke.

Art Wilson jumped to his feet as she entered and

stubbed out his stogie in a big brass ashtray on the desk. "Sorry, Brandy, come on in," he yelled. "I quit these things years ago, but the one right after lunch, well, somehow it's just too good to give up." He shook her hand heartily and motioned her to one of the big leather chairs. "Come and sit, girl. I'm delighted to meet you. Heard a lot about you from John Brandon. He's real proud of you."

Art was a big man with an ugly, weathered face and a freckled balding head fringed in iron gray. The face was deceptively bland and open, but the narrow eyes held that shrewdness she expected; those eyes looked her over coolly and carefully, absorbing her every action. This man was as powerful in his sphere as Walter Lasker had been in his, and she knew it was important to establish herself as his equal.

"Art, I was thrilled to hear you're with us. It's going to make all the difference to our campaign. What can I do to bring you up-to-date at this point?"

"Well, I'll tell you, little lady, the first thing you do is bring me a copy of the campaign plan you've put together so I can see if you're on the right track here. You're pretty new to this state, and we want to make sure you know how we do things."

Brandy bit her tongue to hold back her annoyance. Her uncle and Howie Morrison might admire him, but she suspected already that Art Wilson was one of the goodest of the good old boys and would probably be a thorn in her side for the remainder of the campaign.

"I'm sure you'll like the plan we've put together, Art," she replied coolly. "It's innovative, but it takes advantage of Howie's strengths and the weaknesses of Tom Bainbridge, the Democrat who'll undoubtedly be Howie's opponent."

"Well, that's just fine, Brandy. I'm sure those folks in Washington taught you how they think a campaign should be run, and I'll bet you're a real good manager. But you don't know Montana—things are different here—and that could hurt you in the long run. Those RNC folks who taught you about campaigns have their agenda, and believe me, it don't involve making our lives easier."

Nor are you going to make my life easier, she thought, and she smiled grimly and let him usher her out the door.

Brandy was shocked to find she had little support in her battles against Art Wilson. Even Eila suggested she try to compromise.

"But, Eila," Brandy argued, "the man is stuck in the politics of thirty years ago—he wants us to run a campaign as if television had never been invented—or modern direct-mail techniques. He may be a successful businessman, but he knows nothing about today's political campaigns. If I cave in to him and abandon my campaign plan, we can't win."

"Brandy, he's not interested in jettisoning the whole plan—I've heard him tell Howie you've got a good mind. He just thinks you haven't taken into consideration the things that make Montana politics different. Or at least not enough of them."

Brandy sighed and shook her head. She had been warned that the people of every state insist that their state is different. Her uncle was almost as bad.

"Brandy, don't sell Art short. Yes, he's probably behind the times on the technical things, but he's a wily old buzzard and he knows people. 'Specially Montana people. Stick to your guns on the things that matter, but let him guide you on the local angles. He's been at this a long time."

"But, Uncle John, all he talks about is how the political people in Washington don't know anything about the West, and how their ideas won't work here, while I'm trying to convince people to adopt those ideas."

"You sure they will work here?"

"Uncle John, don't you turn into another Art Wilson." And she changed the subject before he could do just that.

When Greg called her she tried to avoid complaints, regaling him instead with amusing stories of small-town fund-raising events and trips with Howie to places so remote that almost everyone there flew his own plane and the entire population came out to hear a candidate speak. Greg in turn described how wonderful New York was this time of year, what was new on Broadway, and whom he'd just had lunch with. He had taken an interest in New York politics and was convinced she'd fit in much better there.

"Greg, these people you're talking to are Democrats," Brandy reminded him. "I'm a Republican. There's a difference."

"Oh, not that big a difference, Ellen. Actually I think you're right, though—you will have to switch parties if you're going to make an impact in New York politics. But that's no problem."

There didn't seem to be much point in arguing with Greg about political ideology; she would worry about that discussion much later. His attitude was annoying, but for now she had a campaign organization to build.

In the early days of the campaign, before her trip to Washington, she operated out of a corner of Howie's law office. For several months the campaign had consisted of Howie's travels around the district, talking to the key party people, raising money, and just plain touching the appropriate political bases. Her job was to contact the people on the lists Howie passed on to her and line up chairmen in each county. Once the skeleton organization was in place and the strategy and plan developed, they would begin to think in terms of visibility.

Now she was far busier, finding a headquarters location, hiring staff, and identifying volunteers to staff the headquarters. That, of course, was in addition to shepherding the brochures, buttons, and bumper strips through the tedious processes of design and printing. She startled the account rep from the ad agency by saying, "Look, we're not after any design awards here. We want people to know Howie's name, and know he's a good guy. Let's cut out all the fancy stuff."

Finding a headquarters location was easier than she had expected. Business was slow in the area, which was why Howie was focusing his campaign on economic development issues, and Brandy found several reasonably priced storefronts right downtown. Howie was popular enough in the business community that any of the landlords was willing to accept a short-term rental. She chose a space right down from the Northern Hotel, convenient to restaurants and meeting space at the Northern or the Sheraton and close enough to Eila's gallery that they could lunch together when she had time.

She crossed that item off her "to do" list and bravely attacked the next items on the very long sheet. Some days she thought she'd never get to the end of it, but when she called fellow students from the campaign school, all of them were going through the same thing—and she was farther ahead than most. Eila warned her repeatedly not to overdo the long hours but to do what she could and get help with the rest.

"I know how to delegate, Eila, but I don't have a staff yet, and there are a ton of things to do. I can't get behind now, or I'll never catch up."

"And if you exhaust yourself now, you won't be able to handle the problems that come up when we get into the real campaign season. Didn't they tell you in that campaign school that `the winning campaign is the one that leaves the least number of things undone'? You can't do everything you want to do. And I'm talking to a brick wall, aren't I?"

Brandy laughed. "Okay, I promise you I'll at least try to take weekends at the ranch. Most of the time. I miss being able to get out and ride every day. I think riding keeps me from getting so tense."

"And every so often I'll come over there and drag you away for a break. As the candidate's wife, I have that privilege."

She was right, Brandy knew. If she could get some help . . . They would have only a small paid staff, but she began taking a close look at volunteers and found a delightful older woman who offered to answer the phone two days a week and get two friends to cover the other days. She chose a volunteer coordinator recommended by Howie and found a woman who was new in the area and anxious to work as an office manager. Howie had already found two students from the university to drive him. As she had been warned, finding a press secretary was the hardest. Howie had given her the names of some possibilities, but none were available.

Finally one afternoon Howie came into the headquarters. She could hear his usual cheerful exchanges with the volunteers, but this time he poked his head into her office and gave her a thumbs-up sign.

"I've got a live one," he said. "A real live press secretary, and he's perfect."

"Come on, sit down and tell me about him," Brandy said excitedly. "Don't keep me in suspense."

Howie settled himself onto the sagging chair across from her desk. "Wow, this is really uncomfortable," he commented. "I gather you don't want people to stay long?"

"Right. It's a trick I learned."

"Heck, I could have taught you that. And now you want me to make it quick, I gather. Well, the man I'm talking about is Jack Jerome, a longtime newspaper reporter who was press secretary to the governor at one time. Lots of experience, knows his business, and knows all the media types. He's perfect."

"I hate to seem suspicious, Howie, but why does this paragon want to work for a campaign? Not that he shouldn't be thrilled to help you get elected, but it's not exactly a stable job—or high paying."

Howie nodded in agreement. "That's what I wondered, too. But apparently he just lost his business—had some kind of franchise deal—put all his cash into it and just didn't make it. Wants to get back into press work, and the campaign will give him the opportunity to rebuild his contacts. Anyway, I hope you don't mind—I went ahead and offered him the job."

"Sounds fine with me, if he's as good as you seem to think." But when Brandy interviewed him herself, she was not so certain she'd have hired him.

She felt sympathy for him. Lord knew she understood what it felt like to fail. But surely she'd handled her failure better than that. Jack seemed to have a chip on his shoulder, overreacting, assuming her initial questions were criticism. Then once she had assured him bluntly that she was not critical, only interested, his behavior turned almost flirtatious.

"Listen, Brandy, the two of us will get along just fine. We got a lot in common, you know?" Did he wink at her? He couldn't have, she told herself. But she stiffened and her voice turned cool.

"I am certain we will get along fine, Jack, as long as you do the job. I know you're qualified, and I expect you will do your best for Howie . . . and for me."

He lifted his pudgy body straighter as she stared

at him coolly. "Listen, I never minded working for a woman. No sirree, it doesn't bother me at all. The fact you're a female . . . well, I hardly even notice."

Sure you don't, pal. And I'll just bet you don't mind, she thought. One more male chauvinist. That's all she needed.

So Jack was added to the staff, and her concerns about him made that particular day another discouraging one. She still had no allies against Art Wilson and the traditionalists. It was raining, too, a dreary gray day that made her wish she had a fireplace so she could shut out the world and stare into a roaring fire.

Instead she worked until seven o'clock and then went home and put on jeans and a loose shirt. Barefoot, she padded around the small kitchen, tidying up the remains of breakfast, but she couldn't seem to find anything that interested her for dinner. For the third time she opened the refrigerator and stared at its contents, but she couldn't imagine making the effort to cook anything. There was a bottle of white wine chilled, however, so she poured a glass and curled up in the living room with the news magazines and newspapers she needed to catch up on.

They didn't hold her attention, so she picked up the fashion magazine she had bought and not gotten around to reading. Might as well see what I won't be wearing this season, she told herself. But her eyes kept straying to the painting across the room, and her mind . . . her mind kept straying to things she refused to consider. If Jake were here . . .

if his arms were around her, she wouldn't feel so alone, she found herself thinking. Why did she feel so terribly alone?

She leaped to her feet in horror at the tricks her mind was playing. She was only discouraged, she knew. It was only that she was tired and had had a bad day. She moved to the telephone and checked her watch. Nine o'clock. Julia would still be up at midnight in New York, if she was in New York. When she heard the familiar throaty voice, Brandy sighed with relief.

"Julia, it's so good to hear your voice," she said.

"Ellen? My God, I'm glad you called. How's it going?"

"I'm going nuts. I've never seen so many macho male chauvinists."

"More than here in New York?" Julia drawled. "That's hard to believe, my dear."

"Well, maybe not more. Just different." They laughed together. "But I called because you've absolutely got to come out here and save my sanity—you promised to visit, and I've figured out that by the time the primary election is over the first week of June, I will need a break *very* badly, and it would be a perfect time for you to visit the ranch."

"Hmmm. Not a bad idea. I've got some work out west, and I'm dying to visit Montana. I've never been there, you know."

"You'll love it," Brandy assured her, even though she couldn't exactly picture Julia enjoying life on the plains. She did ride, though. Of course she'd enjoy it—she wanted to write an article about it, for heaven's sake.

They made plans for Julia's visit and caught up on the past few weeks.

"You've been very busy, Brandy," Julia commented. "Are you sure you can spare the time?"

"I have to take the time, for my own mental health!" Brandy had completely dispelled by now her depression and the disturbing images it had brought. But another unwelcome problem crept up when Julia slyly asked her pointed question:

"And when is Greg coming out to visit you on the ranch, my dear? I'll bet you can't wait to share it with him."

Brandy couldn't believe how wonderful spring felt. People had warned her that the threat of winter wasn't really over until Memorial Day weekend—and that was no guarantee—but she was sure that winter had lost its grip. The prairie wind was almost gentle now, and the sunshine, which wasn't exactly warm, caressed her face when she went out to savor it during her noontime walks at work. The subsidence of the cold stark days of winter and the promise of warmer days ahead carried a personal message as well. She could see a spring in her own life; the New York debacle was sliding farther into the past, and the campaign was promising a new life of successes and triumphs.

Out on the prairie the calves had been born, and their spindly legs had gained strength, although not grace. During Brandy's weekends at the ranch, the creatures' antics provided many laughs when she and Susie took their ritual rides together. She and the little girl had formed a deep friendship. There were times when Brandy ached to have a child of her own like Susie, but she would pull herself away from the thought, knowing that a family would have to wait for some time yet.

The prairie had come alive. The grass actually was green, and there were puddles and ponds everywhere. Streams appeared where dry, lifeless creek beds had marked the landscape six months ago. Brandy was surrounded by a strange feeling of excitement. Life was good, and she was enjoying it more than ever, although there always seemed to be a piece missing.

As soon as the weather made it possible, she had started walking to work. The brisk exercise first thing in the morning gave her a burst of energy to start her long day, and at night there was always someone to drop her off at home after work was done.

Her uncle had loaned her the money to buy a used car, a heavy sedan similar to his own. "Now look," he said, "you may like walking as much as anybody, and you can walk all over Billings if you want—well, not all of it, but most of it in the daytime—but I don't want you walking anywhere around the city after dark. Folks are pretty friendly around here, but there's still plenty of trouble waiting to happen in a place the size of Billings, and you need to be careful. And not only that—how the heck do you expect to get out to the ranch on weekends if you've got no transportation? I could let you use the Buick now and then, but you need a car of your own. You just go on down to Sam Jensen's and let him pick one out for you."

"Let a used-car dealer pick one out? Isn't that

taking a terrible risk? I mean, I've never owned a car before, but I've always thought used-car dealers—"

"You've never owned a car?"

"Well, I never needed one in New York," she said defensively. "I mean, it wasn't practical. I hired a . . . well, and before that I was always in school."

He shook his head in wonder. "Your first car. Well, I'll be. I'm going to have to go down there with you, I guess. Sam will treat you fair, but I want you to have something real nice."

The dark green Oldsmobile with thin creamy striping had been specially painted and fitted with soft tan leather seats for a wealthy farmer several years ago, and he had obviously babied it. Brandy grudgingly admitted it was a beauty but stubbornly continued to walk to work and leave it in its protected garage stall during the week.

On the weekends, though, when she made the two-and-a-half-hour drive to the ranch, she was grateful for the heavy vehicle and its smooth ride. She now understood why Montanans favored the big American cars; the vast distances they drove regularly made easy handling and comfort a necessity. In a state five hundred and sixty miles across with a widely dispersed population, one or two hundred miles seemed like nothing.

I'm beginning to live like a native, she thought—jumping in the car to spend the weekends out at the ranch, sometimes driving back to town Saturday night for a campaign event, then back out in the morning. She would spend the weekend days riding, going over the house plans or discussing politics with her uncle, or simply relaxing, talking idly with Hattie, reading in her uncle's study.

It helped to separate her life into distinct compartments—her work, her weekends, and, tucked away somewhere not to be inspected as yet, her future plans. Jake was never mentioned, and she managed to keep him out of her thoughts. At the ranch she avoided him; when she did run into him she felt a dull ache in her heart, but she never spent time alone with him, and she never let him know how deeply he had hurt her. She had preserved her dignity, and she was not going to allow Jake Milburn to spoil her enjoyment of her new home and family—a family of sorts, anyway, and the first family she had known in a long time. Her uncle could never match her own father, but he was beginning to play a father's role in her life in many ways.

By early May the workday compartment of her life was becoming less enjoyable and the weekends more critical to her as the stress of the job intensified. What seemed to her—and certainly should have been—a simple management situation became more difficult every day, and there were days when she had to fight to maintain her self-control.

One Monday morning found her making her way around the puddles left from the previous night's spring drizzle, frowning slightly as she considered the day ahead. The campaign organization she had started to develop before her trip east had looked good on paper, but it was not coming together as rapidly as she had planned. With the primary election five weeks away, she still felt things were not totally under control, despite every management trick she could come up with. There was something about a campaign that defied organization. Someone in the campaign school had described a campaign as an amoeba that had to be herded across a bridge, and she was beginning to get the point only too clearly. No matter how carefully she tried to keep it on track, the thing kept slopping over; things were left undone, important deadlines passed unheeded, and she was continually working late trying to catch up on what the others had cheerfully dropped at the end of the day. If the situation didn't improve, she would have to give up all her weekends at the ranch.

Sure enough, the headquarters was still dark when she arrived, despite the fact that she had scheduled an eight-thirty staff meeting and expected the staff to come in early. She hung up her coat and resigned herself to making the coffee again. What a comedown, she thought—she used to have people jumping if she so much as raised a finger, and now she couldn't even get anyone to make coffee for her. And the headquarters was a mess; she resolved once again to put cleanup at the top of the meeting agenda.

By eight forty-five the staff had wandered in—just as the coffee was ready, she noted. She had to rush to grab a cup before the pot was emptied, which didn't help her Monday morning mood. All right, she thought, I'll take a few deep breaths and calm down. She stood a few moments in her office, focusing on the stress management techniques she had learned in New York, before calling the staff together.

What a motley crew, she thought as she faced them across her broad desk. Jack Jerome, the press secretary, Ranny Riedorf, the volunteer coordinator, and mousy little Willa Schrader, the office manager. She had found Willa herself and felt pretty good about her abilities; she was a scared rabbit in the office but was good and stubborn with outsiders when she knew she was right. And she didn't leave with half her work undone.

Ranny was a hard worker, but she hated to argue with any of the old-timers, and the old-timers were incredibly set in their ways. Time and time again she would approach Brandy with a worried look on her face and report that one of the county chairmen had refused to do things the way Brandy wanted because "we don't do it that way here." Since the county chairmen were all volunteers, it was hard to put pressure on them.

Jack winked at her as he settled onto the soft chair directly across from her.

"This was your week to open the headquarters in the morning, Jack. Did you forget?" Brandy asked calmly.

"Couldn't make it this morning," he answered cheerfully. "Had other things to do."

She couldn't believe he'd been out of bed for long, much less accomplished anything before he arrived. He seemed to be wearing the same rumpled slacks and grimy tie he'd sported on Friday.

The shirt was fresh—she could tell because the little wrinkles along the front band and the edges of the cuffs were still white. Later in the day his entire shirt would be trimmed in gray.

"Jack, you are to be here at eight every day this week. Understand?"

"Actually, Brandy, I don't think that's necessary. The volunteers don't come in until nine, and with an easy primary race coming up, no one expects us to spend all our time here." He suddenly seemed to notice the set look on her face. "Of course, I'll be happy to if you really want, even if it isn't necessary. Today I had a breakfast meeting with Art Wilson, that's why I couldn't make it in earlier." He leaned back and smiled slyly.

Trouble, she thought. That was exactly what was wrong with this campaign. Howie had insisted Jack was the perfect person to deal with the press—the jury was still out on that—but she found Jack himself almost impossible to deal with.

"And what was the breakfast meeting about, Jack?"

"Well, you know Art figures it's real important to do newspaper advertising, and we were working out the details on that."

"Jack, newspaper advertising is not in our plan, and you know it. We've been over this before."

"Well," Jack said lazily, tipping back on his chair, "you know an old newspaperman like me isn't going to go along with that, and Art agrees with me. There's no way we're going to win this thing without newspaper ads."

"We'll finish this discussion later. In the meantime, please remember I am in charge, and I will be the one to discuss this with Art."

Jack grinned broadly. "Yes, ma'am, you just do that."

It took an hour after the meeting for Brandy to stop seething with suppressed anger. When she did, she picked up the phone to call Art Wilson and steeled herself for another head-to-head confrontation with the stubborn old man.

That confrontation would have to wait until she was calmer, she decided, or Howie might be looking for a new campaign manager. So she put down the phone and closeted herself in her office to take care of paperwork for the rest of the morning. Unfortunately the volunteer who usually answered the phones was out sick, and her replacement could not seem to understand that Brandy didn't want to be disturbed; she kept transferring calls to her line without even attempting to screen them. Finally Brandy couldn't stand it any longer. She walked out to the front desk and confronted the woman.

"Look," she said, smiling grimly, "I really need some time to get some work done. Will you please just pretend I'm not here and tell everyone I'll call them back later?"

The woman nodded cheerfully. "Gosh, if you *really* don't want to be bothered . . . "

"Thank you. I *really* don't want to be bothered." As she wheeled and started to walk back to her office, she noticed Ranny in conversation with a short, plump woman in a flowered dress, the picture of the old-fashioned farm wife. Ranny was smiling nervously and shaking her head as the woman pressed some papers on her. As the woman became more insistent, smiling and pointing to the papers in her hand, Ranny began to back away nervously.

Brandy wandered, apparently aimlessly, closer to the two of them so she could overhear their conversation, but before she could catch it, Ranny spotted her.

"Oh, Brandy, you're here. . . . I told Mrs. . . . I told her you were out. She has some literature she wants us to put out, and I was explaining we really couldn't do that." She was motioning with her head toward the materials the woman was holding and looking at Brandy meaningfully.

When Brandy glanced at the printed material, she couldn't believe what she was seeing. She had heard about these things but had never actually seen such documents. This was the most rabid, disgusting neo-Nazi material she had ever seen in her life, and this woman actually thought they might help her distribute this filth.

Brandy could feel the anger growing inside her, rising unchecked until she could stand it no longer. Her mouth moved silently at first, and then, face white and set, she threw the offensive literature to the floor.

"You get out of here this minute!" she screamed at the startled woman. "You take your filth . . . no, I'll burn this filth to be certain no one else sees it . . . and don't you ever bring your slimy Nazi self into this headquarters again. If I so much as see you near this doorway, I'll throw you out myself—and I mean *throw*!"

The silence was absolute as Brandy shoved the

stunned woman out the door and slammed it behind her. She turned and looked around, hands on her hips, surveying the observers, who sat frozen in shock.

"All right," she said, voice shaking with intensity. "This is the final straw. I am through being polite. I am through trying to be logical, or sensible, or a good manager. I am fed up with the lot of you. To think that every one of you just sat there and let that woman bring filth like that into Howie's campaign headquarters, and didn't do anything—"

"Brandy," Jack interrupted, "these crazy Aryan nation people are around—mostly up in the northwestern part of the state, I grant you—but when they come around you can just tell them to go away, that's all."

"Shut up, Jack. This incident isn't the whole load, it's just the final straw that broke the camel's back. And this camel is fed up." She whirled and glared at them again. She could see this time that the volunteers were looking very nervous.

"All right. I apologize to all our wonderful volunteers. But I am serving notice on the staff. I am walking out of here right now. I will return in two hours. When I get back this headquarters will be tidied up. You will be ready to fill me in on exactly where we are with your part of the campaign plan. My plan.

"And Jack, you will get that press release out to the wire services and the *Gazette* by the time I get back. *And you will not argue!*" With that, she stormed out the door and walked briskly down the street.

When she reached Eila's gallery, she said, "Close up for an hour. I need to talk to you." Eila took one look at her and swung the CLOSED sign into place. She led the way into her cluttered office in the back and took out a bottle of the wine she kept for special clients in the small refrigerator behind her desk. Without saying a word, she opened it, poured a large glass, and handed it to Brandy. Brandy paced the small room, muttering and clutching the wineglass in her fist.

"Hey, sit down and relax, Brandy, you're going to wear a path in my rug and break the stem of that wineglass. What in heaven's name has happened?"

Brandy threw herself onto a chair and took a gulp of the wine. "I lost it. I damn well went over the edge. I screamed, I yelled, and I threw some Nazi woman out of the headquarters . . . I mean I really *threw* her. She'll probably sue me. Eila, I completely lost control and behaved like a raging tyrant. I proved I couldn't manage this bunch without threatening them."

Eila surveyed her calmly. "It's about time," she said.

"About time! I proved I couldn't handle a campaign with the management skills I supposedly have."

"Of course you can't. A campaign is a different animal. If you want these people to pay attention, there has to be an implied threat. You've shown them what can happen when they don't do the job, and now they'll work harder and do what you tell them, until you need to blow up again."

"But, damn it, Eila, I lost control. I completely

lost control of my temper."

"And how did it feel?"

She thought for a few moments, and then a tiny smile played at her lips. "It felt wonderful . . . I have to admit it. It really felt good."

Suddenly she started to giggle. "Eila, they were scared stiff. You should have seen their faces. I just turned and glared at them, and they looked like scared rabbits. And that poor crazy Nazi woman or whatever she is, why, she almost had a heart attack, she was so scared."

When Brandy finished running through the entire scene for Eila, and finished the glass of wine, she felt calmer—elated now, but not disturbed. There was something wonderfully cleansing about getting all the anger out. Eila was right. It did feel good. And when she got back to the headquarters, the work would indeed be done.

"Do you think you can handle one more step today?" her friend finally asked.

"What now?" Whatever it was, she knew she could deal with it.

"Art."

"Oh, come on, Eila, not Art. I can't deal with another confrontation today."

"Not a confrontation, Brandy. I think it's time for a truce. And I think you have to work out the terms. Art doesn't know modern campaign politics, so he can't do this without you. But you don't know the people and the history of this place the way he does, and I honestly think you can't do it without him. And don't forget," she added softly, "it's my husband who's counting on both of you."

Brandy felt a pang of guilt. All her complaints seemed foolish when she really listened to what Eila was saying. Howie was putting everything on the line running for Congress, and she owed it to him to make sure his campaign was the best possible, even if it meant . . .

"Art really does know a lot about dealing with the people here, and I'm having an awful time convincing some of these Neanderthals to do things my way. If he'd tell them to do it my way, they'd do it." She nodded ruefully. "Okay, I'll call him now, and set up an appointment for first thing in the morning. I need to work up to it." She stood and reached for the other woman's hand.

"Come on, I'll buy you lunch. Now that you've finished psychoanalyzing me and set me on the right track."

"Look, Art," Brandy said, leaning across his desk, "I'm here to cut a deal with you."

"Oh, yeah?" He rolled an unlit cigar around his mouth, his eyes narrowing suspiciously.

"You know more about this state than I'll ever know in a lifetime, and I can't win this election for Howie without your help."

"Been telling you that all along."

"And you can't win it without my help, either, you stubborn old coot."

He dropped the cigar. "Now just a minute . . ."

"No, you listen. I can't do it without you, and you can't do it without me. You don't know a blasted thing about modern campaign techniques, and I haven't been around long enough to know how to get people to do what I want them to without screaming at them, and then they don't do it anyway. We're stuck with each other, and Howie's stuck with both of us. So I propose a truce."

"A truce? Meaning?"

"Meaning you help me bring the organization into line out there in the counties, and I listen to you when you tell me how people think around here. And we preserve the right to argue now and then, with the understanding that getting Howie elected is our first priority."

"That is for sure, young lady. Howard Morrison is going to Congress if I have to work with the Devil himself. And you," he added, grinning, "ain't quite *that* bad."

She held out her hand solemnly. "Shake on it?"

"Shake on it," he agreed. "And now let's talk about the newspaper ads."

"I knew it!" She slapped her hand loudly on his desk. "We no more agree on a truce than you try to take advantage."

He continued to stare at her without speaking. Finally she sighed and flopped onto a chair.

"All right," she said. "Let's talk about the newspaper ads."

And so the campaign proceeded through the primary election and the summer months, not always smoothly, but definitely moving. When Brandy looked back on those days, they were for the most part a blur of activity, crises to be dealt with, mailings to be rushed, deadlines to be met, volunteers to be found, and staff to be motivated. There still were battles with Art Wilson, but they were balanced now by the times he helped her bring the stubborn county chairmen into line. Jack still tried to get by her now and then, but he'd learned not to cross her on the big things.

The long hot summer seemed both endless and only a brief moment in time. Although Brandy no longer fought to hold in her emotions, she still kept her life carefully separated into things she could deal with and things she could not. The summer and fall were a part of the healing process, she felt, and by focusing on something she could do well, a task she could complete, she could prepare herself to deal with the remainder of her life after the elections.

Several times she woke startled from dreams of Jake, memories of their time together, frightening images of fear and loss. She could deal with the dreams better than the reality. Eventually she would be ready for another man—maybe Greg, but more likely someone else, she now admitted. Distance had brought Greg into sharper focus in her mind, and she could see that there was something missing in their relationship.

Once or twice she thought she glimpsed Jake on the street, and her stomach lurched in reaction. But each time when the man turned, he was just another friendly Montanan, tipping his hat and nodding as she passed.

One evening at dusk she was hurrying down a side street when there was a burst of noise from the tavern ahead and two figures staggered out onto the sidewalk, clearly drunk. She stopped in the shadows to avoid attracting attention and watched the man, leaning with his arm across the woman's shoulder while he openly fondled her large breasts with the other hand. She was heavy and tired looking, a cigarette dangling from her hand as she whispered something in the man's ear. He nodded in agreement and threw his head back to take a swig from the bottle of beer he held in his free hand.

As the light struck his face, she recognized him— it was Joe, the ranch hand who made her so uncomfortable. Was this where he had seen Jake, why he could hint with such confidence about Jake's drinking? She shuddered and remained in the shadows until the two of them climbed into a dusty pickup truck and moved off slowly.

Brandy *counted the days leading up to the early June*
primary election and Julia Butler Lee's arrival
the weekend after.

The primary election had been a letdown in a
sense, since Howie had no opposition. It was a
milestone, however, in the growth of the campaign, and a point against which to measure their
steady progress. She and Art Wilson had worked
out their differences sufficiently to develop a stable
if argumentative relationship, and the campaign
staff was, for the most part, under control. Eila was
becoming a good friend, and her deepening relationship with her uncle John played an increasing-
ly important role in her life. She was beginning to
feel the confidence and strength that came from
having a stable base of support—the base that came
from family, friends, and a place to call one's own.

Still, something was missing. Perhaps it was that
contact with another woman who understood her
past and, more important, could understand her
need to return to the East Coast. Julia Butler Lee

was someone she could talk to—someone who wouldn't require any explanations.

Brandy was excited about introducing Julia to her uncle and to the ranch. After a particularly hectic day, Brandy arrived at the airport gate a few minutes late. When she heard someone call, "Ellen! Ellen!" it took a few seconds for her to realize that this was directed at her. She turned and saw Julia standing beside her. The two women hugged enthusiastically.

Julia looked slim and youthful in her soft knit travel outfit, her camera bag slung over her shoulder. It was hard to believe this woman was close to fifty years old—a life of constant activity had kept her muscles taut and her step youthful far beyond those of most women.

"You look great," Brandy said.

"So do you."

"I'm sorry I ignored you," Brandy apologized. "No one calls me Ellen here—I've reverted to my childhood nickname because I haven't had any choice. Actually, I've gotten kind of used to being Brandy."

"Well, it suits you. And you seem to be fitting into Montana rather well. Levi's and boots—I'm impressed. I've never seen you looking so healthy. After all those stress management courses and health clubs and fitness consultants in New York, it's amazing what a little fresh air can do. Out here for less than a year and you look like a million bucks."

Brandy grinned at the compliment. "That's what's so funny—I hardly ever get a breath of fresh air—spend most of my time in an office, operate under terrific stress, have scarcely a minute to call my own, and get almost no exercise. I think I've discovered the real secret."

As they loaded two well-traveled suitcases into the car, Julia gestured at the horizon and said, "My God! Look at the sunset. What colors. It's incredible. You see paintings, even photographs, of this stuff, and in the back of your mind is a little voice that says, 'It's been touched up, it can't be that beautiful.' But this is far better than any representation."

"The sunrises are pretty nice, too," Brandy said with a grin as they got inside the car.

"What! You mean to tell me that you actually get up in time not only to see the sunrise, but to enjoy it, too? I am impressed. Montana's really getting under your skin."

Brandy felt herself bristle inexplicably at this last remark. "No, it's not. I just can appreciate real beauty even in the Wild West. Don't be fooled for a minute. I'm as New York bound as ever."

Julia gave her a wry look but said nothing.

They drove in silence for a few moments. Then Brandy said, "I know, you need to see an old Billings hangout. Let's go get a drink and a snack at the Northern." Julia, who had eaten a dinner of two small packages of airplane peanuts, heartily agreed.

As they walked into the bar, Julia noticed that every head in the place turned to watch them enter. She knew most of the looks were for her young friend. Brandy's new life-style gave her a healthy, effervescent glow. In addition to this, though, she was surprised at how many people spoke to them and called Brandy by name as they wove their way toward a table in the back of the room. In New York heads had always turned when Brandy walked into a room, but few spoke. In New York she generally came across as aloof and unapproachable. Here she was treated like one of the gang; people were obviously comfortable with her.

Brandy stopped and introduced Julia to several people as they made their way through the darkened bar. When they sat down at a table of their own, Julia laughed and said, "How can you look so healthy when you must be a regular customer in this bar? Is that the real reason you go by this new name, 'Brandy'?"

Brandy grinned. "I wondered about Uncle John, too, when I first came here with him. But this is sort of a local hangout. I haven't been here for a couple of months, but most of these people I run into in town a couple of times a week. That's the way it is. It's a small town, even if it is the largest city in the state. Everyone knows everyone else, or at least their family."

It felt so good to Brandy to talk to someone who already knew her well enough that she didn't have to explain herself. Even though Julia probably knew her too well, it was great to share Montana with someone who was seeing it for the first time exactly the way she had—as a shocking contrast to her eastern background. They stopped their chatter long enough to order drinks and potato skins.

"So if you're still New York bound, how come

you look so happy here? How come you fit in so well?" Julia asked.

Brandy leaded back in the lounge chair, her long denimed legs stretched out and crossed at the ankles, her cowboy boots worn and comfortable. She stirred her drink idly.

"I like to think that I've made the best of a bad— well, less than optimum—situation. I've adapted for the moment, and I've profited immensely from my experience here—don't get me wrong. But I haven't lost sight of myself. I belong in New York. Life here is lovely in a lot of ways, but too slow for me. I'd go crazy if I thought I'd have to stay here forever."

Julia did not respond immediately, but after sipping her drink thoughtfully she said, "It's funny, though, I would never have thought in a million years that I would see you living in a place as remote as this and doing so well. That says a lot, Ellen—I mean Brandy. It says a lot about your strength of character, and I think it says a lot about Montana. Don't underestimate the power of its pull or its effect on you. I see a tremendous difference in you already."

Brandy felt a little uneasy again, as she had in the car. Inaccurate or not, her friend's insights were touching some nerves.

Sensing her uneasiness, Julia changed the subject. "Well, now, tell me about this campaign. Is it going better for you?"

Brandy regaled her with campaign stories for the next forty-five minutes and finally noticed the time when she was about to send the waitress away for the third time with "No, nothing right now, we're just fine." She paid the check, left a big tip, and they headed back to the car and were soon on their way on the interstate.

They talked about Julia's life on the Atlantic seaboard. She'd been traveling a great deal and hadn't been to either her co-op in Manhattan or the family farm in Virginia's hunt country. Her traveling and her two homes sounded so exciting to Brandy. Secretly, in her heart of hearts, she envied her friend. Montana was a good place to learn about politics and to build character, but it was so remote. Surprisingly, Julia seemed somewhat disillusioned with her own life-style.

"I've been doing a lot of traveling in and writing about the Third World. It gives you a sense of what's important—basic freedoms, community, the right to say what you think. It's been coming for a long time—I'm tired of Manhattan, Brandy. I'm seriously considering selling my co-op and just using the place in Virginia as a base for my travels. My writing is gaining greater circulation, and there are so many ordinary people who are real-life heroes to write about. I feel so much more attracted to these people than I do to most of the people I meet in New York."

Barely pausing, she continued, "So, is anything settled between you and Greg? He seemed to be pushing you to some sort of decision when you came out to visit this winter. The two of you going to make it permanent, do you think?"

"Well, there's been a tacit understanding between us that when I return east . . . but I'm not so sure now. I want to take my time. It seems like the right thing to do," Brandy said. "I mean, Greg and I both know what we want in life. He's always been very good to me. I like the fact that he's a very practical person like I am. He's very clear about what he wants. I don't have to worry about his moods or if he's going to quit his job, sell his co-op, and move to India. I like stability in my life, and Greg can provide that. The person he was yesterday is the person he'll be tomorrow. No surprises."

"Sounds exciting," Julia said dryly.

Brandy smiled. "Okay, maybe Greg isn't the one, I don't know. But someone *like* Greg," she insisted.

"So you haven't found any potential love interests here?"

"Oh, there was one—but let's face it, they're all cowboys at heart."

"Well, how 'bout this 'one'? What happened? You don't have to tell me if you don't want to."

For some reason Brandy did feel uneasy about telling Julia about Jake but felt she'd better say something since her friend would be meeting him soon at the ranch.

"Well, to tell you the truth, I had a brief lapse from sanity with my uncle's ranch manager, Jake Milburn. At first I was really intrigued by him—a dark handsome stranger, you know—sort of naive and mysterious all at the same time. But he turned out to be just another cowboy with a lot of problems. It didn't take me too long to come to my senses." She heard her words echo with a cheerful bravado she didn't feel. She was surprised at the effect. It was as if she were piercing her own heart.

To ward off the pain, she said to herself aloud, "I need to spend this time getting my professional life together—when I've left Montana and returned east—then I can start seriously thinking about my love life."

Even though it was late when they arrived at the ranch, John Brandon was waiting up for them. The three of them had coffee and Hattie's chocolate cake, and then Brandy insisted that they retire.

"I'm worn out," she told them. "You two may not need sleep, but I've had a tough week."

Julia stood and stretched, stifling a yawn. "No, I'll join you. It's appallingly late by eastern time, and according to your previews, I've got a lot to see tomorrow."

Julia rose early on Saturday, still not adjusted to the time change, so John Brandon suggested a pre-breakfast tour of the ranch. They could drink their coffee now and eat with sharpened appetites when they returned. Tom had the horses already saddled when they reached the barn—a special courtesy for out-of-town guests—and Brandy enjoyed Julia's look of surprise when she leaped onto Sheba's back and called to her to follow.

"Now, wait a minute, Brandy. You're acting awfully casual about this, but I happen to know you never went near a horse in your life. Every time I mentioned the folks' horses and got into a conversation with someone about all those things we Virginians find exciting, you started yawning and changed the subject."

"Eastern riding is different," Brandy replied with a mock sneer. "Sissy stuff. We're tougher out here."

The three of them rode off laughing; it seemed as if they laughed most of the weekend, in fact. Julia had a quick wit and possessed an easygoing nature. She retained an attractive hint of the soft accents of her Virginia childhood and gently drawled droll responses to John Brandon's teasing remarks. She provided a perfect foil for his robust humor.

Brandy couldn't remember when she had laughed so hard.

Sunday evening they sat in front of the fire, sipping their after-dinner coffee. She had hardly thought about the campaign all weekend. The car was drawn up to the door, ready to be packed, and she and Julia were moaning about having to end such a wonderful visit.

"John, thanks for your hospitality," Julia said. "You have a beautiful place here and I've thoroughly enjoyed myself. It's a shame to leave."

"I know what you mean," Brandy said. "I go through this every time I come out here. Thank God I enjoy my job, or I'd just stay here and get spoiled rotten."

Her uncle chuckled. "Never thought I'd live to hear you say that, hon. Next you'll admit you want to stay in Montana."

Brandy shook her head, laughing. "No chance, Uncle John. It's a great place to come home to when I need a break from the real world, but we both know I'd never make it here full-time. I'll be happy if you just keep my room for the times I do come home."

"Home. Brandy, honey, that's one of the nicest

things I've ever heard, that you consider this place your home. I've always wanted a daughter. But let's not get maudlin here, ladies. I want to make a suggestion.

"Julia, we've got lots of room here, and you're sure not in anyone's way. Why don't you stick around for a while? Take some pictures and write a story for one of those big East Coast magazines. Tell them how rugged we are out here, real he-men—they lap that stuff up back there, and it keeps them from moving out here and crowding things." He smiled at her warmly.

Julia for once seemed at a loss for words. "John . . . thank you, but I—I couldn't impose. . . . "

"Julia," Brandy said, "I think it's a great idea. I'll probably be back out next weekend, and if you want to come back with me then, you can. But you'll probably have more fun out here."

Julia made a few more protests, but she was obviously outnumbered by the Brandon clan. She gave up and settled back comfortably into the red leather wing-backed chair. "How long," she mused, "can I stay here and eat Hattie's cooking without bursting the seams of all my clothes? That is the burning question."

Brandy was delighted that her friend was going to stay around a little longer. She knew that her small apartment in Billings would have been too cramped for the two of them to enjoy each other's company for very long—aside from the fact that her schedule made it impossible—and it was clear that Uncle John enjoyed Julia's company. She was surprised, in fact, at how well they got along. It seemed an odd mixture, the tough old westerner and the worldly-wise writer from the East.

But then Julia, she remembered, had always been what Brandy called a horse person, following the results of harness racing and the racing circuit of the East. Perhaps there were horse people and non–horse people, she thought. Although she had come to enjoy riding, she still could not find in herself the rabid enthusiasm she sensed in others.

Brandy left the next morning to drive back to Billings, already excited at the prospect of her next visit home.

With the mounting pressures of the job, however, that visit had to be postponed for some time.

22

One Saturday morning *Eila stopped by the campaign headquarters unexpectedly and, as usual, found Brandy working.*

"All right," she said. "Time for a break. These six- and seven-day work weeks are gonna wear you out."

Brandy blinked dazedly and pushed her hair back from her face. It was hard to refocus her thoughts. Automatically she shook her head."Oh, Eila, I'd love to take a break, but there's just so much to do!"

Her friend firmly removed the pen from her hand and took her arm. "No excuses. Howie specifically told me to get you out of here for the day. You're getting tired and irritable, and it's too early in the campaign for the manager to turn into a tyrant."

Brandy had to laugh, remembering the episode of genuine tyranny that had gotten her started on the right track in dealing with the campaign staff. Eila was right, of course. Her innate perfectionism was still driving her to work longer hours than necessary, and yes, she thought ruefully, she was getting a bit snappish with the staff. They didn't deserve it, either; they had their faults still, but even Jack now did the job with minimal prodding and no argument. Well, *almost* no argument.

She allowed herself to be led to the car. It was a nice day after all, so why not? "Where are we going?" she finally thought to ask as they headed east out of Billings. Eila was dressed in jeans and boots, with a bandanna holding back her curly hair. "Obviously it's not a formal occasion," she added, "since you didn't ask me to change, and you're not exactly dressed to kill."

"It's not a formal occasion, Brandy, but it is special. We're going out to see Thomas Littlehorse. I have to pick up a painting from him, and he said I could bring you along."

"But I thought Thomas wouldn't allow anyone to visit his studio?"

"That"—Eila laughed excitedly—"is why this is such a special occasion. He actually suggested I bring you out—he likes you—said you understand the meaning of his work."

"But . . ." Brandy was puzzled. "Yes," she said slowly, "I do have a very powerful response to his work—it's eerie, in fact. Some of his paintings draw me in so far I almost feel dizzy. But I don't know anything about Native Americans other than what I read in school. I think my response is simply to his talent."

"We'll see," was Eila's reply.

They headed east and south across the brown

landscape that Brandy had once thought so barren. Now, with her new eyes, she could see the colors around her, the shapes hidden in the mesas, the very power of the rocks. The vastness of the vistas made her heart sing. This will stay with me, she thought. Whenever I feel hemmed in by people and places, I will think myself back to this place. She observed the passing landscape carefully, memorizing colors and shapes, imprinting them on her brain. If only I could paint or write, she thought. But instead I'll have to remember it. She concentrated on the feel of the sun on her skin, the heat absorbed by the sandstone, the smell of the air.

Thomas Littlehorse lived in a small frame house set on a dirt track far off the highway. The house and barn could have been deserted but for the chickens that scattered at their approach and the sound of deep barking inside the house. How could an artist like Thomas live in a place like this? Brandy wondered. The screen door squeaked and slammed shut as he strode out to greet them.

A small man, he had a dignity and strength in his appearance that belied his short stature. Today he wore faded black work pants and a neatly pressed white shirt buttoned carefully to the neck. Brandy realized he had dressed up for their visit and felt embarrassed at her jeans and polo shirt. If she had realized—but Eila seemed quite comfortable. Stretching out her hands to him, she radiated a warmth and friendliness that made their dress unimportant. She made it clear this was as special to them as it was to him.

He had prepared coffee and cookies in the tiny kitchen, and they sat in the bare front room to drink and eat before going to the studio. There was no sign here of Thomas's art. Although the stark white of the walls and simple furnishings contrasted sharply with the house's neglected exterior, the room was bare, almost ascetic in its simplicity.

"Brandy," Thomas said in his quiet voice, "I owe you a great deal for introducing my work to Mr. Cavanaugh. I thank you."

"I'm glad it worked out, Thomas. He's quite a prominent collector, and others tend to follow his lead—it should mean some nice sales for you."

Thomas nodded. "Yes, but more important, Mr. Cavanaugh is a man with a real feeling for art. I am proud to have my work in his collection. I know the message of my work will be understood."

What an odd way to talk about his art, Brandy thought. Although—she had to admit it—she certainly got the message herself. Then Thomas startled her—she was to think about it often over the ensuing months—by saying, "I'm glad you have decided to settle in Montana, Brandy."

"But I haven't," she argued. "I'm going back to New York, where I belong. Oh, I love Montana—it's wonderful—but it's not the kind of place where I could live."

He smiled and replied quietly, "You may not recognize it yet, but you have made that decision. Your heart has already taken root here."

Why were these people so insistent? Her vehement denials were met only with silence, and Eila changed the subject to Thomas's paintings. His studio was in the old barn and was again a surprise to Brandy. Although windows and skylights had been cut into the large room to provide light, the view was uninspiring and dreary, an old car parked in the dusty yard.

This time, however, she knew without asking why the view was unimportant to him. He paints what he sees in his mind, she thought, the way I memorize scenery. But he memorizes emotion, and history, and the mystery that he feels in that scenery. Thomas, she realized, must feel the vibration left by centuries of his people's history, of their pain. It must be a wrenching process for him to put it on canvas or carve it in stone.

She looked up to see him watching her with that same strange, knowing look. It was as if he could reach into her mind.

"Thomas," she said suddenly, "are you a psychic?"

"Oh, no." He laughed. "I simply leave myself open to experience and understanding. That's very different from being psychic, but it can enable you to see things that would otherwise remain invisible. There is much around us that we miss because the senses we have been given are not fully used. When we train ourselves to be alive to these things, some people say we are psychic. But, no, I am not a psychic."

A strange answer, she thought. Almost as if by saying no he had said yes. And as they were leaving, while Eila was carefully packing the large oil in the trunk of her car and Brandy was standing chatting with Thomas in the doorway of the studio, he said something that she never forgot.

"You are going through a time of trials, Brandy. Just as the young men in many tribes must go through a series of tests to attain true manhood and acceptance into full participation in the tribe, you are going through very difficult tests. So far, you have done well. But the trials are not complete. There is great pain yet ahead for you. Be strong in yourself, but when the time comes, remember you have friends who will help."

In the months to come, his words stayed with her almost verbatim. She mulled them over in her mind many times. In the end she was glad he hadn't told her more. If she had known the rest, she might not have been able to deal with it.

Brandy leaned back luxuriously in the driver's seat as the heavy Oldsmobile cruised along the interstate. It was a great day for a drive, a clear August sky with the heat tempered by a slight breeze. She hummed along absentmindedly with the country music station and let her mind wander.

She couldn't believe how many weeks it had been since she had been home to visit her family at the ranch. Home! These past weeks she had really begun to reflect on how much it meant to her now. It wasn't simply that it was a place she could always escape to and feel comfortable. She had family there. She remembered in contrast those years after her parents' deaths. The horrible feeling of loss at every holiday. Dreading to spend a special time alone and yet not wanting to be invited to spend that time with a family of strangers— someone else's family. Usually she took the initiative and planned her holidays carefully, filling the time so there would be no spare moments to think about her loss. But that was always a conscious effort on her part, and the effort itself was painful.

It was ironic that she would find her new family in her mother's brother. Brandy had never been that close to her mother—her father had been her shining star. But the three of them had been a family, and Brandy always knew they loved and supported her. It was that love and support that had enabled her to do so well, until . . .

But that was all behind her. She smiled to herself. Now she had a home and a family and a new life. Everything was falling neatly into place.

It meant so much to her that Uncle John had asked for her help in designing the new house. They had looked through tons of magazines, discussed what qualities each thought was most important in a house—agreed with one another, changed their minds a million times. It was going to be a grand house. The only thing they had seriously disagreed about was the direction the house would face. Initially her uncle had wanted it to face west, but Brandy's common sense had prevailed and he'd finally accepted the fact that a western exposure would be unbearably hot in the summer. She had convinced him that waking up to the sunrise every morning and sitting outside on the sheltered eastern side in the dog days of summer would be pleasures to last a lifetime.

It was funny, though, she mused, he had been pretty vague about the details in recent phone calls about the progress of the building. She had considered calling in the middle of the day, when he would be away from the house, so she could talk to Hattie and get a woman's view of the situation. She wanted details—what had the builders done on a particular day, what did she think of the view, did it look like they'd finish on time, or maybe even ahead of schedule. She wasn't able to visualize much from her uncle's standard reply: "Well, honey, it's coming right along. You won't believe it when you see it."

Yes, she should have called Hattie, not only to find out about the house, but also to touch base with her. She was a bit surprised at how much she missed the gruff older woman, especially considering their rocky start. But Hattie was a rock—calm and practical, keeping everything in order. Hattie was a woman of great personal strength, and Brandy respected her immensely for that.

Thinking of Hattie, Brandy's thoughts naturally flowed to Susie, who had much of her grandmother's gutsiness. Susie would grow up to be a real western woman. The little girl had carved a special place in Brandy's heart. Sometimes, talking to Susie, she would forget that she was talking to a four-year-old.

Brandy sighed. In acreage the Rocking B was one of the largest ranches around, but it wasn't nearly large enough for Jake Milburn to remain out of her sight for a whole weekend.

Susie was sometimes more observant than was comfortable. On Brandy's last visit she had asked her why Jake didn't ride with them anymore. Brandy's cheerful reply that since she got out to the ranch so seldom now, she wanted Susie all to herself elicited a penetrating look from the little girl.

"I ride with Jake when you're not here, you know,"

the little girl answered. "He knows everything about riding, and most everything about everything else, too."

"Yes, he's a very smart man." Brandy clenched her teeth.

"He tells really good stories about Indians and things. Can you tell me a story?"

"I'm not as good at telling stories as Jake is." And how true that was, she thought.

She could see the building site on the horizon as she came down the last mile of the dusty road to the ranch. On an impulse, in spite of her eagerness to see everyone, she decided to swing by and assess its progress for herself.

The foundation had been poured, and the workers had about finished framing it in. Brandy was duly impressed and figured they must be at least a few days ahead of schedule. Then something tugged at the back of her mind as she stared at the growing outline of the new ranch house. Something wasn't quite right. What was it?

She pulled the car up next to several pickup trucks and got out. The men watched her get out of her car but continued their work. One of them set aside his tools and came forward to introduce himself as the general contractor.

"I'm Brandy Stanwood, John Brandon's niece," she said.

"Oh, nice to meet you, ma'am. I've heard a lot about you. What do you think of the new place so far?" He gestured at the construction. "Looks good, doesn't it?"

Brandy started to agree automatically, then

stopped herself. Something wasn't quite . . .

She inspected the work on the new house with a growing sense of horror and alienation. It was backwards.

"What's happened here?" she asked. "This isn't right."

"Sorry, ma'am, but this is all according to the final plans," the contractor said as he spread the blueprints in front of her on the hood of his truck.

Brandy looked and blinked. This house was almost entirely different from the one she and her uncle had planned. There were recognizable features—the kitchen, the solarium, and the library with its adjoining office—but it wasn't the same house at all. She left the site baffled and hurt. Her uncle had changed everything without even telling her. That certainly explained his vagueness on the phone. He hadn't wanted to start an argument. Of course, it was his house, and she had been terribly busy with the campaign. Could two months make that much of a difference? What could account for such a change in her uncle? Why hadn't he talked to her?

As she pulled up in the driveway of the old ranch house, Hattie was the first to see her and was out the door to meet her almost before the car could stop. Susie skipped along behind her. Brandy was greeted with hugs and exclamations. Her uncle came up from the barn a few seconds later, and Brandy was startled to see that Julia was with him. She hadn't known Julia was going to be there. They all descended on her with a million questions about the campaign, where she had been, whom she had seen. Caught up in the warmth and genuine love of their welcoming, Brandy forgot about the house for a moment and laughed and returned their hugs and tried to answer all their questions at once.

"This is silly," Hattie exclaimed. "Let's get inside and give the girl a chance to catch her breath. Come on, there's lots of coffee and fresh cinnamon rolls."

As they turned as one to obey Hattie's suggestion, Brandy fell into step beside Julia. "What a surprise to see you here! I figured you were still in Colorado working on that story about the mining camp."

"Actually," Julia said, "that one has been finished for quite some time. I've been researching your capital, Helena, reached an impasse, and thought that a change of scene would be the best way to cure a bad case of writer's block. I got in late the other night, otherwise I would have called you as I passed through Billings."

Hattie's coffee and cinnamon rolls were reassuringly the same—warm and delicious. They lingered around the big table in the kitchen, talking for almost two hours. Everyone at the ranch was fascinated with the inside view of politics and had plenty of gossip to repeat about Howie's opponent and what they'd heard was really going on behind the scenes in the Bainbridge campaign. They listened with keen interest to Brandy's war stories about managing a campaign. It was obvious they were very proud of her, and listening to herself, Brandy was even a little impressed with how far she had come and how much she had learned. A year ago, managing a political campaign was as much of a realistic possibility for her as flying to the moon. In many ways Montana had been very good for her.

After a good hour and a half of their nonstop conversation, Jake stopped in to inform John Brandon about the progress on a new well that was being dug. He nodded to Brandy, and for a moment she thought she saw a longing in his eyes. Her heart warmed to him, but then she remembered her resolution not to be hurt again and turned on an icy smile. He left without saying a word to her, but his presence had disturbed her. She became more aware of the people around the table—until now she had more or less been the center, or at least the catalyst, of the conversation. But now her uncle and Julia were talking about Julia's latest article and how she was planning to do a sequel to it. It was then that Brandy began to notice something different about her uncle. He was beaming, his craggy face flushed with pleasure, his voice full of excitement. There was something about the way he looked at Julia. And what was it about Julia—her usual coolness and wry humor had softened.

Brandy began to wonder idly just how often Julia had writer's block these days and had to seek refuge in the middle of Montana. Oh, my God, Brandy thought with mounting horror. They act as if they're in love. But it can't be. He's too old—he's not her type. And she doesn't belong here, she won't stay. But he called her "Julie," and the looks they were exchanging were suspiciously tender.

The conversation lagged, and Hattie seized the moment to politely but firmly kick them out of the kitchen. "I've got a lot of work to do if you want to eat dinner tonight," she said. Susie had been waiting fairly patiently for Brandy's undivided attention. "Let's go riding," she cried, tugging on Brandy's arm. Brandy laughed and agreed. She gave her uncle and Julia a look of apology and promised to catch up with them later. Secretly she was grateful for this time to be away from her uncle and Julia. She wasn't sure what she should say to Uncle John about the plans for the new house, and she felt very awkward about Julia. This was totally unexpected. She would have thought that sophisticated Julia would find Montana amusing, but nothing more than a passing fancy and material for a few travel pieces. Now she was doing articles about the capital city and making herself at home on a ranch.

The ride with little Susie did Brandy a world of good. It was hard to mope about anything in the face of such unfettered enthusiasm and boundless energy. Brandy felt relaxed and refreshed when she returned. She found a chance to take Hattie aside and talk to her alone in the kitchen.

"Uncle John and Julia seem to be an item," she said, trying to keep her voice neutral.

"Your uncle is smitten, that's for sure," Hattie replied matter-of-factly. "I've known John Brandon for over thirty years—he hasn't been this way since before his Anne died. He's head over heels in love."

"I wouldn't have thought Julia was his type, or he hers," Brandy said.

Hattie looked at her sharply. "Julia Lee seems to be a fine woman. You wouldn't be feeling a bit left out, would you?"

"Don't be ridiculous," Brandy countered defensively, "I'm just concerned about my uncle. I love him a lot and I don't want him to get hurt. That's all."

"John Brandon can take care of himself," Hattie said, "and even if he couldn't, a heartache from falling in love once every twenty-five years can't hurt a soul that much. And, my dear, you'd be doing a lot better if you worried about your own love life."

Brandy pulled back, shocked at the blunt words. But as far as Hattie was concerned, the conversation was over. Brandy beat a hasty retreat out of the kitchen.

At dinner that night Brandy was fairly reserved. She chatted with Patsy and Bobbie and Duke and Tom. Jake made a point of asking her some questions about the campaign—nothing personal—and after she had answered him as briefly and efficiently as possible, they ignored each other, though the silence lay heavily between them. She also ignored Joe as much as possible, although she was still conscious that he was watching her with that dreadful leer on his face. But for most of the meal she observed her uncle and Julia. They really did act as if they were in love. Julia appeared to be just as smitten as he. What could she say to Julia? She felt as if some bond had been broken. Good heavens! Were they sleeping together? She shook her head to get rid of the thought and glanced up to see Jake looking at her curiously. In a moment of weakness and confusion, she smiled at him and then shyly looked down at her plate.

She insisted on helping Hattie clean up after dinner and afterward gave in to the pleas that she join with everyone to play cards. But she felt very uncomfortable sitting next to Julia. She found she couldn't say a thing to her old friend—not that Julia noticed. Her eyes and attention were focused on John Brandon. Brandy retired early with a hollow joke that she had been working too hard on the campaign to keep up with this active night life.

She felt exhausted but slept poorly, tossing uncomfortably and waking frequently to stare into the dark. There was nothing really wrong, she told herself, but everything had fallen just slightly askew, as if she were seeing her familiar world through a distorted glass. Suddenly nothing in the world was quite as it had appeared to be, and she felt a growing sense of unease.

She sat up on the edge of the bed and looked out into the night. The same star-studded sky still loomed enormous over the prairie beyond her window. The same bold sunrise would urge her eyelids open in the morning, proudly parading its glorious colors across the horizon for her approval. But it was all viewed through a funhouse mirror. Everything that had settled into such a solid, comfortable pattern was shifting, alien. The picture she had created of her new home and family constellation—her home here on the ranch, the uncle who loved her, and herself as the center—was suddenly out of focus, off center.

But she would fix it. Surely she could fix it.

She rose early and sought out her uncle in his study. Perhaps a talk with him would help. He was alone, savoring a cup of coffee and glancing through the *Billings Gazette*.

"Hi, sweetie!" His cheerful whisper was almost loud enough to wake the dead. She gave him a hug and then curled up on the couch with her own cup of coffee. Their conversation about the campaign and the ranch felt good to Brandy, but she knew it wasn't the same somehow, any more than the house they had planned was the same as it had been pictured in her mind.

After a while she put her coffee mug on the table and cleared her throat. "Uncle John," she began, "what happened to the plans we made for the house? It's totally different. We worked so hard on them, and now I don't even recognize the place."

"Brandy, you've been too busy to fool around with the ranch house," he said, "so Julie's been helping me. The contractor pointed out some problems with our design, so I showed the plans to Julie and she had some real good ideas to improve it. I think you'll really like the place when we get it finished. Julie's got some great decorating ideas, too."

His words echoed in her ears. She felt tears coming to her eyes. "But you and I worked so hard on it." Damn, she heard her voice pick up a whining note.

"Honey, I'm so sorry. I didn't think you'd be so

upset about this." John Brandon was clearly at a disadvantage before his niece's tears.

"I know. It's your money and your house and you can do what you want with it all, Uncle John. I don't want you to think that I don't appreciate all that you've done for me. I do. It's just that when you asked for my advice on this and let me help, well, it just made me feel like I really had a home here, that I was really family, not a charity case or a good deed for the day."

She was crying almost uncontrollably now. Her uncle sat down beside her awkwardly. He patted her back. "Brandy, honey, don't cry—I'm so sorry. I'll talk it over with Julie and we'll see what we can do to change things. You know, we haven't begun the decorating, and we'd really appreciate your help with that. We'll change it back if it matters that much to you."

Gradually she stopped her crying, and she and her uncle began to talk in more detail about the house—how to decorate it, where to go furniture shopping, carpeting versus linoleum versus tile. It began to feel like old times again, and Brandy left the study feeling better. Her world was falling back into position. At least she hadn't lost her place in the family.

At breakfast Julia looked at her a little self-consciously and seemed to avoid speaking to her directly. As they got up to leave the table, she said to Brandy, "Could I talk to you for a moment?" They went out to the back porch and sat on the picnic table—sitting on top of the table, with their feet on the bench, overlooking the prairie and the river.

"John told me this morning that you were upset about the house," Julia said.

Brandy immediately took the offensive. "Julia, I'm upset about the house and the fact that neither one of you bothered to tell me about this budding relationship of yours. Personally I think it's wonderful and I'm happy for both of you. But why the secrecy? Why couldn't somebody have told me or at least dropped a hint to me? How many times have you been here in the last two months? Not that it's any of my business, but you've only called me once in that time—you've never even swung by for lunch or dinner on your way through Billings."

"Brandy, I'm sorry. We both are. It's just that neither of us expected to fall in love. You're not the only one surprised by this. We were a little self-conscious about it at first, and then you've been so busy with the campaign that while we both wanted to tell you, there just didn't seem to be a good time to do it. We feel really bad about not telling you about the house—I guess we just got caught up in each other. We want to make it up to you—and I would like you to help us decorate the place as much as you can—we want it to be your home, too."

"Well, I'm sorry this had to happen this way," Brandy said. "I'm sorry that I'm not jumping for joy over your offer to share *your* home with me. You have to understand that I'm really hurt by all this secrecy—a person shouldn't have to feel like a third wheel in her own family and her own home. My uncle and I spent a lot of time planning this house, and to have all my work come to nothing . . ."

"Brandy, I'm sorry. We'll change it."

"Yes. Well, Uncle John said the same thing. It's too late to change the foundations, but it's easy enough to shift some interior walls. I just think it would have been easier if you'd kept me informed."

Brandy knew she had won the battle; now she had to extract herself from it gracefully. "Look, I'm still pretty upset. I think I'll go lie down for a while. Then maybe later we can go over the plans for the decorating and I'll tell you what I'd like to see you use." Brandy gave Julia a nod of dismissal and left her sitting on the table.

In her room the feeling of triumph vanished. She had more or less gotten her way—true, the foundation couldn't be redone, they would have to live with that, but at least the inside of the house would look right. But she didn't feel proud of her victory. Something about the situation still bothered her. Yes, she had been open with both of them about her feelings. She hadn't made any wild accusations, and other than crying in front of her uncle—and her feelings *were* hurt—she had maintained her composure. She paced in her room. She glanced up at the wall above her bed. That quilt. Why did it always look so familiar? She was sure she had never seen anything quite like it before. Then, like a lightning bolt, it struck her. A memory of a quiet, soft-spoken woman working on it for hours while a demanding five-year-old girl with brandy-colored hair devised a million schemes to gain undivided attention. Her mother had made that quilt. And as quickly as that realization came to her, so did the understanding of what was wrong with this morning's victory. She had run roughshod over Julia as she had her mother, and she had conned her uncle into doing just what she wanted. Just the way she had behaved as a child. Good Lord! she thought. Can we ever get away from our childhood? She was overcome with guilt over her behavior. My poor mother. Poor Julia. I must have been a terrible brat as a child, but I don't have to be one now. Suddenly the room was too small, she had to get out.

She left the house and headed for the barn, thinking that maybe a good hard ride would clear her head. Maybe she could figure out a way to stop repeating her past.

Brandy clucked a greeting to Sheba, who turned and nickered in response. Brandy reached up to rub behind the creature's ear and was nuzzled in return. The animal's gentle friendliness was too much for her, and the tears came freely now. She rested her head against the horse's neck and sighed. It was silly, she thought, to be this upset— obviously Uncle John and Julia were happy with each other. And it was her uncle's house, after all. He could have it face any way he liked. She'd stay out of the way. Deciding that made Brandy feel better, but she was certain that she had never been more alone.

She had no idea how long she had stood there, stroking the horse's neck. The sound of footsteps brought her back to her senses. She was too embarrassed to turn around to see who had come in, but with any luck she wouldn't be noticed. She didn't want to talk to anyone right now.

Keeping her back to the barn door, she led Sheba from her stall and began to saddle her. The footsteps came closer and stopped, but Brandy pretended not to notice.

"Well, I certainly didn't figure I'd run into you this early on a Sunday morning."

Brandy's heart almost stopped. It was Jake.

"I guess you figured wrong." She kept her voice steady and her back to him, and she tightened the cinch.

"Think maybe we could talk?" Jake said quietly.

"Look, I've had more than my share of hassles today. I don't need any advice about my uncle and Julia, so I'd appreciate it if you would just stay out of my personal life."

She was so angry and afraid that he would interfere in her problems with her uncle and Julia that she forgot she had been fighting depression only a few minutes before.

"I don't want to talk about your uncle and Julia. I want to talk about us."

Brandy whirled around to face him. "Well, I don't think there's much to talk about."

Sheba was saddled by now, and the heat of Brandy's emotions was making the horse nervous; the animal began to prance.

"What is wrong with you?" Jake said. "You moved to Billings and broke off without an explanation, you insist that there was nothing between us, and you refuse to talk about it—it's about time you gave me some answers."

The fury in his blue eyes matched her own, but

she refused to reply. Before the words were even out of his mouth she had swung herself up on the mare and was racing away.

Once she was over the hill she slowed the horse to an easy canter and they loped along. She could feel her limbs starting to shake. The last thing she'd needed this morning was an encounter with Jake. She let her mind go blank and tried to concentrate on the soothing warmth of the summer morning air as it caressed her bare forearms and her face. There was silence apart from the measured drumming of the horse's hooves against the prairie. Then there was another sound. She noticed it almost subconsciously before she could actually hear it. It was the echo behind her of another set of hooves.

24

Brandy looked over her shoulder to see Jake on his
big bay gelding, riding hard after her. She was
stunned and annoyed. Why couldn't he leave
well enough alone? She urged her horse on, snapping the reins and giving a kick. Sheba sprang forward, as if pleased to be given a chance to show
off. They pulled away from the shade of the cot-
tonwoods next to the river and galloped up the
hill toward the open prairie. The trees fell away
behind and the horizon over the hill expanded as
they reached the crest. The wind rushed over
them, and they rode headlong into it; Brandy
leaned close over the horse's neck and urged the
beast to run faster. She didn't know why they were
running, she only knew they had to get away. She
didn't want to talk to Jake, she only wanted to be
alone. Everything was so confused.

The ground sailed by beneath the horse's
hooves, and Brandy knew they were going faster
than they had ever gone before. But the mare's
gait could not compete with that of Jake's horse.

Brandy strained to escape but felt him gaining on her. She leaned low along Sheba's neck and urged the horse on even faster. She didn't think about what she was doing; she just knew she had to escape this man who had hurt her once and now was pursuing her. She heard the hoofbeats drawing closer. Now they were so close she felt his thigh brush against hers. Then she felt him wresting the reins from her hands, and the strength drained from her. She clung helplessly as both horses drew to a stop.

They were hardly stopped when Brandy was down from the saddle, more of a fall than an actual dismount. She turned to run from him, but he was there in front of her, his muscular arms containing her in more of a wrestling hold than an embrace.

"Brandy, stop!" His voice was hoarse with desperation and anger as they tumbled together to the ground, and he pinned her beneath him. "What's wrong with you? What are you running from? Why won't you talk to me?"

"Why won't I talk to you? Oh, please!" She was furious. She struggled to get up, but he held her firm against the ground. Her green eyes flashed. "What a short memory you have. Remember? New Year's Eve and you disappeared without so much as a note or a phone call. I suppose you expected me to wait around until you had time for me again and then just take up where we left off with no explanations. I'm sorry, I'm not that desperate! And this whole macho routine—yes, you can outride me, and wrestle me to the ground, and rape me if that's what you want. But that doesn't make you more of a man."

He recoiled from her as if struck and released his grip. She scrambled to her feet. She didn't run away this time but stood well out of his reach, shaking with emotion.

He looked confused. "But I explained in the letter I left for you. I'm sorry I couldn't tell you in person, but I thought you'd understand. I promised to tell you the whole story when I got back."

"What letter?" A silence stretched between them as their awareness grew. Jake shook his head.

"Brandy, I left the letter at your place at the kitchen table. I couldn't tell you right then why I had to leave, but I told you I loved you and asked you to be patient with me—and trust me. Joe was sitting right there—you can ask him."

"I suppose you couldn't have called?"

"I thought you would understand. I thought you loved me the way I love you."

The words took her by surprise. She wanted to believe them, and at the same time she didn't want to be deceived by them. There were still too many secrets.

"If you really left a letter for me, then what happened to it?" As she asked the question, understanding suddenly flooded over her and she blurted out, "It was Joe, wasn't it? He took the letter."

Jake shook his head. "Why would he have done that?"

"Because there's something wrong with him," she replied. "I can't tell you what it is, but there's something dirty about him, a meanness—he'd enjoy hurting people, you can tell." Her anger grew as she remembered Joe that New Year's morning, smiling smugly and watching her reaction as he told her Jake had walked away from her.

Jake didn't respond for a long time. Did he think she was lying about the letter? When he spoke his voice cracked with emotion.

"What do we do now? We've made a mess of things, and I don't know how to make them right. But I know I love you," he whispered, "and I still want you so badly. . . ."

"What did the letter say, Jake?" she asked hesitantly. "What did you mean to tell me that would have made me understand?"

"It said that I care about you, Brandy, that leaving you even for a moment was painful, but three weeks—almost more than I could stand. These last months . . . they've been hard."

"And did it tell me what you're hiding? What you're keeping from me?"

"No. Not yet."

"Who are you, Jake? What are you? I don't really know you at all."

"I'm the man who loves you. Can the rest of it really make that much difference?"

She stood looking into his eyes, not moving. She had spent so much time hardening her heart toward him, layering on the protective armor so he wouldn't be able to get close enough to hurt her again. She couldn't speak. How could she destroy the wall of anger that she had worked so hard to build for protection? Her heart was secure, but she felt her body weakening as he leaned closer.

"Remember, Brandy? I remember every night. Every moment we had." He swept her into his arms and kissed her. At first she struggled to pull away, but the sheer energy of the passion between them held her. She felt herself returning his kiss with a desperate longing. Her body surged with desire for him. Her tongue responded to his with an urgency that surprised her. He buried his face in the curve of her neck and kissed her more gently but with the same heat. Her hands betrayed her, unbuttoning his shirt to explore his chest and caress the strong muscles of his back, pulling him closer, feeling the pressure of his whole body against her.

His hands on her breasts were just one step beyond gentleness, almost harsh, almost hurting her. The sensation drove her to a higher point of tension than she had ever known. She felt like a wire stretched to the breaking point and held there. Every inch of her body ached for him. They rocked together, their legs intertwined, their bodies melting together as they slid to the ground and lay in the soft grass, the immense Montana sky arching above them, the sun warming their naked bodies as they came together in the familiar heat of their need.

As they lay spent, feeling the light touch of the morning sun, there were no words between them. Later, Brandy thought, she'd deal with it later. She knew that any passion she felt for Jake—no matter how intense—could only be a short-term thing, but how to stop herself from feeling that passion . . . So she savored this one morning, basking in the sun's warmth and in the afterglow of Jake's superb love-making. Jake said not a word about what—if any-thing—he expected from her.

The recognition that she was still so powerfully attracted to Jake left Brandy shaken. How could she feel such a strong, primitive urge for the arms of a man who was so completely unsuitable, so alien to her life and experience? She belonged with someone with a similar background, someone like Greg. Her doubts about her relationship with Greg were growing despite his attentiveness. He called her regularly and sent her amusing notes and weekly flowers. The relationship remained just light enough—and distant enough—to be nonthreatening, lacking the electricity of her relationship with Jake but providing a reminder that there was a world waiting for her out there.

The problem she had to face was that she now knew the only way she could avoid further entanglement with Jake was to return to the East and stay there. If she stayed close to him, sooner or later she would find herself unable to resist his powerful physical appeal. When she tried to explain to him why their relationship simply could not work, he smiled ruefully and replied, "I'm willing to wait a little longer for you, my darling, but I won't wait forever. I know eventually you'll realize we belong together, but please make it soon. I'm a patient man and I know what I want, but we've wasted too much time already."

"But, Jake, I can't," she cried. "I just can't accept the life you live. And you won't fit into mine," she added with a catch in her voice. "We have nothing in common."

"Nothing but our love, Brandy." He grabbed her arm and forced her to look up at him. "Nothing but our love for each other."

She pulled loose from his grasp and shook her head. "No. I can't." And she turned her back on him and forced herself to walk away on leaden feet, his eyes on her back pulling at her at every step. His calm tenacity infuriated her. Why was he so unrelentingly confident that she'd weaken?

She threw herself into her work, spending long hours at the campaign headquarters, avoiding the ranch and the conflicts that lay there. She spoke to her uncle on the telephone often; he never mentioned her conflict with Julia—perhaps Julia hadn't told him. And she always had an excuse to keep her from visiting. Julia was still there, she knew, working toward the completion of the ranch house.

Her time on the campaign was productive, and the staff, while still not what she would call a well-oiled machine, was working together effectively and, with the help of the volunteers, implementing every careful step in the plan. Howie's opponent, Tom Bainbridge, had attacked early, apparently figuring that if Howie were given the opportunity to expand on the positive image he had in his own legislative district, it would be impossible to catch him. In politics, Brandy knew, the rule was that you must establish your own image in the voters' minds before someone had a chance to do it for you, and in a huge congressional district like theirs, there was always a danger that you couldn't move fast enough.

The attack came at a press conference in Great Falls, which was Bainbridge's home and political base. In his prepared statement he accused Howie Morrison of being the tool of the big mining and cattle interests, with no concern for the average Montanan who was worried about making a living. As proof he read out a list of Howie's major contributors, with special emphasis on Art Wilson, whom he called "the Kingmaker."

Brandy felt a thrill of excitement as she listened to the tape one of the volunteers had made at the press conference. From the very beginning they had foreseen this attack, and they were ready. She called Peter Cornish, one of her fellow students from the campaign school, to go over the plan with him. Peter was young, but one of the better strategists in the group.

"Wow, this is really early, Brandy. I think your candidate is the first one to be attacked out of our whole class. I don't know if I'd want to be first in this case, though—how are you handling it?"

"Well, Howie will announce that he's delighted Bainbridge brought up the question of campaign contributions, since he's thrilled to see that people from all walks of life are supporting his campaign. Big money people, average working people, and retired people—Howie has well over two thousand contributors already, and the average contribution is less than twenty dollars. How wonderful, he'll say, that *all* the people of the district are so solidly behind him."

"Great plan—but what about the problem of the campaign chairman? You told me when we talked a couple of months ago that he was a real manipulator, and richer than hell."

"Yes," she said with a hint of embarrassment. "I did scream and yell about Art, didn't I? And yes, he is a manipulator and a power broker. But I have to admit, once I got used to his style he's a pretty decent human being, and he really knows this state inside and out."

"But how will you handle the attack? I loved your stories about him, sitting up there in his big old office with a smelly cigar, like an ugly spider in its web."

"Peter, I have a confession. I did some checking into Art's background, and we can make him sound awfully good. He's a totally self-made man, started with absolutely nothing, made every cent of his money through hard work. And not only that, the man's a war hero."

"Brandy, how do you luck out like this? I'm stuck here in Ohio with a candidate who refuses to ask for money."

It hit her all at once. Now that he'd put it into words, she knew it was the truth. "I *am* lucky, Peter. I am damn lucky. I've got people behind me whom any campaign manager would kill for, and a candidate who's just about perfect. But you'll do just great, Peter. I've got faith in you."

"That means a lot, Brandy. In this business we need friends—it's too easy to make enemies. Your strategy sounds good. Stay in touch, and I'll pass on the news to the rest of our gang."

Our gang. She loved it. It made her feel like a kid again.

Eila was her sole confidante during this time, even when she had to voice her complaints about the campaign. She could never burden Howie with her problems, but Eila had made it clear from the beginning that her role was not only that of candidate's wife, but when necessary, a sounding board for ideas and listening post for problems. She was a good listener, and if she thought Brandy was wrong, she refrained from saying so too directly. She was worried, though, about what was happening in her friend's personal life.

One evening as they sat curled up with glasses of wine in Brandy's living room, Brandy told Eila the whole story of her relationship with Jake, the initial discovery of their mutual passion, of the misunderstanding they had, and of the rediscovery of their undeniable attraction to each other, even though she denied that genuine love was involved.

"The problem is, Eila, I can't see any way Jake could fit into my kind of life. I recognized when I went back east this spring that I really belong there despite the things I don't like about New York. And Greg is the kind of man I understand. Oh, I can see now he's probably not the right man. But he's the *kind* of man I need. He offers the kind of life I want. Sure, I thought in the beginning that I was falling in love with Jake, but that was just my body talking."

"Are you sure it wasn't your heart? I get the feeling you're making all these decisions with your head—and not necessarily wisely, by the way—and you haven't yet faced up to what your heart is trying to tell you."

"No, my heart's not involved. In addition to the fact I can't trust him completely, we have nothing in common, and there's no way I can spend my life in Montana—I'd die if I had to." When she realized what she had said, Brandy threw her arms around Eila and cried, "I'm sorry—I didn't mean— you know what your friendship means to me, and of course you and Howie are important. But don't you see—you'll be living in Washington after November. I'll be out there, too, and things will be just the same as they are now."

"Will they?" Eila asked. "Washington is going to be a big change for us, I know, and I can't help but think that no matter how much you've changed in this past year, you still aren't finished changing. No"—she raised her hand to stop Brandy's denial—"I'm not going to argue with you. I'm just telling you what I think. I'll be your friend whatever you do, but I think you're wrong about Jake. He's a sensitive, intelligent man, and he spends his life the way he does not because he has to, but because he thinks it's a good way to live. And I agree with him."

Brandy thought often about what Eila had said, but she still couldn't agree. The only route for her was eastward, and her home was at the end of that road.

Jake was patient with her. He wrote beautiful letters to her, describing life on the ranch, phoned her to ask how the campaign was going, but surprisingly he refused to see her. "Brandy, I am not going to accept your crazy idea that this is some kind of sexual attraction that will eventually go away. I want you more than I can stand, but I want more than you want to give right now. I can't give up all contact with you—I admit that—but until you can come to me without reservation, I can't see you."

"Without reservation?" she said angrily. "That's asking too much, Jake, when you won't be open with me. But why argue—it won't get us anywhere. Let's just accept the fact that there's something purely physical between us, and leave it at that."

But one memorable evening, when the night was full of stars and the silence was almost unbearable, he appeared on her doorstep, looking tired and very serious. It was late; she had just bathed and donned her robe when she heard his knock.

"I had to see you," he said. "It just hurt too much not to." Brandy couldn't help herself. With a moan of pleasure and pain she fell into his arms, reaching for the strength of him, holding him tightly as if she could stop her hurting by hurting him.

"Jake, I need you so. I can't think about the future when the present is so compelling. Just this once, love me the way you did that first night, so I'll never forget."

"You'll never forget," he murmured, "nor will I." He lifted her lips to his, and they sank slowly to the floor, mouths joined in passion, whispering together the words of passion as their bodies touched, pulling at each other's clothing.

The light gleamed on her body as he opened her robe. He looked down at the moisture-dewed breasts, then kissed each lightly, worshipfully, on its rosy tip. "Your body is so beautiful, my darling. I want it to be mine forever."

"Oh, Jake," she cried, her eyes wandering over the sinewy body that loomed above her. "Take me now. Make me yours."

The sky was beginning to glow along the horizon when they finally fell into a deep slumber, their bodies sated from hours of lovemaking, nestled together as they drifted into that brief oblivion.

Never had Brandy felt such fire in her veins, the exquisite torment that had filled her that night. Never had she known the release, the fusion into one body that had occurred. They were truly one and forever joined. She knew that even after she left, even after she returned to another life, she would forever be fighting the pull of Jake's arms.

Her birthday was in September, and her uncle insisted she spend it at the ranch. "The house is almost done," he said, "and I really think you'll like it once you see how it turned out. At least let us help you celebrate your birthday."

"But the campaign is really heating up," she argued. It's past Labor Day, and we don't have much time left." She had not seen Julia since their talk, and she didn't feel ready to see her now. Jake would be there, though, and she hesitated, thinking of nights spent in his cabin, exploring the delights of their passion.

"You have two months left, hon, don't lose your perspective. If you don't take some time to relax now, you aren't going to last that long. You haven't ridden Sheba in weeks, and Susie thinks you're mad at her. And if I do say so, it's about time you got your head out of the sand and dealt with some of your problems."

She wanted to say, "Like what?" but she was afraid of his answer. Jake, of course. He didn't know what had happened between them, but he was perceptive enough to know there was a situation to be resolved.

I t had been a long day at the campaign headquarters. Brandy had always felt that one of life's greatest mysteries concerned the way smooth, well-organized work weeks often deteriorated into mayhem on Friday afternoons. In a three-hour block of time she had had to deal with ten thousand brochures returned from the printer done in two colors that no one on this planet would ever have agreed to; a well-known congressman from another state who decided that although he was scheduled to be the keynote speaker at an upcoming fund-raising event for Howie, he was unfortunately forced to cancel (with two days' notice); and a hysterical volunteer whose wife had informed him that she would not tolerate another Montana winter.

It was now four-thirty, and Brandy knew she wouldn't be leaving the office until well after sundown. She sighed. So much for an hour of work after lunch, a leisurely drive to the ranch, and a nice dinner. She picked up the nearest phone to call her uncle to tell him that she was going to be late but was interrupted by the UPS delivery man pushing a clipboard under her nose, demanding a signature and pointing to an enormous box.

"Sign here," he said, shifting his chewing gum to the side of his mouth.

"It's for you, Brandy," Martha the receptionist cried excitedly. "It must be a birthday present."

The staff gathered around her, watching curiously as she cut the tape and slit open the box. It was from New York—must be the birthday gift Greg had sent. He had mentioned on the telephone the day before that he was sending something he wanted her to use as soon as possible, but he'd refused to tell her what it was. There was a card inside, with a brief note:

Ellen:
   This was so elegant it reminded me of you, my dear, and I hope it reminds you that I am waiting for you. Use it soon!

All my love, Greg

Brandy pulled back the tissue paper to reveal a matched set of luggage, sleek and expensive in its coat of creamy leather, totally impractical but very, very rich looking. She felt a flash of annoyance; the perfect gift that sends a message, she thought, clever—and guaranteed to make an impression. But it had never occurred to him to think about what she really might want. Her Louis Vuitton luggage was perfectly good. Perhaps she should exchange this set for a good saddle, she thought. That would show him.

Willa reached out to stroke the soft leather as the others let out a joint sigh of awe. "Wow, what a present," the young girl said. "I never saw suitcases that nice."

Brandy smiled and accepted their congratulations distractedly. I must be more tired than I thought, she told herself. Why does it make me so angry that he sends something I don't need just to make his point? Unbidden, a picture entered her mind: Greg dictating to his secretary, saying, "And pick up the most expensive, impractical set of luggage you can find. Send it to Ellen Stanwood with the note I'm leaving for you." And sitting there smiling smugly to himself at his cleverness. No, I'm not coming back to you, she responded mentally. But where am I going?

She asked Martha to repack the luggage and store it in the back room, then threw herself into another two hours of hard work, putting out the fires of the day and laying the groundwork for all she would have to accomplish on Monday. Finally, with a sigh of relief and without a glance back at the office, she got in her car and started for the ranch.

The heavy Oldsmobile purred under her touch and leaped into the open streets with a burst of power. Even the car was happy to be set loose, she thought. It would be so good to be out in the open again. A long ride tomorrow morning would work off all the pent-up energy the afternoon had produced.

And, she had to admit, it would be nice to spend some time with Jake. She had missed seeing him, and she knew it was time for them to talk. There was nothing in the world she wanted more than to feel his muscles under her hands and his arms around her, his hands exploring her, his kisses penetrating her very soul. The intensity of her feelings unnerved her; she had never desired anyone this way before, and it scared her as much as it excited her. The problem with Jake, she thought, was that she couldn't control what she felt. It was as if she were always watching herself in a mirror, as if she weren't in charge—not a comfortable feeling, and so different from the relationship with Greg. Life with Greg would have been much simpler. It was a shame it wasn't to be.

She turned up the radio and pushed a little harder on the accelerator.

John Brandon and Julia were waiting up so they could show her around the new house, which was now complete except for the finishing touches on the decorating. It was clear that they were both proud and excited, and Brandy had to admit, grudgingly, that it really did look wonderful, much better than she had imagined and perhaps even better than her own plans would have made it. The exposed-beam ceilings and hand-pegged oak floors contrasted drastically with the cathedral ceilings and Berber carpet Brandy had originally suggested. The new house was at once simpler and more elegant than anything she had envisioned. Yet despite its elegance it was warm and inviting, with the kind of comfort John Brandon's friends were used to. There were potted trees to soften the rough stone and wood. Brandy smiled at that touch of California style. Julia's influence, undoubtedly. Plenty of bright tile in the bathrooms and the kitchen. A kitchen designed for ease and comfort. Hattie must think she's in heaven, Brandy decided. There was a breakfast nook built into a corner window, and Brandy could imagine herself daydreaming the morning away, sitting there with a cup of coffee and a cinnamon roll or visiting with Hattie. All through the house the colors were bright and warm against the rough textured white walls.

As she wandered through the house, Brandy found she had to admit to herself that Julia really did seem to be good for her uncle. This romance had been going on for about six months and seemed to be not only lasting, but growing strong. He continued to have that new spring to his step, and he looked younger. And now he even had a home he could truly be proud of.

The house tour ended at a large suite that had clearly been designed just for her use. It was beautiful. A sliding glass door opened onto a screened private deck. And it faced east. The room was huge, actually more of a suite, with a fireplace and built-in bookshelves in the sitting area and her own private bath and dressing room. Brandy almost cried. She hugged the two of them, but she couldn't find the right words to say.

Her uncle said only, "This is your home, Brandy, no matter what. Please remember that."

After they left her she sat silently, absorbing the luxury of her new surroundings, her mind still in turmoil. She did remember with a twinge of loss the shabbier room in the old house that had become her first home in so many years. So much had happened since then, and now she thoroughly enjoyed looking out at the vast prairie. It didn't intimidate her at all anymore—it welcomed her. Suddenly something in the room caught her attention. On the mantel over the fireplace was a small package in gold paper with a green velvet bow and behind it a card propped up against the wall. Brandy's heart skipped a beat when she saw her name on the envelope in Jake's handwriting.

She tore open the envelope and pulled out a plain white card on which Jake had written: "Brandy, I hope this is a special birthday. No matter where you go, or what you do, my thoughts and my love will go with you, but my hope is that you will be beside me. All my love, Jake."

Brandy's hands shook as she opened the box. Inside were a pair of jade earrings wrapped in gold rope, a perfect match for the pendant he had given her. She felt a pang of guilt. She hadn't worn that pendant since he had left in January. She knew that if she did, he would see it as a signal, and of course, she knew it would be. If she wore the pendant, they would both forget they had no future together. But the earrings were beautiful; she traced the simple design with her fingers.

Despite her late arrival, Brandy was dressed and saddling Sheba by seven o'clock the next morning, determined to get in a good, long ride before preparations started for the birthday party. She'd just swung into the saddle when she heard her uncle's voice calling as he rode into the yard.

"Well, you did sleep in." He grinned. "I've been up for hours—care for some company?"

"I'd love it," Brandy returned, and they rode out together.

They didn't talk much at first; they simply enjoyed each other's company. The morning was crisp and clear, with just the slightest bite of fall in the air, and Brandy knew that if she tried to describe just how blue the skies were, her friends in New York would think she was exaggerating. New York skies didn't come that blue. When they had ridden in silence a while, Brandy began telling her uncle about the campaign and asking his advice. His perspective was valuable to her, making things clear that she had not understood on her own. She'd learned the value of mature judgment, she told herself wryly.

They lapsed into silence again, hearing only the gentle thud of the horses' hooves, the call of the birds, and the rustle of the breeze through the dried grasses.

"Brandy, what are you going to do about Jake?"

She had sensed it was coming, but the bluntness of her uncle's question startled her. This time she would not get defensive; she knew that her uncle was only concerned for her and Jake.

"I don't know," she said, "There are so many things I just don't know. We're so strongly attracted to each other, but how can anything ever come of it? I'm going to move back east, and he certainly isn't going to join me in Washington or New York. We come from two different worlds, Uncle John, and those worlds just won't fit together. I don't belong here, any more than he belongs on

Wall Street. I've thought and thought, but I just don't see an answer."

To her surprise, her uncle snorted in disgust. "Dammit, Brandy, I'm sick and tired of hearing that craziness from the two of you. You don't belong here . . . he doesn't belong there. Don't you two ever *talk* to each other? Maybe if you did, you'd find out you don't have such a big problem. But no, that would be too easy, and too sensible for you two.

"God knows you're made for each other. You're as stubborn as a pair of mules. Well I've just about had it with the both of you. If you keep this up, you'll get just what you deserve—he'll live his life like a damn monk and you'll marry some sleazy character with a fancy Manhattan address."

With that he wheeled his horse around and rode away at a gallop, leaving a stunned Brandy staring after him, mouth open.

27

he following afternoon, work on the Rocking B ground to a halt. The barbecue pit had burned down to perfect coals and huge slabs of beef were roasting over a spit operated by an engine that would have put Rube Goldberg to shame. It apparently had served the ranch for years, although no one was certain how it had managed not only to survive with minimal repairs, but to escape the ravages of modernization. A huge pot of beans hung suspended from a tripod over a smaller pit. The very air was saturated with the delicious aroma of wood smoke and roasting and simmering food. Neighbors began to arrive, bringing salads and desserts. A keg was set up.

Brandy was surprised that her birthday celebration would bring out such a crowd, but then remembered that there had been few parties since Christmas. The ranchers had been working hard taking care of newborn calves, pasturing their herds, branding, haying, and now many of them were just finishing their wheat harvest. There hadn't been much spare time for parties, and people were ready for a good time.

This group was not the Billings crowd, or her uncle's political friends from Helena. These were the "neighbors," the ranchers and farmers from across the eastern part of the state who had in common their way of life. Wealthy cattlemen and small landholders, all had a mutual history of wresting a living from the earth and fighting the whims of a sometimes fickle nature. Strong but uncomplicated, Brandy thought. She admired them even if she could never live the way they did.

She was surprisingly glad to see everyone. Most of them were people she hadn't seen since the Christmas party last year, but they remembered her and greeted her warmly. Several of the men clapped her on the back cheerfully, and women gave her the big, smothering hugs of honest affection.

"Brandy, honey," Ed Schroeder's wife scolded, "we haven't set eyes on you since last winter. You turning into a city gal again now you're living in Billings?"

"Not hardly, Bess." Brandy laughed heartily at the idea of Billings representing the temptations of the big city. "I'm sorry I haven't been around here much. Susie complains nobody is taking her to see the buffaloes anymore."

Bess shook her head. "Those silly beasts. Ed's so proud of those durn things. Well, you just listen to Susie when she tells you you should spend more time out here, and stop over for a good meal on a Wednesday when I bake my bread. You could use some fattening up."

Brandy smiled fondly at the retreating back as Bess walked away, a short, rounded figure who looked as if she feasted often on her home-baked bread, but who, like the other local women, was probably as strong as many of the men.

The men gathered to play horseshoes. Some of the women joined in, too, but most sat in the shade and talked about their families and the ranch routine. It had been weeks since they had really had the chance to sit and talk without feeling as if they should be doing something else. Many of them thanked Brandy warmly for providing them with an excuse to get together.

Surrounded by the women, Brandy was surprised to find herself fighting a rising discomfort, almost a sense of panic. These women were pleasant and friendly, and faces were familiar now, but an entire afternoon sitting in the shade drinking beer and discussing the finer points of canning and child care loomed like a dark shadow over her. This is my limit, she thought. I can stand only so much Montana girl talk! She managed to catch her uncle's eye.

"Come on, Brandy!" he bellowed. "I'll show you a real sport."

Brandy had never in her wildest dreams imagined wanting to learn to play horseshoes. But right now it looked very good, and in no time at all she was laughing and joking with the men. She was a natural athlete, with excellent eye-hand coordination. Riding and working out at the health club in Billings had helped her build up some strength in her upper arms, so that pitching the shoes wasn't nearly as difficult as she had thought it would be. Although she never came too close to winning, she certainly didn't stand out as a failure.

Jake was always there—never close enough for her to touch or even talk to, just close enough to make her ache to reach out for him. He appeared to be having a good time. Sometimes Brandy wondered if he was too much of an introvert for her, but seeing him in the crowd of people reminded her that there was indeed another side to this strong, silent cowboy.

Occasionally their eyes would meet and he would give her a smile. Her longing for him became almost painful. She tried to concentrate on what others around her were saying, to actively engage in the five or six conversations that surrounded her. But she couldn't hear them. She wanted to be alone with Jake.

In desperation she excused herself and left the crowd. Maybe Hattie could use some help in the kitchen. She just needed to get away from the guests and Jake for a little while. A little work would help her relax and give her the strength to deal with the party and her own feelings.

Hattie looked up and grinned at the sound of the screen door banging shut.

"I wondered how long you'd be able to stand the crowds without a break. You're getting better. Here. Start chopping these veggies."

Brandy was startled. "How'd you know?"

"Honey, why do you think I stay in here fussing with salads and homemade ice cream when they've already brought more than enough food to feed an army? There's only so much silly chattering I can stand. I spend days and weeks canning, and it's a job that ain't a bit of fun. I don't want to spend an entire afternoon talking about it. If you're going to talk, there must be other subjects than what you spend your life doing."

She glanced at Brandy and laughed. "So make me happy and tell me what you're doing. Tell me about the campaign."

Brandy was more than happy to oblige. Hattie was a good listener, and her common sense often provided Brandy with insights that she could take back to Billings.

So they talked and sliced vegetables and drank coffee. It struck Brandy as strange that she avoided the company of the other women only to seek the companionship of this one. Were the others so different from Hattie? She didn't know.

"Well, tell me, did you hear anything from that city slicker of yours for your birthday?" Hattie asked.

Brandy sighed. "As a matter of fact, he sent me an entire set of new luggage. Something to carry me back to the East Coast, he said. I guess I'll just have to leave for the East earlier than I planned."

Brandy spoke in her most saccharine voice. Some people would not have heard the heavy sarcasm behind her statement, but Hattie knew her well. Brandy was about to follow up with an elaboration on Greg's insensitivity, but she never had the chance. Jake stood in the doorway, looking shaken. As if he'd seen a ghost, Brandy thought.

"Just thought you two might like to know we're

going to start serving in fifteen minutes." His voice was harsh and his grin seemed forced.

What was wrong with him? Brandy wondered as she and Hattie began to take the salads out to the barbecue area. She was only joking. She'd have to take him aside after the party and explain.

28

Brandy cupped her hands around her eyes to try to peer through the rain-lashed windows, but the night was too dark, and she only saw her reflection staring back at her. The storm had blown in while they were eating dinner and had quickly built into a torrent of wind-driven rain and hail. The guests had dispersed early, exchanging worried looks as they hastily gathered children, dishes, and utensils and hurried to their cars.

Jake had excused himself from the table, looking worried. "Better check the stock. The river's high already, and I want to be sure we don't have any strays down that way. Could be some flooding tonight."

Now Brandy waited for him to return, pacing the floor in her uncle's office, now and then throwing herself on the big leather couch to leaf through a magazine. Her uncle poked his head in a couple of times to check on her, and around ten-thirty he began to look worried.

"I'm worried, too," she told him. "I think I'll go

out and see if maybe he just slipped over to his cabin when I wasn't watching. He may be avoiding me, but I'm determined to talk to him. And you know I don't give up easily." She smiled.

"Nope," he said, "that's for dang sure. You're the stubbornest woman I ever saw."

She grabbed a slicker from the back porch and hurried through the downpour to Jake's cabin, a flash of lightning briefly illuminating the yard. Water cascaded everywhere, and the area around the barns was a sea of mud. She splashed through, oblivious of her sodden jeans, and ran for the shelter of the cabin porch.

How strange, she thought. The cabin was dark, but a small gleam of light seemed to be flickering within. Perhaps the electricity was off and Jake was using a flashlight. Wiping her feet, she threw open the door without knocking and stepped inside, not intending to give him a chance to rebuff her.

But it was not Jake who whirled to face her, flashlight beam dropping as he reacted with a surprised grunt.

"Joe. What are you doing going through Jake's things?"

"Hey, don't get excited, girlie. You didn't exactly knock before you walked in here yourself, you know." He straightened and moved closer to her, grinning slowly, his narrow eyes glittering in the half-light.

"Glad you stopped by, though," he whispered. "Guess since Jake ain't here to take care of you I'll just have to fill in for him, won't I." Before she could move away he had pinned her to the door with his body. She could smell his foul breath on her face and feel the rough stubble against her cheek.

"Joe, you're drunk! Let me go!" She twisted wildly, trying to free herself.

"No, you don't. Not when I got a chance like this, honey. I been watching you for a long time, twitching that little rump, sticking your snooty nose up in the air—think you're too good for us, don't you? Well, I'm gonna give you what you deserve this time—actually more than you deserve, if I do say so myself." He cackled with drunken laughter.

"My uncle," she cried. "He won't stand for this—you'll end up in jail."

"Bullshit. I'm taking off tonight. I'm fed up with this dump, and with snooty babes and phony ranch managers. Real men don't have to take that shit."

"Jake fired you, didn't he?" Brandy suddenly realized Joe would be with the other hands if he hadn't been let go—something must have gone badly wrong. "Where's Jake? You know, don't you?"

"Naw, he's out there somewhere. He headed down toward the river—maybe got into trouble, I hope. Said I wasn't doing my job. Bullshit. I'll show him a man's job."

He began to drag her toward the bed as she struggled wildly against his sinewy strength. Her eyes searched vainly for a means of escape, a weapon, anything, but there was nothing within reach. This couldn't be happening—it had to be a nightmare. She felt herself falling backward, and suddenly he loomed over her, smiling horribly as he tore at her clothes and rubbed against her.

She turned her face away from the fumes of his

breath, almost ready to stop fighting the unrelenting pressure of his strong body. But she remembered suddenly—there was a chance. With her one free arm, and the last of her dwindling strength, she groped in the dark for the brass lamp she knew sat on the bedside table. Grabbing it by its base, she raised it quickly and, with all her strength, brought it hard against the side of his head.

He went limp, grunting once as he fell senseless across her bruised body. Thank God, she thought. I may have killed him, but thank God! She pulled her torn shirt around her and picked up the slicker. It was ripped badly, so she rummaged in Jake's closet until she found a replacement, too big, but dry and warm. As she donned it she glanced at the figure on the bed, barely visible in the dark, but clearly not moving.

She'd check later to see if she'd killed him. Right now finding Jake was more important. She slammed out of the little cabin with Joe's flashlight pointing her route to the barn. Sheba was quickly saddled as Brandy talked nervously to the excited mare.

"Come on, Sheba, you've got to help me tonight. Jake's out there somewhere, and he may be in trouble. You know Jake, Sheba. Help me find him—I'm so crazy about him, I can't lose him now." She leaped on Sheba's back, and the horse quickly broke into a gallop as they left the barnyard and headed for the river.

"Careful, girl, you don't want to slip." Still, the horse moved rapidly, surefootedly, toward the sound of rushing water that Brandy had never heard here before.

The river, usually placid and brown, had risen rapidly and was now a torrent of water lapping over its banks and rushing, filled with debris, carrying away anything in its path. She saw no signs of cattle along the banks, but she followed the river downstream along the fence, checking for signs of activity or breaks in the fence. It had washed away in several places, but there was no sign that Jake had been here. The rain could have washed away the tracks, of course.

After about forty minutes of searching the riverbank, she began to despair. Maybe Jake had gone somewhere else—maybe he was back at the ranch house already. She was soaked through, her hair plastered to her neck and her hands swollen and red from the chafing of the wet reins against her skin. They were almost to the point now where the river turned away from the property line, and she had seen nothing. Perhaps she had ridden in the wrong direction. She pulled Sheba up and started to head back the way she had come.

Sheba whinnied as she pulled the rein. "What's wrong, girl, sore mouth?" The horse whinnied again, and suddenly through the roar of the water she heard an answering cry—a horse somewhere out there in the night. "Sheba—let's go," and they turned toward the sound.

For a long time Brandy could see nothing, but as the horse's frantic cries became louder, she spotted movement down a newly cut steep bank. Near the edge of the rushing water, Jake's horse's reins were tangled in the branches of a fallen tree, which was now partly covered by the rapidly rising stream. The horse was struggling but could not escape the relentless river.

"Oh, Cherokee, you poor thing." She quickly waded to him and broke apart the network of small branches that held him to the tree, pushed him toward safety, and started to clamber back up the bank when she saw a dark form half in, half out of the rising water.

"Jake? Oh, my God," she cried. His face was out of the water, and he appeared to be breathing, but he did not respond to her touch and his face was deathly pale in the light of her torch. Brandy pulled at him, trying desperately to drag him out of the water. He was so heavy, and the mud so clinging.

Finally she slogged up the bank and untied the rope coiled on Cherokee's saddle. Holding her breath as she groped under the rising water, she managed to tie it around Jake's waist, her stiff, bleeding fingers fumbling to knot it securely. If only she'd paid attention in scouting, she thought hysterically. Now that she needed to make a knot, she didn't know how. But she tied and retied the rope, and it seemed to be strong.

She removed her torn wet shirt and tied it carefully around Jake's head to save his face from mud and bruising rocks as much as possible, then took Cherokee's reins and urged him to move slowly away from the river.

"Come on, boy, you've got to help me. Slow and easy does it, I know you don't want to hurt him.

Please don't hurt him." They inched back, and the rope tightened, but the still body did not budge. His legs might be held by something under water, she realized. But she couldn't get down there to see. If she injured him . . . but if she left him, he'd die. She'd have to take the chance.

"Okay, Cherokee, a little harder now." She gritted her teeth. The horse pulled, and the rope went taut. Gradually Jake's body began to pull free of the mud, bit by bit, until he was on the bank above the rising water. He was so heavy and so still. She knew she couldn't get him on the horse, but away from the river he would be safe until she brought help. She removed the yellow slicker she was wearing and carefully tucked it around his body—a signal to the rescuers at least, if a vain attempt to protect him from the rain.

"Take care of him for me, Cherokee," she cried. "I'll be back—I promise." And she leaped on Sheba's back, spurring the horse toward the house's lights, yelling as she drew closer, praying that someone would hear.

"Uncle John, somebody—please help, oh, please!" She tumbled off Sheba's back as the ranch house door opened and figures ran toward her. Suddenly she was exhausted. Her uncle supported her as she gasped out her story.

"Please—it's Jake—he's hurt. Down by the river." Her voice gave out, and she simply pointed. Tom and Duke had reached them by this time, drawn by her screams, and they quickly took off for the barn to saddle up while Hattie helped her into the kitchen and her uncle ran to call the ambulance.

Hattie told her later that she had never seen such a sight.

"Why, Brandy, I thought you was a ghost or something. All covered with mud, yelling. I never saw nothing like it in all my born days. I got to tell you, Jake owes you his life. But it's just lucky," she added firmly, "you had all that mud plastered all over you. Why, child, you didn't have a stitch on above the waist when you rode in here."

Brandy had meekly allowed Hattie to help her bathe and bandage her hands, and it was not until she was wrapped in a robe and blanket in front of the fire, still shaking as she tried to drink a cup of bourbon-laced hot tea, that with a sudden pang she remembered Joe out in Jake's cabin and told her uncle what had happened. She was calm now. It seemed so unreal as she looked back.

"I may have killed him, Uncle John. What if I did?"

"I hope to hell you did," he replied, face red with anger. "I hope you did. And if you didn't, I'll see him in prison." He ran to the back door, not even stopping to don a coat. As he opened the door, Brandy could hear a siren fading in the distance. The ambulance had arrived, and Jake was, she hoped, on his way to medical treatment.

If only the weather had been better so they could have used a helicopter. As it was, they'd fly him into Billings, but the ambulance ride to the airstrip would add so much time. She wanted to be with him, but she was so tired, and her bruised body was already beginning to ache. She was gripped by a terrible lassitude; she simply could not move.

In the morning she would be by his bedside. A few hours of sleep, and she could start the drive into Billings by daybreak. She knew her uncle would let her know if there was any word on his condition in the meantime. And tomorrow would bring another difficult task—the phone call to Greg, to let him know finally that it was over between them.

How could she ever have planned a future with Greg? She admitted to herself openly now that she could not imagine life without Jake. All of the months without him—wasted months—were enough loneliness for a lifetime. Greg could give her all of the excitement of New York, the luxury of wealth, but he could never give her what she needed most.

Somehow she and Jake formed two perfect halves of a circle that must never again be broken. Without that other half, she would remain forever an incomplete person. They would have serious adjustment problems, she knew, but this time she was ready to give—and to compromise.

She could hear her uncle calling to Tom and Duke out back, and then the sound of Duke's pickup truck heading into the night. John Brandon looked grim when he returned to the house.

"Well, you didn't kill him," he said. "He's gone. Blood on the bed and on some towels in the bathroom, but no other sign of him. Doesn't look like he took anything, but we'll have to check with Jake about that."

"Did you send Tom and Duke after him?" she asked.

"Yep. And I've just phoned the sheriff. He'll be out looking, too. Looks like Joe took off in his old Ford pickup, so they're going to put out an APB on the license number."

He sat down heavily beside her and took her hand. "God, I'm sorry about this, honey. I just never would've hired the guy if I'd had any idea he was this kind of trouble. How can you ever forgive me!"

"There was no way you could have known, Uncle John. Please don't feel bad about it. It's over, and I'm okay. Right now all I care about is Jake, and I'm worried sick about him. What if something happens to him? After I've wasted all this time. It's my fault, you know. It really is my fault." She burst into tears, sobbing deeply and painfully as she recalled Jake's pale face and labored breathing.

Her uncle took her in his arms and patted her helplessly. "Brandy, don't cry. He'll be okay—he has to be okay. We both need him too much. Besides, he owes it to his public to keep on, doesn't he?" They sat that way a long time, her uncle rocking her lightly as her tears subsided, then finally wiping her eyes with his big handkerchief and leading her to her bedroom, where he tucked her in like a small child.

It was quiet in the ranch house, and John Brandon sat by himself in the big living room, watching the dying fire, waiting and hoping against hope that the news would be good. He'd had a chance to look closely at Jake's still form as he was carried to the ambulance, and what he saw was not encouraging. He had seen the paramedics shaking their heads when they checked his pupils for response to light. He was well aware that Jake might not make it, but Brandy must not know, at least not until she was stronger.

Julia had promised to call when she knew anything. She had slipped away to ride into Billings with Jake since it was clear to both of them that Brandy was too exhausted to make the trip. Tomorrow morning he could tell Brandy how Julia had ridden out to help bring Jake in and had gone with him in the ambulance to the hospital. He hoped this would bring the two of them back together, because these two women were the most important people in his life, and he didn't think he could stand it if they remained apart.

"John," Julia had said, "Brandy's had a rough time. She and I will get over our misunderstandings, but she'll never get over it if anything happens to Jake. I don't care how many mistakes she's made, she doesn't deserve to lose him. You take care of her, and I'll do what I can for Jake. The two of them are very important to you, and that means they're very important to me, too."

"Julie," he had replied, "I hope Jake cares about Brandy as much as I care about you, but I don't know that that's possible. I don't know what I did without you in my life."

She had smiled up at him and touched his cheek lightly. "I love you, John Brandon. And don't worry. You're going to have a hell of a time getting rid of me."

29

Brandy woke slowly to a gray morning. At first she was puzzled by the soreness of her body, but then, with a rush, it all came back. Jake—oh, God, she had to see Jake. Swinging her legs over the side of the bed, she winced at the pain. She felt as if her whole body had been pounded—muscles shrieked, and joints groaned. And I thought I was in good shape, she told herself ironically.

She threw on a robe and hurried down the hall. She had overslept. "Uncle John, where are you?" she called. Hattie came bustling out of the kitchen to intercept her.

"Brandy, honey, your uncle's out checking fences. He called the hospital a while ago, and Jake's still the same. They operated on him, but there's no word yet." She put a kindly arm across her shoulders and drew her toward the kitchen. "Honey, you come on and have a nice cup of coffee while I fix you a good breakfast. Then you can get dressed and head for Billings."

"I'm not hungry, Hattie. And it's late."

Hattie took her arm and steered her firmly to the kitchen table. "None of that stuff, child. You've got a tough day ahead of you, and you're starting it with a hot meal. Jake ain't going nowhere. He'll be there when you get there."

Brandy fell meekly onto the chair. The coffee did help, but the oatmeal and fruit tasted like cardboard. She itched to get behind the wheel and on the road, but Hattie was standing over her, arms folded, watching her eat.

"All right, Hattie." She smiled wanly. "I'll eat up like a good little girl."

Hattie leaned over and enveloped her in a tight hug. "Oh, child, I'm praying for you. You think I'm an old busybody, but I care about you, and I don't know no other way to show it."

"Oh, Hattie, I know that." Brandy turned to hug the older woman in return. "This morning your bossiness just makes me want to cry, and I can't cry—I've got to be strong for Jake."

"Honey." She handed Brandy a tissue. "Wipe your eyes now. Just look at the two of us, two grown women sniffling together over breakfast! You go get dressed now and go on."

She wiped her own eyes surreptitiously and busied herself at the sink. Back turned to Brandy, she added, "I'll be praying for him. You tell him that, okay?"

Brandy ran from the room before her emotions got the best of her. She showered hurriedly and threw on jeans and a shirt, scarcely stopping to run a brush through her hair, but by the time she was dressed and ready to leave, her uncle was sitting at the end of the big kitchen table, warming himself with a cup of coffee.

"Damp out there, hon. You'd better take a raincoat."

"I've got one. How are the roads?"

"Sit down, Brandy," he said. "You don't have to worry about the roads. Jim Dahlberg is going to fly you over in his Cessna. I'll run you over to the airstrip when I finish my coffee."

She was flooded with relief; everyone was being so kind. But Jake—"Uncle John, what about Jake? Have you talked to the doctors? Is he better this morning? Did he come through the surgery okay?"

"No, he's not better. Not yet, at least. He was in surgery for several hours last night, but I don't know the details. You'll have to ask Owen Beeman when you get there. Good surgeon, by the way. Best there is around here."

Was that good enough? Brandy wondered. Was Montana's best enough to save the man she loved? If not, what irony—that a man who loved this country so could lose his life because of it. She knew she had to go to him, to share her strength with him.

"Uncle John, can we go now? I can't stand thinking about Jake lying there alone. It's wrong, he needs someone with him."

"He has someone with him, Brandy. Julie's been with him all night. She's called regularly with reports, but I couldn't see any need to wake you if we had nothing new to tell you."

Julie—with Jake? She felt a burst of jealousy. Why should Julia be by his side when he needed her, Brandy? But as suddenly as it had come, the emotion faded and was replaced by a sureness she had never felt before. She knew why Julia was there—because she cared. Everyone was showing her how much they really cared about Jake and about her. For the first time since her parents died, she knew she was at the center of a caring family who would stick by her no matter what, who would buoy her over the toughest times, and whose strength was her strength. With these people around him, with this love to support him, she knew Jake would recover. All of her anger at Julia faded, and she reached for her uncle's hand.

"I'm sorry about the way I've acted," she said. "Julia has been such a good friend, and I've been so selfish. That's why I stayed away, I guess—I didn't like what I was doing. You've been so wonderful to me, I didn't want to share you. But you need someone to fill the empty places in your life, I know that now. And I think Julia will fit just fine."

"Brandy, that's all I ever wanted to hear, that the two women I love most care about each other. Now, you go get in the car and I'll be right out. Julie's refused to take a break until you get there, and she's about worn out."

She was indeed worn out. Dark circles ringed her reddened eyes, and her face was pale above the stained and wrinkled clothing she had worn since last night. When she saw Brandy, she ran to her and enfolded her in her arms. They wept together, two women who needed each other.

"Come sit down, Brandy. I'll tell you everything I know, and then you can see him."

"No, just let me look in on him first. So he knows I'm here." Julia watched her pityingly as Brandy entered the stark, quiet room.

The pale figure on the bed, eyes puffed shut and darkened under a crown of bandage, tied by thin tubes to a seeming maze of monitors and plastic bottles . . . could that be her Jake? Brandy moved closer. His breathing seemed shallow, but he was alive. She leaned over to kiss his cheek and squeeze the limp fingers.

"I love you," she whispered. "I'll be waiting for you."

Julia filled her in on the events of the night. "It was a crazy trip to the hospital, I'll tell you. The storm, and I was scared stiff. Honestly, I thought the plane would fall out of the sky, we got tossed around so hard. Poor Jake, I kept trying to keep him from getting jolted. The doctors were waiting when we got here. They'd been told it was a probable head injury, so they were prepared in case he needed surgery. Dr. Beeman is wonderful—so calm, but he moves so fast.

"The X rays showed a depressed skull fracture, quite severe. Must have hit his head pretty hard. He was in surgery several hours, came through okay, but they still can't tell about brain damage. Not till the swelling's down, at least. Or until he wakes up."

"He will wake up, won't he?" Brandy asked anxiously.

Julia took her hands. "Brandy, I don't know. You can ask the doctor yourself, but I couldn't get a clear answer. He says there's no way they can tell at this point."

As Brandy walked with Julia to the elevator, two women in stiff white uniforms at the nursing station followed her with their eyes. "Hasn't she got gorgeous hair?" one of them whispered. "It's really going to be hard for her. He's never going to be anything but a vegetable even if he lives, you know. And he must have been really good-looking, too." They shook their heads sadly. But Brandy didn't hear them.

So the vigil began. Julia went back to the ranch to change and rest, and Brandy spent the first of many hours at the quiet bedside. The hospital smells and sounds were strange to her. It was a new world, and the beginning of a new chapter in her life. But first she knew there was a chapter that must be closed, and perhaps by closing it she could make things right—a superstitious idea, no doubt, but compelling. By ending her tie to Greg, she was convinced her tie to Jake—and his to life—would be strengthened.

She went to the bank of pay phones near the reception area. She reached Greg at home. She told him about her realization that she loved Jake and her determination to make Montana her home.

He refused to believe her. It was incomprehensible to him that anyone would want to live in such a place. Or without him, as it turned out.

"Ellen, you're obviously distraught. You're not making any sense at all. I think you should call me back when you've calmed down."

"Greg, I am perfectly serious. Life with you would be exactly what I thought I wanted. You're attractive, intelligent, successful—the kind of man most women would give anything to meet. But the spark is just not there between us. Love."

"Love?" Greg laughed. "Come on, you've been reading too many books. We're sexually compatible, you're smart enough so that we can hold an intelligent conversation, you look spectacular, we're comfortable together—that's what makes a relationship. And," he added, "you know everyone thinks we make a great-looking couple."

How could she not have seen how shallow Greg was? But, of course, her own eyes had been closed for so long. She felt sorry for him.

"Greg, I'm sorry. I'm really very fond of you. But my future is here with Jake. I hope you'll forgive me."

He finally believed her. "Wait until our friends hear about this one. Ellen Stanwood gone native, living with some illiterate cowboy out west. I can picture you in a few years—stringy hair, wrinkled face, in a polyester pantsuit—what a sight! I knew you were acting strange, but I didn't realize you were too far gone to get back to normal. Now I'm sorry I tried."

As she hung up the phone, Brandy thought about what he had said. "An illiterate cowboy." Something stirred in the back of her mind. Jake was far from illiterate, she knew that, but it was something more, something her uncle had said to her when she was so emotionally racked that she could hardly focus. Something about the public . . . Jake's public. She thought about his letters, the wonderful way he had with words, the word pictures . . .

Oh, my God! The memories came flooding in. T. J. Three in New York, talking about the writer Jay Mills, living somewhere nearby. Jake's secretiveness, his disappearances. Susie prattling on about the wonderful stories he told. Something her uncle had said . . . She turned back to the phone, hands shaking, and quickly dialed the ranch, hoping he would answer.

"Hattie! Oh, Hattie—is my uncle around? No, Jake is the same, but I need to talk to Uncle John right away. It's very important." She felt almost hysterical.

"Uncle John," she burst out when he came on the line, "am I just stupid, or what? Jake is Jay Mills, isn't he?"

Her uncle laughed. "Whew, when Hattie told me you said it was important, I thought Jake had taken a turn for the worse. Of course he's Jay Mills. I can't believe you never figured it out sooner."

"But why didn't he tell me? Why didn't *you* tell me?"

"Now, Brandy, you know how stubborn that man is. He had some romantic idea about making sure you loved him for himself. I told him it'd be a hell of a lot easier for you to love him for himself if you knew who the hell he was, but he made me promise—I tried to hint, you know!"

"Oh, Uncle John, we were both just too stubborn to listen to anyone. You should have just shaken us both and told us to shape up. Does Julia know?"

"Of course she knows, and she'll be pleased as punch that you finally woke up. I'll tell her—and I'll give her your love, okay?"

"Give her a big hug for me, and thank her again for being the best prospective aunt a woman ever had." They laughed together, the first real laughter Brandy had felt since her nightmare ride. There might be tough times ahead, but with her help she knew Jake would pull through.

In the weeks that followed, Brandy spent every moment she could at Jake's bedside, completing her long day at campaign headquarters in time to grab a quick snack in the hospital cafeteria and spend the evening visiting hours at Jake's side. With a lot of help from Eila and the staff, the campaign was moving well, but she knew that her own work was not what it should be. Often she found herself just staring into space, too frozen by worry and exhaustion to make the simplest decisions. All she could think of was Jake, the man she loved so much and was so close to losing.

Art Wilson, that crusty, cantankerous old man, came to her rescue. With Eila's help, he quietly kept things on track, stopping by daily to check on the staff, keeping things moving, and bringing tears to Brandy's eyes when she overheard his gruff commands.

"Now you listen up, group. Brandy may not be watching you so close as she did, but I'm filling in for her, and don't you think I'll let up on you, because I won't. We're sticking to Brandy's campaign plan, by God, and there'll be no arguments from any of you. Is that clear, Jack?"

Brandy felt a catch in her throat, but she had to laugh. Ornery old Art, defending her plan and pretending she was the fierce one. Why, the poor staff were so frightened they ran like rabbits trying to keep ahead of him. But they did their jobs, and now and then they let her know they cared.

"Er, Brandy . . . " Jack stood in the doorway late one afternoon when she was sitting at her desk, staring into space. "Brandy, can I get you something cold to drink? Or maybe a cup of tea?" He looked at her anxiously.

"No thanks, Jack, but it's nice of you to offer."

"I . . . I really do hope everything will be okay, Brandy. I mean, you and me, we haven't always gotten along too good, but you know I don't mean anything by the things I say, just can't help myself, somehow, you know?"

He was so nervous, poised half in and half out of the doorway, that she had to smile. This was as close to an apology as she was going to get, but it was clearly meant, and it meant a lot. She rose from the desk and went over to him. "Thanks, Jack." And she enveloped him in a big hug.

She told Eila about it later. "That poor man," she said. "He just turned to stone—stiff as a statue and white as a sheet. I think he thought I was going to attack him."

Eila came by every day late in the afternoon to tidy up loose ends and see how things were going. Her quiet warmth counteracted Art's abrasiveness and reassured the staff. Between the two of them, Brandy was bolstered and kept going, watched over by her friends as she in her turn kept her own lonely vigil over Jake.

How could she have been so foolish as to try to convince herself that she didn't love Jake? To think that she could really live without him? And now he was hanging on to life by a fragile thread and she could not imagine life without him. How ironic that she had once sworn she would never speak to him again! Now that he might never be able to hear her, she spoke to him constantly.

She had heard that coma victims could actually hear and even understand what they heard. Keeping her voice soft and low, she told Jake how much she loved him, what their life was going to be like when he woke up. She told him stories about her childhood and memories from college. She told him how sorry she was that she hadn't realized sooner that she loved him. She held his hand and stroked his arm and only left his side when the nurses drove her away and when her uncle insisted that she eat or rest, or when the office called begging for her decision on something that couldn't wait.

Sometimes, though, she sat by his bed and simply held his hand and gazed at his closed lids and bandaged head. He looked so young and helpless; she could imagine how he had looked as a child. Sometimes, as she gazed at him, she would feel a stirring in her mind, a feeling that he was calling to her in a faint whisper, trying to respond. But when she looked closely at his face, there was no sign of awareness, and his hands remained limp and unresponsive.

One Saturday night the nurses had kicked her out as usual, seemingly more concerned about her health than that of their patient.

"You get out of here and get some rest," the youngest one said. "You're just wearing yourself out for nothing. He's not going anywhere."

No, he wasn't going anywhere. Brandy looked at her face in the mirror of the ladies' room and understood why the nurses were acting concerned. She had lost weight, more than she could afford. There were terrible circles under her eyes, and her face had lost its color. She looked and felt ten years older.

Time passed very slowly, and the days continued in the same painful pattern. Good news at the campaign headquarters was followed by bad news at the hospital, day after day, and it became more difficult to remain optimistic. From time to time she saw Dr. Beeman in the hallways or when he stopped by Jake's room, but he remained noncommittal.

Then one day the doctor's secretary called to ask her to come to his office for a meeting. Could this be it? she wondered. Had Jake's vital signs finally shown the changes that meant he was coming out of the coma? Excited but apprehensive, Brandy sat in the doctor's familiar office, shivering; the air-conditioning was too cold, and she was anxious to get back to Jake in case he needed her.

Dr. Beeman strode in. "Sorry to keep you waiting, Brandy."

She nodded and looked at him expectantly, anxious to hear a report on Jake's progress. Surely there had been some improvement by now. Yesterday—she was certain that yesterday he looked better.

He shuffled his papers on his desk, leaned back on his chair, and looked beyond her out the window at her back.

"I'll try to keep this as simple as possible. Mr. Milburn has suffered a severe head injury. He's been in a coma for quite some time, and we haven't had a sign of any change. It's true that a person can be in a coma for a long time, longer than this, and come out of it. But the longer it goes on, the less likely that will happen. And the longer it goes on, the more likely it is that if they do come out of it, they will be seriously brain damaged."

Brandy looked at him through a veil of tears. She blinked to clear her vision.

Dr. Beeman's voice went on. "You need to start thinking of yourself and your future, Brandy. It's difficult to let oneself experience a loss when there seems to be a shred of hope that it isn't so. But the chances are virtually nil that you'll ever have him back the way he was. You need to come to grips with that as soon as possible and get on with your own life."

"But he's better," she cried. "I'm sure he's getting better."

"Brandy, we all want to think that, but there's simply no evidence. Sometimes we hope so much that we convince ourselves that it's really happening. But this time . . ."

He shook his head and continued to speak. His

voice was gentle. But Brandy wasn't listening to the words anymore.

She didn't remember leaving the doctor's office or even saying anything to him after he told her about Jake's condition. She found herself back at Jake's bedside, staring at him, her mind empty of all but the shock. Gradually a picture began to form—Thomas Littlehorse's studio, the miles of brown grass surrounding the little house, and Thomas's face.

What had he said? Something about the young braves who were tested, that she was to undergo similar trials. Was this the test? Watching Jake wither away while she sat by helplessly?

"Brandy?" Susie stood hesitating in the doorway, a bunch of daisies clutched in her small fist, eyes wide and uncertain. Blindly Brandy reached for the little girl and held her tight.

"I brought some flowers for Jake. I thought they might make him happy. When's he going to come home? I miss him. I want to ride the big horse."

Brandy started to explain to Susie what the doctor had told her. No point in the little girl hanging on to false hopes, either. But when she looked in those deep, solemn brown eyes, Brandy knew it was wrong to deny the child hope.

Susie seemed to sense something of the struggle inside her. "Don't worry, Brandy, he'll be all right. You know nothing can really happen to Jake. He loves us too much to die."

Brandy reached for the little girl and held her tight. Thomas's voice came to her, and this time she suddenly remembered the rest of his prediction—he had said she would pass these tests, that she would make it through her trials. She knew it was wrong for her to give up; she couldn't live without Jake, and if she was destined to come through this, then so was he.

Brandy smiled. Susie was right. He did love them all too much to die. Brandy had been up against overwhelming odds before. She didn't always win, but she never gave up without a fight. And she wasn't going to give up on Jake.

"Susie," she said, "you just practice your riding. Because Jake's going to want to see how much you've improved when he gets home from the hospital."

*T*he night before the election, everything seemed to be running smoothly. After months of frantic activity, Howie's campaign appeared to be a well-oiled machine. Phoners in the headquarters were contacting voters, reminding them to go to the polls tomorrow, and the headquarters was abuzz with scurrying volunteers checking lists, tallying favorables contacted in all the targeted precincts, and answering phone calls about where to vote, how to get rides, and what the latest polls showed.

The polls looked very good. Although Howie's opponent was respected in the community, he couldn't overcome the reservoir of goodwill Howie had built up in his years in the legislature. Brandy and Eila sat in Brandy's office sharing a bottle of wine at the end of a long but satisfying day. Brandy's desk was piled with papers as usual, but this time they didn't have the urgency of the past months, and she shoved the clutter to one side to make room for their glasses.

"Can you believe this will be over tomorrow?"

Eila said. "What a year this has been! And it looks—cross your fingers—as if we're going to win, thanks to the hard work you and your staff have put in."

"I hope so," Brandy said anxiously. "I keep thinking . . . maybe we should have done one more mail piece, or put just a little more into radio. I don't know. . . . "

"Well, you did do Art's newspaper ads, and he insists they're going to make the difference," Eila said laughingly. "Yes, and you know, Art was right—we did need to do newspaper ads. Not because they'll win it for us, but because it's important to support the local papers—let them know we care about the community. At any rate, you've all done a wonderful job, Brandy, you and Art and the whole staff."

"Don't kid yourself, Eila, our success is all Howie's. If he wasn't the special person he is, the best campaign in the world probably couldn't elect him. And you, my good friend, have been a godsend to both of us."

"Hey," Eila said, "being the candidate's wife isn't that hard."

She looked so fresh, Brandy thought. After all these months of grueling work, she looked as warm and cheerful as ever.

"You're a lot more than that, Eila. I may have set this operation up and written the plan, but these last few weeks, if it hadn't been for you and Art filling in for me when I couldn't handle it, propping me up when I was ready to break down and bawl—you were wonderful, and I'll never forget that."

"Hey, you're our friend, and we care about you. You'd do the same for us, after all. I'll miss you when we leave for Washington," she said quietly. They looked at each other for a long minute, then Brandy leaned back on her chair and sighed.

"So you know."

"How could I help but know? Howie and I have talked about it already. You can't possibly go to Washington with us. It's hard enough for me to leave Montana and my business, but at least Howie and I will be together. You and Jake—well, I can't see you wanting to leave him now."

"But I promised Howie, and I feel so bad about it. Is he upset with me?"

"Of course not," Eila said impatiently. "Don't be silly. He'll find someone else, and you can help set up his office here, maybe run it if you feel you can." Between them was the unspoken knowledge that she might not have time, that she might continue indefinitely her hopeful vigil beside that cold and narrow bed.

"Jake's going to be okay, Eila. Really, he is." But tonight it was almost a question.

"Of course he is." The older woman smiled. "Let's drink a toast to your future and Jake's. And to our friendship. Tomorrow night you can toast Howie and me." She lifted her glass and they both smiled, thinking back over the months that had cemented their friendship.

Brandy set her glass down suddenly. "Oh—I had a wonderful idea! All the things I have stored in New York—the furniture, linens, china—you and Howie can have it for your house in Washington, so you don't have to move anything."

"Don't be silly, Brandy. Your things are worth a

great deal of money, and besides, you'll need them. You can't just give them away."

"Eila, I *have* to give them away, or at least *get* them away. Those things are part of a life I'll never go back to. They're things, just things and nothing more, and they mean nothing to me except as reminders that once that was all I cared about. Please, won't you and Howie at least use them, make them worthwhile again? If I thought my things would be a part of your life in Washington, I'd be so happy."

"We will need to furnish a house, I suppose," Eila mused. "And it would be wonderful to have something to remind us of you. I know, we'll take care of your things until you and Jake need them for a place in the East."

Brandy wrinkled her nose. "Ugh. Do you think we'll have to have a place in New York, just because of his writing? Well, we'll see. Jake and I will see." A warm feeling stole over her as she realized for the first time she had talked openly to her friend in terms of "Jake and I."

"But what about the gallery?" Brandy asked. "You aren't going to close it, are you?"

"Oh, no," Eila replied with a firm shake of her head. "That gallery's my baby. I'll get someone to run it on a day-to-day basis, and I'll still make the big decisions—Washington's not *that* far away. You could keep an eye on things for me, too, couldn't you?"

Brandy smiled broadly. "Yes, if it means I'd get a discount on Thomas Littlehorse's work—his prices are going up like crazy now that New York has discovered him."

Eila drained her glass and, setting it on the corner of the desk, said very casually, "Oh, by the way, Brandy. Thomas Littlehorse will be stopping by the hospital tonight to see Jake, if it's all right with you."

"Why, of course it's all right. Why wouldn't it be? I'd love to see Thomas, too." She thought ruefully of Thomas's predictions; he was right about Montana being her home, but at what cost had she found out. She could only hope against hope that the trials he saw would soon be over. Perhaps she could ask him. . . .

Eila stopped her with a hand on her arm. She seemed to hesitate before speaking. "Brandy," she said, "we're all praying for Jake. But the doctors say they have done absolutely everything they can. Sometimes you need to stretch your understanding a little, and look farther for an answer."

"What do you mean? I don't understand." Brandy was puzzled by her friend's serious gaze.

"Just go and talk to Thomas. He'll tell you what I mean."

Brandy mulled over Eila's words as she drove to the hospital. The night was clear, and for the first time in days the stars were unveiled in all their proximity. Their glow seemed to light the sky even as the moon was still hidden behind the mountains on the horizon. Leafless trees stood sentinel, unmoving in a night that was totally windless. Traffic seemed to move silently, the heavy stillness broken only by the clear call of an owl.

It's eerie, she thought. I have this strange feeling of expectancy, as if something is about to happen. Maybe it's a storm coming in, ozone in the air. But

it felt totally different, as if she were moving inex-
orably toward something unknown . . . and yet
she felt so calm. As she made the familiar turn into
the hospital parking lot, she thought she heard the
sound of drums in the distance.

You're imagining things, she told herself. That's
thunder across the valley somewhere. And she
continued to move eagerly toward what awaited
her.

When she arrived in the waiting area near Jake's
room, a slight, dark-skinned figure stood up to
greet her. Thomas was dressed in neatly pressed
khakis and a blue cotton shirt buttoned carefully
at collar and cuffs; he had removed a baseball cap
from his head. He was the picture of the modern
American Indian, civilized and polite, dressed in
the way of his neighbors.

But there was always something about Thomas
that puzzled Brandy, some quality that made him
very different from everyone around him. At first
she had thought it was that he was an artist, but it
was more than that—it was the same dark and hidden power that lay beneath the painted skin of his
oils and fought to escape from his sculpted pieces.
Thomas always looked as if he would be more at
home wearing deerskin and feathers, moving quietly through the Montana night.

Tonight that feeling was more pronounced. As
he stood proudly, his hand reaching out to her,
she felt his touch was the connection to some
mysterious force she did not understand. She
reached gladly for his hand.

"Brandy," he said in his soft voice, "I hope you

don't mind that I came. I have been so concerned."

"Oh, Thomas, that's so good of you. I'm afraid things aren't very hopeful right now."

Thomas drew her to a chair in the far corner of the room. "I'm here because I know that. I've thought about this for a long time before coming to you. You've been a friend to me, and Jake is a good man. I don't know him well, but I sense that he is in tune with the earth and the forces around him. He would understand what I want to do for him."

"What you want to do? Thomas, the doctors say there is nothing that can be done, that only a miracle will bring him back now."

"Then perhaps I can help you make such a miracle." He spoke slowly and thoughtfully. "I don't know how much you know about my people, and about our beliefs. We have our own medicine—not the medicine of doctors, but a greater healing power that has its roots in the world around us. It cannot be used only as a treatment, but is a way of life, a mystery. Perhaps you have sensed some of that mystery in my art."

"Yes," Brandy said excitedly, "I have sensed that, but how can it do anything for Jake?"

"My father is an old man, wise in the lore of our tribe, and trained in the healing arts. He has taught me to follow him, but I am only a beginner with many years of study ahead. We do this to preserve our heritage, but also because we believe in this power, and believe it must not be lost."

"So it's a kind of religion, isn't it?"

"In a way, but greater than that. Brandy, I have

brought my father here tonight. I would like him to see Jake."

"Oh, Thomas, a medicine man? I can't see . . ."

He took her hand and caught her gaze. "Please, listen with your new heart. He is a healer."

At once she was calm; she could see the rightness of it. As her mind filled with a strange peace, she heard again the faintness of drums in the distance, calling. And yet the drums were inside her head, the pounding of her heart.

An old man stood in the doorway, dressed in a black suit and white shirt and bolo tie. His wispy white hair was long, and he wore a band to hold it in place. A medicine man, a shaman? Outwardly he looked as ordinary as Thomas but had that same strange aura about him. He gave a questioning look and, in response to Thomas's brief nod, lifted his large black bag in salute and entered Jake's room.

Brandy wondered why the nurses had not interfered. They had given him a quick glance and gone back to their work. Had he been here before? Thomas continued to reassure her.

"I must join him, Brandy, to assist him with the ritual. When I return, I will take you in to see Jake. If he responds, he will sleep deeply tonight, and tomorrow will bring the changes we are looking for. Keep your mind tuned to our work, and you will help us in our task."

She had no sensation of time passing. When at last Thomas led her into the small white room, his father was gone, though she had not seen him leave. The only sign of activity was a single long feather lying on the bedside table. She leaned over Jake and kissed the pale cheek. His breathing was deep and quiet, for the first time like that of normal sleep.

Tomorrow she would know.

In the morning when she returned to the hospital, Thomas was still there. Sitting in the corner of Jake's room, face impassive and figure stiffly upright, he looked like a carving of an Indian brave.

"Thomas? Have you been here all night?" Brandy peered at him in the half dark of the room.

"Yes. He might have needed help. It is a difficult thing, calling himself back from the darkness. The spirit does not always want to come back."

"But Jake has so much to come back for," Brandy cried. "He is coming back, isn't he?"

"Look, and tell me what you think."

She leaned over the quiet bed. He was half on his side this morning, one arm flung out as if he had been restless during the night. Every few seconds he seemed to sigh, and his eyelids fluttered.

"Thomas, he's waking up!"

"Not yet, but soon. The doctor has been in this morning. He tells me that his medicine seems to have worked after all." Thomas smiled wryly at her.

She rushed out into the hall. "Is Dr. Beeman

around?" she asked the nurses at the desk.

"No, he's on his rounds," one answered, "but he was here earlier. He says it's a miracle—your young man is coming out of the coma."

"Yes," she replied, "it certainly is a miracle."

"Isn't it amazing what modern medicine can do?" the nurse asked.

Brandy looked at her for a minute. "Somehow," she said, "I don't think this particular medicine was so modern." She turned and went back to the room.

"Well, Thomas, they all seem to think a miracle of modern medicine has occurred. Shall we let them think that?" she asked. "And tell me, will he be all right? I mean, can your magic—and don't deny it, it is a form of magic—can it tell you what our future will be?"

"Now you ask too much, my friend. Only you can see your future. I can only tell you Jake is coming back to you. If the two of you search together for your future, perhaps you will have that vision."

What a strange answer, she thought. And what a strange experience she had had. Did she believe it, or did she believe the doctor's explanations? She would have to tell Jake about it when he woke up. Perhaps he would know.

But it was election day, and another important milestone in her new life. The day that was to have marked her return to the East Coast now would be memorable for a completely different reason. She would have to leave Jake until after the election returns were in, because there was a great deal left to do in last-minute preparations for the victory party, and she had promised to be with Howie and Eila in their moment of triumph.

And triumph it was. Tom Bainbridge capitulated early in a truly moving concession speech and surprised them by vowing to support Howie despite their party differences. The hotel ballroom was crowded with cheering supporters and those who simply wanted to be remembered as friends of the new congressman. Brandy moved through the crowd, festive in a creamy wool dress, her thin cheeks glowing with new color, accepting the congratulations of everyone she met. At one point she found herself facing the woman she had met at her first Billings political event—what was her name? The one who had been so vicious about Brandy not belonging?

"Oh, my dear," the woman gushed. "We are all so proud of you. Our very own Brandy Stanwood running a superb campaign, helping dear Howie win his seat in Congress. You won't be leaving us now, will you?"

No such luck, Brandy thought. You won't get rid of me that easily. Outwardly she smiled and thanked the woman sweetly. Why not? She had won, after all.

And she had won in so many ways. Howie's moment of triumph was a wonderful moment for her, too. As he and Eila stood on the stage, waving together to the cheering crowd of well-wishers, she felt a burst of pride greater than any she had ever known. This time she had done a good job. This man, this couple, would make Montanans proud.

Art Wilson brought a lump to her throat when

he gave her a hug and congratulated her.

"You're a tough lady, Brandy. I'm proud of you. It wasn't easy for you dealing with a bunch of narrow-minded old fogies like us, but you did a great job and you taught us a lot."

"Oh, Art, you don't have to be so nice. I know I made a lot of mistakes, and without you I would have made more. I didn't know anything at all about Montana politics."

"That's why we made a good team," he answered. "Next time we'll just get off to a smoother start."

"Next time?" Yes, there would be a next time. She narrowed her eyes and gave him a stern look. "I want to tell you one thing, Art Wilson. Next time *I'm* in charge, and no arguments from you."

"The hell you say," he shot back. "This is one place where age and cunning win every time, and you just try it."

They both collapsed in laughter, two stubborn battlers who in this moment knew each other well enough that no more words were necessary. What a combination, she thought—we'll fight each other on the details, but when the chips are down we're right in there together—and nobody better cross the two of us.

Brandy was proud of her part in Howie's success. Maybe Montana wasn't the center of things, but if she could make a difference here, it was worth sticking with it. She glanced at the figures on the stage—state house member Sharon Walters stood next to Howie. Hmm, Sharon ought to be looking at running for the state senate pretty soon. . . .

Before Brandy left the party to return to the hospital, Howie and Eila took her aside. "You did a great job, Brandy," Howie said, "and no matter what you say, we couldn't have done it without you. I know you're planning to stay here, and I'll miss having you with me in Washington, but I understand. Just promise me one thing—that you'll keep on with politics, once you and Jake get settled. We need people like you badly in this business—people with the skills and ethical standards to help us restore the public's faith in the profession."

She couldn't speak. It had all come round at last. She, Brandy, the same Ellen Brandon Stanwood who had disgraced herself on Wall Street, was held up as an example of honesty and ethics. How ironic it seemed! But of course, she really had tried to live by those standards; she knew that her only lack of honesty had always been a lack of honesty with herself.

"Brandy wants to get over to the hospital to see Jake," Eila interrupted. She turned and grasped her hand, then spoke with a conspiratorial note in her voice. "We don't know how it happened, of course, but we're delighted to hear that Jake seems to be coming out of the coma."

Brandy smiled back at her. "Yes, it is strange— almost like a miracle. However it happened, I owe a great debt of gratitude to someone . . . or something."

Later she sat by Jake's bed, in what she was sure was the last of her long vigils. His face had color now, and he moved about in his sleep. What would he think when he woke? she wondered. Would he know she had been here? Anxiety gripped her as she realized he might not even want to see her.

"Jake," she said, "please wake up. I need to talk to you. I need to explain to you. . . ."

"Brandy?" The weak voice startled her. "Brandy, you're back."

"Jake?" She leaned over him. His eyes were still tightly closed, but his mouth was moving.

"I need a drink of water," he said. "My mouth is so dry."

Tears coursed down her face as she held the glass for him, placing the bent straw in his mouth. As he sipped, his eyes slowly opened, and he pushed the glass away.

"You look good," he said. "I've been waiting for you all day. I tried to say something this morning, but it wouldn't come out." He reached up and cupped her face in his hands. "Just let me look at you. I love you so."

"I love you, Jake. I've been telling you that for weeks, but you didn't answer."

"I think I heard you," he said. "I remember hearing voices . . . I remember something strange happened. When I woke up, at first I didn't know where I was. What I still don't remember is how I got here."

It was not until the following day that Jake heard the full story of his near fatal fall and Brandy's wild ride to the rescue. She and her uncle talked about whether to tell him about the incident with Joe but decided against it. Eventually he would be told that Joe had disappeared; and in fact, Joe was never seen again. His old pickup truck was found abandoned beside a dusty road between the ranch and Billings, but no one ever located him. The warrant for his arrest remained open, but no one from the Rocking B ever commented on it or wondered aloud where he had gone. Tom and Duke told those who asked that they simply must have been too far behind Joe to find him in the chase that ensued that night.

But tonight was a new beginning for Brandy and Jake. She was prepared to correct a lot of misunderstandings and explain so many things, but Jake insisted he already knew; he had heard all of this before. And he had apparently, over the past few weeks. Thank God I talked to him, she thought. We have gotten so many things behind us. Now we can start looking at what's ahead of us.

She hushed him when he berated himself for not telling her sooner about his identity. "It doesn't matter now," she assured him. "We were both a couple of stubborn idiots."

"You understand why, don't you? I wanted to be certain you cared about the person I really am, the Montana person. You were so anxious to return to New York, and I was afraid you'd only care about the Jay Mills side of me."

"Don't be silly," she said. "Jay Mills is a brilliant writer, but he's a bit long-winded for me."

"Brandy, don't tease. I want to be sure. I don't want any more misunderstandings. . . ."

"Don't worry. All that's behind us. As long as there are no more secrets between us," she admonished.

"No secrets," he assured her. "Somehow I get the feeling I'll never be able to keep anything from you again."

33

T*his morning Brandy handled early press calls from the East Coast with a new lilt in her voice.* "Representative-Elect Morrison's office." Wonderful words, wonderful day.

In between congratulations, press inquiries, and the amusing calls from those supercautious souls who had simply "forgotten to mail" their contributions to the campaign until after the election, Brandy worked her way down her own list of important calls, starting with Peter Cornish and the other fellow members of her training class for whom election day meant the difference between an end and a beginning.

She had watched the late returns from Ohio, but the results of Peter's campaign had still been up in the air earlier that morning. When she finally reached him midmorning, it was still not definite, but things looked good.

"They're still counting absentee ballots," he told her tiredly. "What a night—but it looks as if we did it. We're ahead right now, and Republicans generally take a larger share of the absentees in this area. God knows we worked at it."

"Peter, I know how hard you worked and I'm sure your lead will hold. I'm thrilled for you, friend. Are you going to work in the congressman's office in Washington?"

"No, I think I'll help him set up an office here in the district and then look for another campaign. Can't see getting out of the campaign business yet. I assume you're staying with it, too—at least I hope so. You're kind of a role model for the rest of us, you know. In fact, I'll send you a resume just to remind you I'm available for your next campaign. I've always wanted to see Montana."

"I'll take you up on that, and thanks . . . for everything."

"Hey—you take care."

Brandy's happiness kept bubbling over. She managed a long talk with Meg and left a message for Barney that he later told her absolutely made his day—he must have told everyone on the floor about the protégée who had made good in politics. Carey Steele had sent a gorgeous bouquet of roses that had to have been ordered before the election was even decided—only Carey would be that efficient and that confident.

Already Brandy was beginning to feel the sadness involved in dismantling a good campaign organization. Months of hard work putting it together, and just when it's running perfectly, you have to tear it apart and discard it. But she knew already it could be put together again, and perhaps it would—not in exactly the same form, but in other combinations and other circumstances the people she had grown to know so well would once again herd the fabled amoeba across the bridge, sometimes making it to the other side, sometimes sliding over the edge, but always caring and always vowing it would work better the next time.

So today was an ending for this campaign, but an auspicious beginning for her own future—her future with the man she truly loved. There were no more parts of her life she was afraid to face or unwilling to deal with. How could she ever have thought the pieces of her life had to be separate? she wondered. She needed every one of them—including her past.

She called Jake just to be sure nothing had changed since last night, and the sound of his voice touched her heart. "I'll be there in an hour, as soon as I can get away," she told him.

She couldn't resist running home to change into a light-colored silk dress that made a perfect background for the jade pendant and earrings. Her green eyes, reflecting the deep color of the jade jewelry, seemed larger and more brilliant than ever in the finely drawn oval of her face.

"You're awfully thin," Jake said. "We make a great pair—probably have to prop each other up."

She leaned over him, frowning. "Now you listen to me," she said. "I may be skinny, but I'm tough enough to handle you. And you said it just right. We're a pair and we're going to stay that way."

"Well, at least we'll be a pair some of the time—when I get back east, or you come back to visit the district with the new congressman. It'll be hard, but I guess a lot of people make it in long-distance relationships." He sighed.

"Jake," she said, "I'm afraid it's not going to work that way. I talked to Howie last night, and he's taking someone else to Washington with him." She tried to look downcast and almost succeeded.

"You're kidding. You didn't get the job?"

She leaned over and kissed the end of his nose. "No, you idiot, I turned it down—told him I'm too much of a Montanan to live in the East. Surely you don't think I'd lose out to someone else when I really want something."

"Don't do that, Brandy, it hurts to laugh," he croaked. "No, I can't imagine you ever losing when you really want something."

They sat together as the sun continued its trek across that great Montana sky and dropped to touch the wide plains that looked so lonely but teemed with hidden life. Finally she stretched and looked beyond their little world, sterile and forbidding no longer.

"Look at the sunset, Jake—the color, the way it spills across the plains. You'd never see a sunset like that in the East."

"Wait a minute," he cautioned. "I've got bad news." She turned to him, startled.

"I'm afraid, my love, you'll have to leave Montana for a while. My agent called this morning, and we've decided to do a pre-Christmas tour to promote my new book. I told him my wife and I would be ready to leave by Thanksgiving. Think you can make it?"

Her heart nearly exploded with joy. "Well," she said seriously, "it'll be tough, but since you need someone to take care of you, I guess I can put up with those crazy easterners for a while."

As darkness fell, and the love and laughter of their friends and family gathered them in, they turned their eyes together toward the future, and they saw it clearly. As Thomas Littlehorse had promised, no matter where their lives took them they knew they would be together, and this great, wide, exciting country would always be their hearts' home.

MARGARET CARROLL is a pseudonym for the writing team of Carol Whitney and Peg Dawson. This is their first book.

PEG DAWSON currently works in the office of Health Policy Fellowships of the Institute of Medicine of the National Academy of Sciences. She resides in Arlington, Virginia.

CAROL WHITNEY is a political consultant and professional trainer headquartered in Washington, D.C. She is a native of the Pacific Northwest, and now makes her home in northern Virginia.

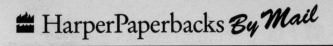